Praise for Tony Romano's previous works

When the World was Young (novel)

"Compelling...breathtaking. Romano is a careful and evocative writer who takes time with his descriptions to give his fictional world depth and texture. As adept as he is at rendering visual images, Romano is even more skilled at presenting his characters' psychic landscapes...a most-accomplished first novel, rich in characterization, setting and psychological acuity."
—*Chicago Tribune*

"Tenderhearted... Romano describes the mourning process in heart-wrenching passages even as he relays the love and the secrets...that bind and separate family members."
—*Booklist*

"[This novel] refuses to sentimentalize the Italian immigrant life that it explores. It pulls you deeper and deeper into this life through a series of wonderfully disturbing surprises that will make your heart ache."
—Robert Hellenga, author of *The Fall of a Sparrow* and *The Sixteen Pleasures*

"Tony Romano creates this story of an Italian family in the 1950s with a perceptive eye and a compassionate heart. The story moves with vitality and a flair for language. As with all good storytellers, his characters and the way they seek to resolve their dilemmas, remain with the reader long after the book is closed."
—Harry Mark Petrakis, author of *A Dream of Kings*

If You Eat, You Never Die (stories)

"The overwhelming themes of love, loss, grief, struggle
and isolation are expressed in unsentimental and
sometimes even desperate prose. Dreams, and the
failure to reach those dreams, choices, risks and settling
(or not settling) permeate this moving collection
of tales that will stay with the reader
long after the book is shut."
—*Publishers Weekly* (starred review)

"Romano illuminates a Chicago neighborhood and an entire
universe of dreams and disappointments...Romano narrates
fluently from different points of view...[He] has a penetrating
eye, respect for life, poise, and deep understanding of how
helpless we are when emotions and actions betray reason."
—*Booklist*

"The author's depth of feeling for his characters,
combined with his ability to follow their subtle
transformations through the decades, is affecting...
A spirited evocation of a complex immigrant culture,
willing to show the scars its characters bear."
—*Kirkus*

"A delightful and dark collection of stories about family in
its most loving and bitter sense. The chronicle of an Italian
immigrant family, these are portraits of the people we
simultaneously love and hate: our mothers, our fathers, our
siblings. Tony Romano's gift for finding the perfect voice, the
nuance of detail, is terrific. A fine collection."
—Bret Lott, author of *Jewel* and *Dead Low Tide*

Also by Tony Romano

When the World was Young (novel)

If You Eat, You Never Die (stories)

WHERE MY BODY ENDS AND THE WORLD BEGINS

Tony Romano

 ALLIUM PRESS OF CHICAGO

Allium Press of Chicago
Forest Park, IL
www.alliumpress.com

This is a work of fiction. Descriptions and portrayals of real people, events, organizations, or establishments are intended to provide background for the story and are used fictitiously. Other characters and situations are drawn from the author's imagination and are not intended to be real.

Book and cover design by E. C. Victorson
Front cover image: Victor Tondee/Shutterstock

ISBN: 978-0-9967558-7-0

Library of Congress Cataloging-in-Publication Data

Names: Romano, Tony, 1957- author.
Title: Where my body ends and the world begins / Tony Romano.
Description: Forest Park, IL : Allium Press of Chicago, [2017]
Identifiers: LCCN 2017043766 (print) | LCCN 2017046512 (ebook)
 | ISBN 9780996755887 (ebook) | ISBN 9780996755870 (softcover)
Subjects: LCSH: Our Lady of the Angels School (Chicago, Ill.)--Fire,
    1958--Fiction. | Italian-Americans--Illinois--Chicago--Fiction. |
    Families--Illinois--Chicago--Fiction. | Disaster victims--Fiction. |
    Psychic trauma--Fiction. | Domestic fiction. | GSAFD: Historical
    fiction.
Classification: LCC PS3618.O57 (ebook) | LCC PS3618.O57 W49
2017 (print) | DDC 813/.6--dc23
LC record available at https://lccn.loc.gov/2017043766

In memory of Marilyn Stoltman Konwinski

1

⟡

Summer 1967

Neighbors gather. A familiar voice calls out, *We need an ambulance.* I've heard this before. The sky opens. Limitless. Vast.

Why do I always forget this part? White fire seizing my leg. I'm twenty and lying in the street and I've injured the same leg three, four times now.

"The sinister left leg," Nonna calls it. She's seventy-one and lives in the flat below us and wears black—for me?—and points to my cursed leg every time I limp. She calls up to her Christ for guidance and understanding, pleading, but quickly waves the plea away, knowing her prayers won't be answered. Then she turns and reaches, as if for a cane, which must be for me, to mock me, because she refuses help of any kind. She lost her own cane after a few weeks but not the habit of reaching for it. Now I'll have to face her again.

Mr. Lipschultz. It's his voice I hear. He leans and blocks the sun and studies me, then my leg. I think I detect shock in his glare. And this is what tightens my gut—his grave reaction. Mr. Lipschultz's the sonofabitch on our block who calls the cops if someone's washing his car with the radio blasting. He's an ex-cop himself, retired three years ago, so he knows how to talk to them. "An ambulance," he says again. But there's no urgency in his voice. He shifts to the right and the sun blinds me.

"Don't move," he says. As if this is a possibility. I dare a peek, thinking I'll see blood. Because I felt the crunch, heard the dull snap. I swear I feel a wetness, but this must be my head playing tricks, because there's no gash, no pool of blood. Just my leg twisted at an impossible angle, a thing apart. Gory and satisfying. Something's oozing on the inside maybe, the tibia in pieces.

You learn the names of bones when you break them. This time I'm pretty sure it's both the fibula, which could fracture from an off-balance sneeze, and the tibia, the shin bone, more substantial. With my fingers, I venture down my thigh and wonder if I shattered my femur, too, this time.

Just out of reach is the baseball I'd been gripping, a black bruise on the leather.

"What the hell is wrong with you?" Lipschultz asks. "What kind of goddamn klutz... If I didn't know better... What, do you fall on purpose? Is this some sick way of getting attention?"

I know he means from my dad, to get the attention of my dad.

Other neighbors are behind him, keeping their distance, because Officer Lipschultz is on duty now, out of retirement.

What is this hold he has on everyone? Why does that steely gaze seem so...protective?

He picks up my baseball, turns it in his hand, lays his fingers across the seams.

"Go fuck yourself," I mutter under my breath.

"What?" he asks.

"The ball. Hand over the ball," I tell him.

"I got your ball right here," he says, and tosses it away from me.

"Yeah, go fuck yourself," I say clearly.

I take in his canvas shoes, the thick wool socks. In the middle of summer. The crazy old bastard.

He bellows over his shoulder in his usual boom, "Has anyone called?"

I hear a distant siren then, as if on his command.

They'll send me back to the shrink now. Either that, or they'll think I'm trying to dodge the draft because my number's coming up. That's how everyone puts it. *Dodging.* Like thousands of guys like me are faking left, then darting right, leaping. Like going to war is fucking dodgeball. If you're quick enough, you get to shatter your bones on a one-way street in Chicago rather than on the fields of Cambodia or wherever the hell they're fighting.

The throbbing is a sound now, like it's coming from outside. From one of the cars gliding by I hear, "One pill makes you larger and one pill makes you small." I close my eyes to steel myself but worry I'm going to pass out, so I force one eye open. Beyond Lipschultz, neighbors line the sidewalk on the other side, trying to catch a glimpse of that lanky stupid klutz Anthony Lazzeri, who can't cross a street without incident, the gimp. *What happened?* they all want to know. *Did a car swipe him? Is this some kind of hit and run? In our neighborhood? With Mr. Lipschultz on watch?*

What will I say when people ask? What will my story be? I can live with hit and run. Because Lipschultz's cop pals will have questions. *Make of car? Description of driver?* More important, what do I say to Nonna? To my mom, who has suffered enough?

Suddenly, tiny Mrs. Mazzolini is in my face, a biscotti in her bony hand. I might be dying, but I still have to eat before I get there. *"Grazie,"* I tell her and take it. The biscotti is warm and, what the hell, I take a bite, as she backs away. The glazed sweetness coats my throat and somehow eases the pain.

I search through the crowd for my sister, Ellie, who's only eleven but seems much older, like she's ready to run the world. She'll shake her head, the way she's seen Nonna do, then she'll nurse me back to health, ordering me around when I start to feel sorry for myself.

I swallow and the biscotti falls from my fingers. Then I do pass out. But it must be for just a second or two because when I open my eyes, nothing has changed, except that I realize, as if for the first time, that my leg is shattered. *That would be hell*, I think. To pass out every few minutes and to come back having forgotten, with the realization of...*this*. My leg seizes up. I spot a red halter top across the street, and I squint hard to see if it's my sometime girlfriend, Maryann, who lives next door, which would be impossible because she's at school, taking finals for two summer classes at Loyola so she can graduate in three years. *What's the hurry?* I always ask her. She could be *here*, in the street, holding my hand and forgiving me for being such a jerk the past few months. The past few years?

I glance back at our apartment. At Nonna's window. I think I spot the curtain flutter. I picture her rooted there seconds before, glaring out, then turning in disappointment.

I didn't break my leg to slow me down or because I wanted to kill myself or to gain Maryann's sympathy or anyone else's. I broke my leg, the left one, because the entire length of it, or nearly, inside and out—the bones and tendons, the muscles, the skin, the sparse forest of hair—none of it belongs to me.

2

⬦

At the hospital, I flirt with the nurses. They usually come in twos, the lead nurse doing all the talking while the trainee lurks behind, trying her best to look sober, like she just found out she was being audited, which happened to my old man once, which is how I know that look. The trainees are younger, though not always cuter, and my IV-induced flirting is meant for them, but they don't dare step out of the shadows and give me a smile, which isn't too much to ask, I think.

Nonna, shrunken, in black, sits in the corner, eyes shut. She's a fixture, unobtrusive as a light switch. Her leathery face is crossed with deep lines that make her seem ancient, but I know the skin is baby soft. And those marvelous hands, the fingers thick and nimble. With those hands, her bare hands, she removes hot trays from ovens. Right now, they stitch their way through a white rosary, fifty-four gleaming beads. She's probably wishing she was in church, where she goes every morning for hours and sometimes twice a day if there's a traveling shrine for Our Lady of Fatima or some other holy big shot.

"Nice try," says my roommate when the nurses leave. He's an old geezer named Harold, who coughs up a lung but who's here for his hip. "They got them nurses running scared. They're afraid they're going to get wrote up. My granddaughter's a nurse is how I know. She says it's the worst here."

Here is Cook County Hospital, a teaching hospital, and my mom, who once worked at this place, used to complain about the same thing. The sight alone was enough to keep me away. At night, from the road, the building looks like a gothic asylum, the concrete-gray cornices taking on the shape of gargoyles. At least I have the bed near the window, though the blinds are never cracked.

On the third day, visitors start pouring in like it's a wake. Apparently, the story in the neighborhood is that I was nearly killed, and everyone feels lucky to be able to see me one more time. I must admit, I'm touched by all this, even though some of them would barely notice me otherwise. Every time I open my eyes, a new visitor is standing over my bed.

My boss, Freddy Corsini, on his way to work, gets there early. He draws the linen curtain between the two beds. "We're saving a job for you, Antney. Don't you worry." Freddy's my supervisor at Streets and San, which means he drives around in his metallic gold Eldorado, clocking in everyone else's hours. How he can afford a '65 Caddy is a mystery. He never walks if he can drive, never exerts himself, yet his wide chest still hasn't sunk into a low pouch, a source of pride, especially now in his mid-fifties. The only time he exerts himself is during elections, collecting signatures, promising new trash cans for votes. Sometimes just the lids are enough incentive.

"So how you holding up?" he asks, grabbing his crotch.

"I'm okay," I tell him. I begin to return the gesture but remember the catheter and wince just thinking about it.

He glances toward a young nurse passing in the hall. "That's what I'm talking about. You oughta marry one of dem." He reaches in his shirt pocket for a cigar, inserts it in his mouth, but doesn't light it, not because he's in a hospital but because he never lights his cigars. Just chews on them, which is satisfying enough.

"I thought you said there was no such thing as a happy marriage."

"I didn't say nothing about happy."

He's on his fourth marriage and thinks everyone should be as miserable as he is. Or so he says.

"How's the arm?"

"It's the leg, Freddy."

He makes a pitching motion. "The arm...the arm. I can give a shit about your leg. But that beautiful arm."

"Okay, I guess."

"Nothing ever come of those two scouts, huh?"

"I guess not."

"Your old man..."

My old man played two seasons with the Detroit Tigers. For their farm team. I always pause before I add that last part, just to see people's faces. He got pulled up twice but only for a couple of days each time. Everyone thought my dad had paved the way for me, that I'd pick up where he left off.

I shake my head.

"Well, when you see him," he says, "bust his balls for me, will ya?"

"I will...for getting me a job with *you*."

Inevitably, he starts in on the big election next year. "Back in '60, we were the ones who pushed Kennedy over the top, you know. Without the commonwealth of Chicago, he's just a good lookin' Irish senator. You know this, right?"

Only because he never tires of reminding me.

"We did that. Me and the other precinct boys."

"The machine, I know."

"Yeah, I like that. The machine. Well, you watch. Bobby's going to throw his hat in. And then he'll be next. He'll destroy Nixon. We'll make sure."

I've thought about this. But, because I like Freddy and because I like my job—always outside, usually in a truck—I've never said anything. Until now. Though I'm not sure why. Maybe because I'm bored stiff from lying in a hospital bed all day. Maybe because of the drugs clouding my veins. Anyway, here's what I tell him. I tell him, "Let me run something by you. Maybe we would've been better off if Kennedy had lost in 1960. Now, hear me out on this. Maybe if Tricky Dick had won, then there wouldn't've been bullets flying in Dallas, and then Kennedy could've run again in four years and *he* would've been president. Now, right fucking now, he would be president." I won't add anything about Vietnam because Freddy has a son there, but I can't stop thinking that if Chicago hadn't put JFK over the top, who knows if Nixon would've ever sent troops. Not that I ever want to imagine that sonofabitch Nixon as president, but who knows. Maybe things would have turned out different.

Freddy pulls the cigar out of his mouth for a second and moves closer to the IV bag and squeezes the liquid inside. "What the fuck's in here that's making you so goddamn crazy?"

He chomps on his cigar and talks a while longer and then he's a blur at the door. He says something about finding the cocksucker who did this to me, or maybe I imagine this.

❖

When I open my eyes, I expect to find my sister, Ellie, staring at me. But it's someone else. I see her thin wrist before I feel its warmth. Miss G…Cecilia? She's touching my hand, and for a heartbeat, and then another, I don't know where I am. I must have dozed off in her class, I think. Social studies, government. Miss Gyerson. Miss G. Shortly before graduation, I began calling her by her first name, Cecilia—because she looked so young, because she *was* so young, we were her first students— and she said that no one besides her mom had ever called her that. Because this pleased her, I never stopped, though *Miss G* sounded right, too, and what I usually resorted to. My first thought is, *Where's Freddy?* To have them meet! I've imagined the scene, the two of them talking about trash can democracy in Chicago, Cecilia letting him have it. She's the only teacher at William H. Wells who's ever gotten me to think—not only about the global machine but about the politics in my own neighborhood.

She kisses me on the forehead and pinches my hand. "You look good," she lies. That voice. High pitched like a girl's, but scratchy, as if she's had a cough, but it's just her normal healthy voice, which thrills me.

I'm grateful that she's standing opposite the catheter bag that hangs to the side. She would have had to walk around, which I'm certain she did for my sake because nothing shocks her.

"If you'd gone to college like I kept telling you...you wouldn't be here." She hasn't let go of my hand and I think, *I can get used to this*. She smells vaguely of peppermint, and I wonder if it's her hair or her skin or if the source is somewhere darker. Sitting in my little desk at school, I've imagined those dark places.

"So, this is like karma or something? My punishment for not going to college?"

She smiles and twists her neck, so that one thick strand of hair falls behind her shoulder, but the hair returns just as swiftly. It's straight and brown and frames her tiny face.

"No, not like that. What I meant is that if you'd gone to college, you probably wouldn't have been standing in the street at that moment."

"So I would have gotten hit on another street." I'm amazed that I've already gotten used to the lie. *I got hit*.

"So it's fate, is it?"

How do I tell her that it wasn't karma, that it wasn't fate, that I'd done this to myself? "Just a freak accident," I insist. "I don't remember much." Which is what I told the cops when I arrived in Emergency.

I battle a yawn so she doesn't think I'm tired and that she's keeping me up. "So you think I'm college material, huh?" I ask, because I know what she's going to say.

She brushes my arm. "You were my best student my first year. Without a doubt." A wistful look fills her eyes. "On the days you were gone, the class seemed different. A little empty."

She's never added that last part. I feel a stirring beneath the sheet and twist to hide that. *This is wrong*, I say, but it's just a whisper in my head. And then I think, *Shouldn't this be her thought? Shouldn't she be the one reminding me that she's four years older, that we were once teacher and student, though that seems so long ago, over a year now. Why do I have to be the one to bring this back safely to our usual, harmless flirting? Probably because of Nonna.* Though she is more or less blocked from my view, my grandmother is dutifully sitting there like a statue, her eyes shut, judging without judging. Even Miss G has forgotten she exists.

I don't know how to respond, I don't know what I want, so I shift in my bed, which creates a dull itch where they stitched me after surgery. But I soon realize, again, why Miss G's gaze is so unwavering, why she's still touching my hand. She thought I nearly died on Paulina Street. I'm part ghost to her. A wave of guilt hits me, but passes just as quickly, because suddenly I feel the magnitude of this gift I've been given. And maybe my gift back is to allow her to *believe* I'm lucky to be alive. *Besides, this is how we should live every day*, I think. *Fuck the truth.*

"You're smiling," she says.

"Am I?" I don't need to explain. After all, it's a miracle I'm even breathing.

We reminisce about our class. I talk about the baseball team I miss and the coach I don't. She asks me about my old man, like she always does when we're talking baseball, like she's waiting for some happy ending for us. Father and son putting aside their differences and walking toward green grass and an infield with a pitcher's mound, where the father will pat the son on the back, and they'll play catch together, or some bullshit scenario like that. I don't say much. She looks concerned.

I ask her about the classes she'll teach this year.

She doesn't answer right away but then she tells me about her schedule.

"How's Mr. Sack?" His real name is Zak, but I always mangle it. He and Miss G team taught American Studies. One time I caught them teaming up in her dark classroom after school. I didn't actually catch them. Sack was leaving as I was approaching the room, and I didn't think anything of it until I opened the door, surprised by the dark. I was about to turn away but then spotted movement and called out her name, like it was a question—*Miss G?*—then felt instantly stupid because I realized what I'd almost walked in on. Her hair was frazzled. I think I heard her mutter, *Oh shit.*

"Mr. Zak is fine," she says.

"Are you still…teaching together?"

"No, that was a one-year thing."

"That must have been tough. Making lesson plans together. You probably had to spend a lot of extra time. After school and stuff. Late nights."

She punches me in the chest with a loose fist. A playful punch. "Anthony Lazzeri, you are a bad person."

Nonna bristles. She doesn't understand sarcasm. No one is going to call her grandson a bad person. But her eyes remain shut.

"I should go," Cecilia says. "I'll be at school the next couple of Mondays getting ready. If you're feeling up to it, stop by."

"I'm afraid I wouldn't be much help."

"Keep me company." She says this innocently, without a trace of suggestion. And then she's gone, promising on her way out to call, to drop off catalogs for DePaul and Loyola, and threatening to break my other leg if I don't apply.

❖

After lunch, my catcher, Perez, stops by. The first thing he does is crouch down to signal a curve ball inside, his game smirk on. Then he breaks out into a wide grin. The only time I've seen him without a smile was when we were freshmen, after his older brother shot himself in the heart. I had never heard of anyone aiming there and not the head. Most guys would crawl inside themselves after something like that, but Perez went the other way. He became more of himself. Wiry and compact, he'd always been intense, but now he strutted with the fuck-you confidence of someone with nothing to lose. If he had any real rage in him, he would have been in jail by now.

"When do you ship out?" I ask.

"Couple weeks."

He's almost a year younger than I am. When his number didn't come up, he took the CTA to a marine recruitment center on Irving Park and enlisted.

"I wish I could go with you."

"Yeah, right, man. Gimp or no gimp, you wouldn't last a month, you pussy."

He rolls his neck around, a habit he picked up from watching Roberto Clementi in the batter's box, but Perez does it all the time now.

"I do. I wish I could go with you. But not to where you're going. We should have gotten another season. With some semipro team, maybe." I want to add, *Where grades don't matter,* because Perez was barely eligible each spring.

"Yeah, well, I gotta go protect us from them commie bastards, you know. Otherwise, they'll be crawling up the curbs on Ashland Avenue tomorrow."

We both roll our eyes at this. "So, you're willing to get shot at. For what?"

"Just something to do, man. A job. Maybe I'll get to jump out of a plane. What else I got to do? Visit some gimp asshole in the hospital? Besides, no use thinking about it anymore. I pissed and coughed and passed my medical. All clear, man. And, if I change my mind, I can always throw myself in front of a car."

Perez is the only guy I've told about my leg. After what happened to his brother, I've always felt a strange obligation to be straight with him. Besides, all the times he's seen me barrel into second base or home plate like a torpedo, my little obsession would've been hard to hide. But I only meant to punish myself, not the fielder, who I always managed to avoid by contorting my leg in unusual ways, which raised the odds of injury.

Perez wants to know how I hurt the leg this time, how I managed not to kill myself. He stands there with his broad smile and bronze skin—he likes to remind you he has Cherokee blood in him—and he waits, because he knows I'll tell him. He knows I won't tell many people...but I will tell him.

With a nod, I signal him to lean closer, so that Nonna won't hear. Then I whisper. I tell him what I've told him before, that when I was a kid, I used to imagine throwing my leg out in front of a passing car.

He rolls his eyes. "Crazy fucking shit, man." But, because he's heard this before, that's all he says because he wants to keep me talking.

"So, I don't know...I was coming home from work, crossing the street, and I see this big Lincoln or something big like that coming my way, and I get the old urge to stick my leg out. But it's more than that. I feel like I have to. Like this is way overdue. It feels right. So I stop. In the street, I come to a dead stop. I'm pretending that I'm waiting for the car to pass so I can cross. I'm timing it. Because if I do it too soon, the car will just swerve away."

"Yeah, you don't want that screeching shit. You crazy fucking bastard."

"I'm waiting...and waiting. And I start to hear this small voice telling me, *You can't do this, man.* It sounded a little like you, Perez. *You can't do this.* My head's down. I can see my leg, and then, a second or two later, out of the corner of my eye, I see the grill of the car right there in front of me, and I know I have to go. Right now. But that voice. *You can't do this.* It kept insisting. I want to throw my leg out but instead I plant it, right there on the asphalt, and it's like bolted there. Nothing's going to move it.

I'm safe, I think. But I still want to shove my leg out, like you can't imagine. So I twist, I do this little twist, because I *have* to lift my leg but I can't, because, you know, it's planted, and I twist some more, and I feel something snap. While I'm fucking standing up, I feel the snap, and I realize...I realize that, by planting my foot, I broke my leg. Standing up. On my own. The car didn't touch me. *What a stupid asshole*, I think. And then I fall, the car long gone."

"They ain't never gonna let you out of here, man. They're going to send you straight to the cellar and lock you up in a rubber room for your own good." He says all this through a bright smile, a gleam in his eyes. "But don't worry, man. I'll visit. I'll bring my glove and you'll get that slider moving again."

He stares at his hand, as if a mitt's there. He pounds his palm with his other hand and bounces on the balls of his feet, like he's ready to play, though I doubt anyone else would have noticed the bounce.

He looks stricken with worry, suddenly, and I instantly know why. Amid his joking, he realizes what we've both known for a while. That we'll never play together again. The reality of his leaving, and my fractured leg, overshadows our talk of insane asylums and self-inflicted injuries. With any luck, he'll return home whole, and my leg will heal, but we'll never be what we once were, two guys on a sandy diamond surrounded by a blur of dust, the short path from the mound to the plate the only thing real to us. That we had those days seems like a dream to me.

He slides to the nightstand and opens the drawer.

"What are you looking for?"

He finds a deck of cards.

"Listen," he says. "If you feel like throwing your sorry ass in front of a car again, take this instead."

A shiny square appears in his palm. It looks like a tattoo of a cartoon cat. He slips the square inside the deck and closes the flap.

"Just put it under your tongue and let it dissolve. Make sure you got nowhere to go for a few hours."

I start to protest. But I figure I can bury his little gift in the trash after he leaves. He tells me to take care. I tell him the same, though we both know it's too late for that.

❖

After dinner, Mom brings me a bag of Hershey's Kisses, licorice strings, and two newspapers—one early and one late edition—so I can read Royko first, then check sports, a habit I picked up from my old man. If someone on the Tigers or Cubs is a home run leader, I'll go straight to that, then the box scores. I can tell Mom won't stay long by the way she hands these things to me, like obligations. Or maybe she thinks I'm turning into my father. Which is why she's hardly home anymore. She stays most nights with her sister, who lives closer to work.

She looks ready to collapse. She's been a nurse all day. Her chestnut hair is matted, her powder blue scrubs smudged, one heel of her hospital shoes splashed with what might be Mercurochrome or blood.

"How's the leg?" she asks.

I push aside my annoyance—or try to—that it's taken her, *a nurse*, five minutes to ask. I keep looking at the door, expecting Ellie to show up.

Where's Dad? I want to ask. But it would be a cruel question, intended to aggravate her, because this is not the life she envisioned for herself.

My mother's family was connected. Not in the usual way most people think about that. Her father was editor-in-chief for the *Daily News*, when that meant something in Chicago. She and her sister would tag along with their parents to dinners downtown in high-ceilinged ballrooms to honor hotshot guests that Mayor Daley felt deserved hotshot dinners. When she met my dad, who was selling beers out of a tray in the stands at Wrigley Field, her parents made it clear she could do better. He tried to tell them the vending was temporary, that one day he'd be *on* the field. But they dismissed this as a boyish dream, which, in the meantime, wouldn't bring in a single red cent.

He never got the chance to show them. After two years in Detroit Triple-A, and one day before being called up his first time, both her parents died instantly in a head-on collision on South Lake Shore Drive, on their way home from a reception. When the story is told, another detail, delivered with a sneer, is always thrown in. The reception was for some junior statesman from a small country in South America hoping to open a factory in Chicago—as if to highlight some cruel irony, like it would have been worth dying on the highway if the dinner were for the prime minister of Great Britain or something.

My old man, having gotten called up, couldn't make it back for the wake or funeral but promised to take care of my mom. It looked for a while like she wouldn't have to rehabilitate him after all, that he was going to make something of himself. But he'd already begun his boozing. I don't have any proof of this, but I think the drinking took a serious turn around then because he couldn't believe that something good was happening to him. He had to find a guarantee he'd fail.

I must admit, the way Mom glides around the room now is reassuring. She checks the connections on my IV bag, follows the line down to the back of my hand and inspects the needle. She takes my temperature, feels my pulse, and I feel like a boy again.

She stays longer than I expect, looking less exhausted than when she arrived, as if being in a hospital room rejuvenates her. What prompts her leaving is the bolt of pain that seizes my leg, followed by a warm rush through my arm that will soon put me out for a while. I wave and follow the movements of her mouth and feel the warmth of her kiss on my forehead. I almost ask, I almost say this aloud, *Is Ellie coming to the hospital tomorrow?*

3

⬦

amn him, I whisper. It's afternoon. Nonna is at the kitchen counter chopping onions with a wide butcher's knife and doesn't respond. Not that I want her to. Not that she's within earshot. Except that this is Nonna, whose senses have improved with age. I'm at the far end of her apartment, and this is day three on the couch in her living room, which is on the ground floor of our two-flat, and I'm turning a little batty, saying things I don't intend. But I'm not ready to climb the stairs to my own living room and will have to stay a bit longer. I think worse thoughts than *Damn him*, but I bottle these tightly. As in, *Fuck him, who can't even visit his son, who was almost killed by some lunatic driver.* Which could have been true. Even my mom has stopped defending him, though I can see this pains her. And Nonna won't weigh in at all. Because this is her son, Frank, or Francesco to her, who has abandoned his family, and she sees this as her own failure. She seems determined to watch over me as atonement. But then she'll appear out of nowhere to scold me.

I hear a knock at the back and squint to focus. Mr. Lipschultz is at the kitchen door and pokes his melon head into the screen. His smooth head glistens, the silver beard and mustache neatly trimmed, the eyebrows darker, ash gray, like filaments in a light bulb. That's what draws your attention, the way they angle down into a scowling V. Nonna doesn't invite him in. She doesn't say a word, just signals for me to gimp over and shut the door on the bastard. "Damn him," I say loudly. And Nonna—I want to say she scowls, but her face is a permanent scowl—she sneers in agreement and returns to her onions.

Soon, because it's Monday, Nonna will shuffle to the A&P with her pull cart, even though I offer to go for her. She wants to return a sack of flour because it made her bread taste like soap. She will bring along a small loaf as evidence of her case. When Ellie and I were young, we'd help make the bread on Saturday mornings. Since Nonna never measured anything, we'd have to watch closely and approximate what we saw, mixing in handfuls of flour, folding in the oil and yeasty water and eggs, and finally kneading, the most satisfying step, breathing in the aroma with each deepening punch. Before long, we were making bread without Nonna.

I return to the couch and peer out the front window. I can see the spot where I broke my leg, a canopy of branches from the catalpa tree framing it like a stage. No one in Chicago knows the names of trees, but my old man, who got me the job at Streets and San, used to trim branches from the bucket of a cherry picker and, when I was a kid, he'd teach me the names of the trees on our block. That and how to throw a two-seam fastball.

After a while, Mrs. Mazzolini steps out of her house with her own loaf of homemade bread wrapped inside a dish towel. I can tell it's still warm by the way she holds the bread with two hands. She crosses the street and makes her way toward Mr. Lipschultz, who sits on his front porch and now greets her warmly. Madelina, he calls her, though I'm pretty sure that's not her name, the crazy bastard. Mrs. Mazzolini, dressed in her usual mourning black, keeps the entire neighborhood stocked with bread and soup and summer tomatoes from her backyard.

I glance at the clock. Mom is at work. Ellie's at band camp, I imagine. I hardly see her or her clarinet anymore. With the drugs I'm taking, I can't be certain of anything. It's Monday, that I know. The first Monday after my surgery. The last Monday before school starts. Not for me but for Maryann, who arrives an hour later at 3:02. She slips through the front door with a greasy paper bag in hand.

"How's the gimp?"

I hold out my arms for a hug. I'll take a pity hug if that's what it takes. She ignores my outstretched arms and sits on the floor. She touches my leg. I want to touch her sandy hair.

"Stop looking at me like that," she says. "Lately…"

But it's not lately. We've seen each other almost every day for twenty years—minus seven months, since that's how much older I am—and I've always been glad to see her, even when I've been the target of her wrath, which I have well earned. When she went through her pudgy chin and flabby forearms stage in sixth and seventh grades, I didn't defend her from the other boys' taunts. Not ever. Yet, when she thinned out and filled her tops in the right places—and the boys noticed, becoming all awkward around her suddenly, unsure if meanness was the best strategy anymore—I was the one she clung to, the only one who hadn't been outright cruel. She forgave me for my cowardice, which she understood. She still dresses modestly, wearing muted colors, t-shirts a size too big, as if she shed the pounds all those years ago but not the bloated image in her head. How I mistook her for the red halter top the other day in the street, I don't know. I must have been delirious. Or maybe pain makes me horny.

"You know, you should think about a halter top. It's ninety degrees out there. You'd look good in one."

She gives me a little curl from one corner of her lips. Maryann doesn't smile easily. I want to tell her she should get a job as a nurse's aide at the hospital.

"You better get your mind on something else," she says.

We've had sex five times, back when we were seventeen. I still remember the way she gazed at me while she was on top, her shimmery hair tickling my face. There was a yielding in her eyes, but a boldness, too, like what we were doing was an act of defiance. But, after those few times, I couldn't return the solemn promise in that gaze. And I've never told her why.

"Here. I brought you a beef from Santo's. Sweet and hot peppers, juicy."

I tear open the bag and pick at strips of beef pushing out from the bread, then inhale the entire sandwich in about five bites.

She rolls her eyes toward the kitchen. "How is..."

"Nonna? She's fine."

Worry crosses Maryann's brow, then hardens into tired resignation.

"Did you have the phone thing with the shrink?"

I nod.

"So you talked? What did she have to say this time?"

She is Joyce, my pale, anorexic shrink. Sometimes I think she's thirty-eight, other times fifty-eight. If I'd never met her, on the phone she'd be twenty-five. I started seeing her three years ago at the insistence of my mom, who thought I was depressed about my old man's disappearances from our lives, not to mention the real reasons. No, never mention the real reasons. Before today, I hadn't spoken to her in months.

"We talked mainly about my leg and—"

"Does she still believe—"

"She does."

My shrink thinks I suffer from the some kind of "philia" thing, which caused me to blow up in her office the last time I saw her. Like I get off imagining myself as an amputee. And the sooner I come to terms with that, she suggested—very subtly, so tactfully—the sooner I can deal with the desire. "Desire?" I shouted. "Desire?" None of this gives me a second of pleasure. I'd been going to the library myself, doing my own research, and I told her it was like a phantom limb pain, only the opposite. Like my leg is a ghost. If I had a sick obsession to be an amputee, like she was claiming, why didn't I ever think about chopping off my right leg or one of my arms? Why is it always the same leg? And how do I know exactly where the ghost part begins? Give me a black marker and I'll draw a line. The line never changes. But we didn't talk much about this, not this time. I spent most of the call trying to convince her that I wasn't trying to kill myself, that I didn't need to be locked in a padded cell.

"Her latest theory is that it might have something to do with my dad. That my hurting myself over and over again is a metaphor for how I feel about him. That I feel cut off by him. And that makes me want to cut off a part of myself. Literally."

Maryann scratches her cheek, considering. She doesn't want to commit to any one diagnosis because, as much as I've tried to explain this to her, she doesn't understand. I don't understand.

"It all sounds so logical, doesn't it?" I say. "Such a tidy fucking explanation. She can move on to her other patients, now that she's figured this out. But it's all a load of bullshit."

"She's trying at least. And what she said—"

"Is bullshit. I should see an exorcist instead."

"It makes sense at least. What she said is true, right? Even if it doesn't have anything to do with your leg."

"Which gets me nowhere if the two aren't related. Like when she spent months trying to convince me I was identifying with my sister's—"

"Post-polio syndrome."

"Yeah. When I told her I had these thoughts about my leg even before Ellie got sick, I could tell she didn't believe me."

"Did she connect what happened with…anything…or anyone else?"

"Like who?"

"Anyone."

I give her a look, which I don't intend to be mean but must be good at, because she backs off. It seems, sometimes, that she knows what I'm thinking better than I do.

"Let's go for a walk," she says and hands me my crutches.

We step outside and I ease myself into the wheelchair my mom borrowed from work and she pushes me down the block, which turns out to be more treacherous than we imagined, every line in the sidewalk sending a jolt up my spine.

We pass Maryann's ordinary frame house next door, and I think of her mom inside, probably cooking, stirring a wooden spoon, her fingers splotched with acrylics. She paints all morning, then cooks and cleans. Maryann's father, who will arrive home no later than five thirty, is a claims adjuster. How they met and married, I'll never understand. Next door, that sonofabitch Lipschultz, with his tweed shirt, is sitting on one of the squat columns that flank the front steps of his brick colonial, smoking a Lucky Strike. He looks smug, as usual, even more so now as he blows smoke over his shoulder. He doesn't quite stare at me as we pass, he looks a little beyond me in fact, but he knows he's in my head.

Little Marilyn and Rosemarie are playing hopscotch up ahead, and I think we'll have to maneuver around them, but they stop and stare at me, and then at my leg, without a word. As soon as we clear their chalked HOME space, which tugs at something inside of me, they resume their game, and I envy their hopping. Across the street, Jack Hoffman is sitting cross-legged on the sidewalk, throwing lit matches into the parkway dirt and watching each stub burn out. He moved in during the middle of fifth grade and, with his unfortunate name and one poorly timed hiccup during introductions to his class, he never gained footing. Whether it's true or not, that's the story everyone's heard. Jack Hoffman must have seemed an ordinary enough name to him, until he blurted out, "Hi, I'm Jack-off Man." Maybe one day his mistake will seem amusing to him.

Mrs. Weed is in her garden tending to her geraniums and doesn't look up as we pass. I don't know her real name. Her crazy sister, Mildred, lives in the apartment above her, but we haven't seen her in years. When we were kids we used to climb the steep stairs and knock and run. One time, as we were tearing away, I swore I could smell her crazy sister's rancid breath over my shoulder but I didn't dare look back. Every once in a while, when I pass her house, I can still smell that hot breath.

At the end of the block, the kid with the pointy teeth is playing mumbly peg by himself with a pocket knife. He's only a couple of years older than Jack-off Man, and I know that Maryann is thinking that the two of them should play together, while I can see how that would never work.

We cross to the other side and double back, providing entertainment to anyone who happens to be gazing out their window—as I have to push myself up to one foot, hop down the curb, all while holding the arm of the moving chair. Maryann suggests a few alternatives, like her returning to retrieve my crutches, but I ignore her. Soon enough, we pass old Lipschultz again, so I reach across and put my hand on Maryann's, smiling through each jolt from the sidewalk, to let him see she's still my girl, which may or may not be true. He smirks right at me, then slowly surveys the block up and down, all calm and cool.

Poor motherfucking Anthony, he's probably thinking. A big rock through that picture window of his would rattle him, shattering his wife's old chandelier lamp, sending him on his knees looking for clues.

"Stop glaring," Maryann says.

"I'm not."

"What do you have against that guy?"

I always tell Maryann everything, which is usually a good idea. But I can't bring myself to tell her about Lipschultz.

"Nothing," I say.

"Tell me."

"He's an asshole, that's all."

What I don't tell her, what I can't, is what Lipschultz revealed to me years ago, over a period of weeks. Because that's how he works. He drops a casual remark that you barely take in and then another offhand comment days later. He lets it stew until you put the clues together yourself while you're taking a shower or tying your shoes. And what you put together, what you conclude, might not even be true, but it doesn't matter because the idea is in your head now, slowly poisoning you, and you put it there, not him. He just got you thinking about what you knew all along. At least that's how it feels.

We were having our Avers Avenue block party a few years back, and he must have noticed, maybe for the first time, that Maryann and I were more than childhood buddies, because this was around the time we were in each other's pants and could barely hide our pawing.

I was reaching for a grape soda from the cooler and out of the corner of my eye, I saw an arm and a hand and an icy can of Pabst, which I didn't regard as any kind of coincidence at the time, both of us reaching.

"You make a nice couple," Lipschultz said.

"Couple?"

"You and Maryann."

I should have acted amused or mildly surprised. Instead, I pretended to be disgusted by the thought. I played it up. And then he knew.

"Is she Italian?" he asked.

"Croatian and German and something else."

"Because she looks Italian. The same olive complexion as you. The dark hair. I just assumed."

A few days later, I was walking home from summer league practice. Lipschultz was outside as usual. Watering his lawn with a wand sprinkler.

He made small talk about baseball, while all I wanted to do was rush inside to shovel in the stuffed peppers I could smell from Nonna's kitchen. It was a game I played, seeing how soon I could detect what we'd be eating that night. And now Lipschultz stood there, the stench of cigarette smoke in his silk shirt battling with the sweet aroma of tomato sauce drippings.

"Ever imagine what it would have been like if your dad had made it? In the majors?"

"Not really," I lied.

"That kind of life would have suited him well, I think. He's a bit of a...a—"

I eyed him closely, daring him to say *wanderer* or anything close to that truth. Because my old man had been home for a good stretch at that point.

"The other day, at the block party," he said, "I should have minded my own business. About you and Maryann. I just thought...I notice things, you know, that was my job for thirty years, I can't help it...the way you *were* around each other just seemed, you know, like you were together. But, hey, I made a mistake. Sue me."

I waited for him to stop, just a little lull. "Something smells good," I said.

"Oh, that's your dinner, right. Go. I had another thought, but I'll talk to you later. Go on." He turned back to his wand, moving it back and forth so that the water curved in gentle arcs.

"What?" I asked. "What other thought?"

"Nothing. Some other time."

"What? Something about me and Maryann?"

"No, no, no. It's just that a long time ago, I made the same mistake."

I knew he was reeling me in but I'd taken the bait and had to see this through. With my cleats on my shoulder and my mitt tapping my thigh, I waited.

"I shouldn't even be telling you this," he said, and repeated this, as if trying to convince himself. "But one time, oh I don't know... fifteen...sixteen years ago, after your dad had come home from a long trip—this was when he was in the farm system, for Detroit, wasn't it?—I could have sworn that he had a thing for..." He nodded toward Maryann's house. *My father had a thing for Maryann's mother!* "But I was mistaken," he added quickly. "I know that now."

25

He turned to me and our eyes met. He tried to rein in his smug smile. "Just like I was mistaken about you and Maryann." He pointed to his giant head and traced a circle with his finger to indicate what a crazy thought this was, then added a shrug.

"I gotta go," I told him.

And that's what I did. I walked away, not thinking much about what he said because I was so hungry. But when I got inside and started forking down dinner—I was right, stuffed peppers, I can still taste them—I thought, *What an asshole. Why bring up a stupid idea he had fifteen years ago?* And the thing is, he liked my old man. Because of this, I didn't give him, or what he said, another thought that night or the next. None of my damn business anyway what happened fifteen years ago. My dad was home now, he and Mom were getting along. But then my mind started doing its tricks, tunneling back to all the times when my dad and Maryann's mom had talked. He'd call her Mrs. Stitchner, which is what we kids called her, but I never read this as flirtatious at the time. When they were in their backyards, talking across the fence, their voices would become hushed. Or was this my imagination now? Had Lipschultz seen them necking one time? Because he's not the type to speak without evidence, even if it was his own twisted eyewitness account of what he *thought* he saw. Not that I was going to press him.

And then the other remark he'd made. What I'd almost forgotten. That Maryann looked Italian, that we looked alike. *Did he say that exactly?* And the number he threw out, casually, as if to test his memory, fifteen was no accident. He wanted me to know exactly what he suspected, that Maryann and I were more than neighbors, which suddenly seemed plausible and which caused me to lock myself in the bathroom on the edge of the tub, where I could think uninterrupted and piece this thing together, searching in my mind for other evidence while simultaneously trying to dismiss the ridiculous possibility that Maryann and I were—but I never quite allowed myself to finish that thought.

The idea, the suggestion, though, remains a dull impression, restraining me when I reach for her hand. I'm able to push it aside most times and convince myself that what Lipschultz suspects is preposterous. That's the word that always pops in my head. *Preposterous.* I love the sound of it, like I'm spitting and hissing at the same time. Then I tell myself that I don't care what anyone thinks, especially that asshole. But convincing myself becomes a job.

"Fuck him," I tell Maryann now.

She waits a beat. "Yeah, you're right," she says, then leans into me. "He's got some nerve sitting outside his house like that." She turns the chair toward the curb, squaring us toward Lipschultz's house. "Let's go tell him off. Right now."

Suddenly, from across the street, we're facing him. He's gazing straight at us. She pushes me forward a step, then another, waiting for me to joke back. When I don't, she begins to pull back so we can finish our walk. But I grab the wheels and lock us in place with my grip. I haven't seen our houses from this angle since I was a kid. My apartment is the tallest of the three, but Lipschultz from his attic, his little spy loft, would have a good view of our backyards. He could have seen my dad and Mrs. Stitchner down there one sticky night, when they thought they were alone. My old man's not the most careful guy in the world.

I meet his gaze, determined not to look away. "Let's go," I say. "Let's go talk to the old bastard."

4

⬥

"hat did you see, you old bastard?"

I've crossed the street and I'm at the foot of his concrete stairs, gazing up. I can feel Maryann tugging at the chair. Lipschultz doesn't respond. He doesn't move. Only his eyes shift, from the wheels of the chair, to my eyes, then to Maryann.

"Fifteen years ago, what did you see?"

From behind me I hear, "Anthony…stop." Like a mother scolding her child.

"Out for a walk, are you?" His voice is gravelly, like these are the first words he's spoken all day. "Good to get some fresh air. Must be hell, cooped up all day."

He does something with his eyes. He shifts them back and forth again, but more deliberately, with a message this time. He's saying, *Do you really want to talk about this in front of her?*

"Don't change the subject, you sonofabitch."

"It's the medication," Maryann calls out.

And, in part, she's right. The drugs have fogged up far corners of my mind having to do with inhibitions—I say whatever the hell I want, though I already want to apologize to Maryann—but they've also cleared away a layer of murkiness that I was never fully aware of. Sitting there, I realize with a clarity that astounds me why no one shuns the old bastard and his petty bullshit. Because they're afraid of him. Because they don't want to become targets themselves. Better to placate, to take his side.

"Go ahead," I say. "Tell her. Tell her what you saw, what you think you saw."

It's not fair to drag Maryann into the middle of this, I think. But I can't stop myself. It's like I believe the stories about me nearly dying on the street behind me. And now I have nothing to lose, which is liberating. But Maryann, full of life and all its confinements, *does* have something to lose. She can't know what I'm feeling.

I turn my head toward her but won't meet her eyes. Do I tell her? "He said that he thought my dad...and your mom...that there was, you know, something between them." And there it is, out in the open, with barely a stammer or catch in my throat. I'm heartless. I turn back to Lipschultz to see if he'll deny this.

He doesn't say anything at first, probably hoping I'll dive on my own grenade, which in fact concerns me, so I wait. Maryann doesn't say anything, either. I imagine her steady gaze on Lipschultz's bald head, though I don't dare look.

He takes a short drag and lets out a stream of smoke that doesn't seem proportional to what he inhaled. "I said what... when?" he asks.

"At the block party," I blurt out, and realize my mistake right away. I'm not as bold as I thought. I'm not ready to dig that up, the time when Lipschultz insinuated that Maryann and I looked alike. It's a natural mistake, I think, because the block party is woven in my mind with this other instance I meant to bring up. I ignore the warmth radiating at the back of my neck and plod ahead. "No, I was coming home from baseball practice." I describe every detail I can recall, even the smell of the stuffed peppers, and I realize I'm trying too hard and sounding desperate. Because I have to stifle my fury. Because if it weren't for this rat-faced sonofabitch, I wouldn't have to pull away every time Maryann and I start our whispering into each other's necks, which rarely happens anymore.

"So, you were coming home from baseball practice," he says, "and you stopped? To talk? And, allegedly, I said something about your dad...and Mrs. Stitchner? Do I have that right?"

Allegedly. One of his cop words. He's already writing up the report in his head.

"So you didn't say it? Is that what you're saying?"

"You expect me to remember everything I said…what…about something that happened, fifteen years ago, Anthony?"

Don't use my fucking name. Because that's how he softens you, using your name over and over again, like he has this deep understanding of what troubles you.

We go back and forth like this. Maryann steps away from the chair and inches closer to her house. She's ready to leave me there.

"You mentioned the block party, Anthony. Why'd you bring that up?"

You expect me to remember everything? Yes. Because he thrives on remembering. He remembers and tallies up everyone's weak spots. He's counting on me to back down.

I can lay this out in the open and be done with our little secret, but I know I won't. Because I still hold out hope that I can push his little suspicion about Maryann and me out of my own mind. But I don't think Maryann could ever do the same. Plant the idea that we're related in her head, and she wouldn't be able to look at me. And definitely not touch me.

"Let's get out of here," I say, puffing my chest but sounding small. What would Perez say? *This piece of shit ain't worth my time.* But I know I can't pull it off like he does, so I wheel back and feel Maryann's hands take charge. She has a few questions, I can tell. One being, why didn't I tell her what Lipschultz said before? Also, I fear she heard the retreat in my voice when Lipschultz mentioned the block party, and she'll want to know why.

She wheels me to my house but doesn't help me inside. She barely says goodbye. A muttered "See you," is all I get. All I deserve.

5

❖

as it been two weeks or three? I'm not sure, but I'm striding catlike on my crutches now. At least that's how it feels on this Sunday morning as I glide from room to room in Lipschultz's house. The gliding reminds me of a baseball swing in reverse. One long lunge with the crutches, my arms straight and stiff, my body swinging forward, then the loose curling into myself, ready for the next thrust. I try to imagine that all this happens in time with my heartbeat.

The rooms are more cramped than I pictured, or everything looks that way because I'm feeling lightheaded, wondering what the hell I'm doing there. And I'm out of breath after playing dead on Nonna's couch for so long. I take in everything in flashbulb glimpses. The linoleum kitchen floor, a single sheet designed to look like flecked mint and cream tiles, something you'd see in a barber shop. On the counter is a pot of coffee and a jar of instant Coffee-mate creamer, two half-eaten green bananas, and a loaf of homemade bread with the heel torn off. The refrigerator has an arched door that reminds me of Nonna's old icebox, with not a single magnet attached to it. On the wall next to the fridge hangs a tear-off calendar from Giuseppe's Shoe Repair with a picture of a kitten toying with a ball of yellow yarn. Tacked next to the calendar is what looks like a drawing of our street, boxes with all our names on them, first and last, a kind of map, which both puzzles and excites me because I'm looking for—

I don't know what I'm looking for. All I know is that I've been feeling the press of Lipschultz's thumb on me for too long, and I yearn—I don't think that's too strong a word—I yearn for something on him, some piece of dirt that will turn our block against him. Or maybe I'm just paranoid from barely having slept for days. But I already sense I'm wasting my time. Because it's just a stupid map. He's old and senile and needs to keep track of who's who, that's all. I've seen the confusion in his glassy eyes as he searches to ground himself.

I swing into the living room. No question it was his wife's room, left untouched after she died. It smells of polished wood gone sour. I'm not sure why, but I take in everything more slowly. The chandelier lamp with a lace doily underneath. A china cabinet filled with cups and saucers and other porcelain pieces that I've never known the names of, not to mention their purpose, all of which have probably never been used. Some of the cups have eggplant purple leaves painted on them. On an end table, next to the colonial-looking couch, sits an emerald-colored glass ashtray, which is clean. Connected to this room is a den. This is clearly where he spreads his fat ass, on the large cushioned couch facing the television, which also affords him a glimpse of the sidewalk and street. These three rooms—the den, living room, and the kitchen—form an L.

A short hallway off the kitchen leads to the bedrooms, but I realize I have to piss. I glance at the back door, my escape, which looks inviting. I can slip into the alley and be home in under a minute to piss and forget this craziness. Some people might call it breaking and entering, which is what Perez called it when I asked if he would help. "A Puerto Rican kid caught inside a cop's house? I don't think so," he said. I asked if he would be my lookout then, just wait in my room and call if he saw Lipschultz coming home. He eyeballed me like I was out of my mind, a look I've seen before, so I backed off because I didn't want to strain our friendship weeks before he left for training. I didn't ask Maryann, who would be all logical and levelheaded. She'd want to know what was really bothering me. She'd want to talk to me about my *alleged* comments to Lipschultz.

What I did instead was this. I forgot about it. I really did. But then this morning, after the third restless night in my own bedroom, I glanced out the window, wondering what day it was. Along the street, everything was still. And all I felt was a numbness. After a while, a sound began to register, the church bell from Our Lady of the Angels was ringing, had probably been ringing for some time now. Only now was I becoming aware of it and then realized it was Sunday. That's when the idea hit me, maybe I'd been dreaming it, I don't know, but it seemed like divine inspiration, which was fitting. The idea tumbled out of me fully formed. The bell clanged at nine o'clock. Lipschultz had been an usher at the nine thirty Mass since forever. When he left for church, I thought, I would make my way into the alley, and as long as no one was pulling a car out of the garage, I could easily sneak into his backyard, where I'd find a key in a flower pot or under a mat, somewhere obvious, because no one would dare violate his privacy. I sat down on the cold radiator, trying to calm my nerves, because I knew that once the idea floated there in my thoughts it would be hard to dismiss. I stared at the floor, letting my eyes blur. After a while, the image of Lipschultz's bulldog son, George, took shape in my mind. I remembered him reaching high, straining to reach the ledge above the window for the back door key. I must have been sitting in Nonna's kitchen that day and stored away this little secret. Old Lipschultz probably never even knew the key was there.

In the hall, I passed my sister, Ellie, who was reading, and asked her to play a game. To sit near the front windows and look down at the street and to call the number on the sheet of paper I gave her if she saw Mr. Lipschultz coming home. She smiled and nodded, but said nothing, looking forward to this game we were going to play. She had on her school uniform, a plaid skirt and white blouse. I wanted to remind her it was Sunday, but she seemed content with her book of saints she'd gotten one Christmas, so I didn't say anything. I knew I wouldn't get a call, but I felt assured anyway to have her looking out for me.

Five minutes have passed now, but it seems like another day.

A splash of sunlight pours through the crescent window in Lipschultz's kitchen door. I have to leave or piss. I take a couple of weak strides toward the door, feeling like an idiot for getting this far and giving up because of my bladder. But I know if I leave I won't return, so I head back toward the hallway leading to the bedrooms to find a bathroom. Everything smells stale here, and it brings to mind boiled cabbage and unmade beds. I squeeze into the narrow bathroom and don't quite close the door behind me and sit on the toilet, which is habit for me, even when I'm only peeing. I discovered many years ago that if I sat, I wouldn't have to stop reading. The stench of stale cigarette ash cuts through the smell of aftershave cologne and copper plumbing.

I have to piss so hard that the initial blast offers no relief. I sit there in the partial darkness with my eyes closed, trying to will myself to piss faster so I can have a look around and get out of there. That's when I hear something at the back door, a small rattling, followed by a creak. What the hell. They're not even at the homily yet. A light step, which is small reassurance because there's nothing light about Lipschultz. But, fuck, I'm dead. A bright thought hits me. At least I'm in the bathroom. I can claim I was passing by the house and couldn't wait, what with my crutches, which is more than ridiculous but it's something. I should have listened to Perez. I'm not able to stop peeing, that's how full I am, but I direct the flow to the side of the bowl to silence it and I hold my breath and wait for someone to slam open the bathroom door. I will myself to stop finally and shake myself off because I refuse to get caught with my pants down. Balancing on one leg, I gather myself and zip my pants, all without a sound, and wait, ready to use my crutch as a weapon. Against what? A cop's gun?

"Anthony?" A small voice, a whisper. But full of reprimand. Please be my imagination, I pray. Please be my sister. But another soft step tells me it's Maryann. Will she be madder knowing I broke in or that I didn't confide in her?

My first impulse is to wait her out, let her think she's mistaken, but she must have seen me.

What else can I do? I flush.

"Just a minute," I call, relieved that my voice doesn't waver, though it sounds a little pinched.

I flip on the light switch and glance in the mirror. My hair is disheveled, my eyes are rimmed red. I touch my bristly chin and vow to shave when I get home. My right brow always rises higher than the other, like I'm trying to be a smart-ass, but it doesn't match how I feel, though it may serve me well now. I try to relax my face to see what Maryann will see in a second, but it's no use. She will never see what I see.

I wet my hands and dry them on the hanging towel and wonder if the towel will still be wet when Lipschultz gets home.

"Did you need to use the bathroom?" I call out mid-stride, as I turn the corner and meet her eyes.

"What the hell are you doing here?" she asks. She's not as angry as I expect. Surprised, yes, but if I'm reading her correctly, thrilled a little, too. Her voice is the one that wavers, which stirs and excites me. For a flash, I imagine us entangled on the colonial couch, tugging at our clothes, rushing to finish before we get caught. *Pray for us sinners.* I glance directly at the couch now because I can't recall if it has plastic cushions, which it does not. I keep all this to myself, of course. I'm crazy but not stupid.

"Would you like something to drink?" I try.

"Anthony, stop. You have to get out of here."

I open the fridge, more out of curiosity now than to deflect her pleas. I steal a glance at a stack of TV dinners, a crusty bottle of mustard, a half loaf of Wonder bread, two cans of Schlitz, before Maryann pushes the door shut again.

"If my grandmother saw what was in there, she'd have a heart attack."

She pulls at my hand, gently, as if she's trying to coax a small child to follow her. "Come on, let's go."

The black hour blades on the copper-rimmed wall clock read 9:51. No second hand. Lipschultz is walking around with his basket about now, collecting envelopes and crumpled singles, along with the occasional five. I imagine him stealthily pocketing a handful of bills before dumping the basket in the iron strongbox at the front of the church.

"Anthony. Do you understand? You could go to jail for this."

She mouths each word slowly so I'll feel their gravity, and I'm moved by this.

"Hey, when I go to confession, I'll have new material," I tell her, though I haven't been to confession in years. "I'm getting tired of the same old sins. Disobeying my parents, lying. I think the priests are getting tired of my lame list, too. So, what I'm doing here, this will be good. I won't tell them which house I broke into, of course, 'cause no way they're going to keep that to themselves. But you know, I didn't technically break in because the key was right there, above the door. How many Our Fathers and Hail Marys just for looking around, do you think?"

"Anthony, please."

With Maryann here, I feel confident. If it weren't for her, being there for me all these years, I'd probably be locked away in some institution by now.

"Did I ever tell you…" I sag into the crutches and dip my head so that we're close to the same height. "That you have sad eyes?"

She becomes exasperated, which is much less alluring than the sad eyes. I want to tell her about her smooth, creamy neck, too. And her high cheeks shaped like apples, her curves…that I want to caress. Actually, I don't want to tell her this last part, I just want to do it, to reach and cradle the side of her face. I'm beginning to realize that my breaking in has something to do with boredom, with my need to feel…something and, with Maryann standing next to me in this strange kitchen, whatever excitement I happen to feel I direct at her. Whenever I can put aside my stupid apprehension, about *us*, and simply want her, I mark this as a good sign. Which helps me realize another thing—that the reason I've come here is to look for clues that Lipschultz is full of shit. Because if he is, then I can dismiss anything he's ever said to me about anyone I care about, namely Maryann. But what clue could possibly tell me this? Don't I already know he's full of shit? Sure, he's a fuckhead but he's a particular kind of fuckhead, who doesn't need to invent hurtful stories because the world is pretty much screwed up as it is.

"Can you tell me?" she says.

"Tell you what?"

"What it is you're looking for."

I glance around, as if I'm trying to decide, which is not inaccurate, and start to sing. "Feed your head…feed your head."

"Anthony."

I keep singing.

"It's not feed, it's *keep*. Keep your head." Correcting me is a ploy. She thinks I'll get distracted and stop this nonsense.

"That doesn't make sense," I say. "It's *feed*. As in, feed your head…with dope."

She bristles and tugs at my arm again. "No, *this* doesn't make sense. Standing here in this kitchen makes no sense. Let's go."

I hobble away from her and make my way to his bedroom, where pajamas and buttoned shirts and wads of tissue are strewn along the scuffed pine floor. On the nightstand is a glass tumbler that looks to have some kind of solution in it, for dentures maybe. Next to that is a taller glass with a swallow of whiskey left in it. I expect another tug, but I glance behind me and discover that Maryann hasn't followed me. I slow my breathing to listen, hoping she hasn't left, but I hear her pacing from the kitchen to the front window. My lookout.

Poking out from beneath the bed is a baseball bat and a Playboy. If Maryann weren't in the kitchen, I'd study the centerfold. I turn to the double doors of the closet, thinking as I ease them open that they're booby-trapped. Inside is nothing unusual, other than a carton of bullets on a high shelf, which chills me. I push aside the row of pants hanging on the lower rack and, at the back, on the floor, are two plastic boxes, the kind that hold file folders. I crumple down and sit and slide the first one toward me. I'm about to open the lid when I notice the stack of Playboys in the back. I thumb through the dates, realize they're not in any order, then stuff one of them in the back of my pants, and return my attention to the box. The file folders are cadet blue with a Chicago Police Department seal on the outside and scrawled handwriting on the tabs. I open one, and a mug shot of Mrs. Weed stares back at me. Apparently, she got her nickname from something other than planting geraniums. Two separate arrests for possession and distribution of marijuana. Another folder tells me that little Jack-off's father likes to exceed the speed limit. No pictures this time. Just the citations. I stop and turn to the alarm clock on the nightstand and tell myself to breathe. The clock's ticks are heavy. How the hell does he sleep with those ticks next to his pillow? I have maybe ten minutes.

I rifle through a few more folders and realize he has the whole neighborhood in here, if not for violations, then notes he's written down about everyone. Which would include me. Why this doesn't dawn on me immediately I don't know, though my slowness might not surprise anyone else. I pull out "Ant Lazz" and tear it open and find that it's bare. I shake it out and feel like an idiot because there's nothing to shake out. Instead of relief, I'm filled with dread. His suspicions about me are so dark, he can't put them in writing. I hear the damn clock ticking and find my mother's folder, which is light. A ticket for blowing a stop sign, another one for running a red light. My father's is more sturdy. Drunk and disorderly. A sheaf of moving violations. Drunk driving. I'm familiar with his work, so I stuff the file back and push the box back to where it belongs amid the cobwebs.

I pull the second box out. Inside, there are no names on any of the tabs. And I soon realize why. Every one of the files is about me.

Maryann

❋

With Anthony, you have to be patient. You can't scream at him to get out of the house already, because if you do, he'll get this faraway look and shrink into his shoulders and move slower. So, you coax and plead and try to kid around, but he still won't come out until he's good and ready. But at least you haven't upset him. Because the last thing you want to do is upset him, after all he's been through. You never lose sight of that.

So, you stand in the living room that smells faintly of liniment and dried sweat and become his lookout and hope he has enough sense to find what he's looking for fast and get out. You think about bluffing, calling out that you see someone coming, but you don't want to alarm him.

When he finally scrapes around the corner, his eyes full of worry, you want to ask what's wrong but you head for the door instead and peek outside. A sunny day. Everything still. You feel the throbbing of your heart in your wrist as you reach toward the screen. And you pause, your hand poised on the handle. Because, if someone spots you, how do you explain this? But you step out anyway because you have to, you can't very well stay, and you hold the door open, hoping Anthony will follow, which he does, thank God. He locks the door and returns the key to the high sill.

You go to his house because no one's home, no one's ever home, and you pace while he locks himself in his bathroom, the sound of ruffled papers scratching your curiosity. He comes out empty-handed.

"What's going on?"

"Nothing."

"What did you take?"

"Nothing."

"Anthony."

He looks defeated because he knows he can't hide anything from you, then turns back to the bathroom. The linen closet door opens and closes, and he returns flashing a *Playboy*, hoping this and his sheepish grin will appease you, but it does not because you don't care about that.

"What else did you take?" you demand.

He stammers and balks and swings to the window and shoots a glance at the street, and when you insist, he slips away again and returns a second time with a file folder, which he places on the bed.

And then you understand. Then you wish you hadn't asked.

※

Bad things happen. And usually there's no one to blame. Even when there is, you still have to live with the bad thing. Which is hard enough without getting into why.

But it's a favorite topic for Anthony. If there is a God, he wants to know, why does he allow bad things to happen? To you, it's not a question worth asking because you can't come up with any real answer. Besides, Anthony's pretty good at twisting anything you say. If you give him the standard line that he wouldn't appreciate the easy times if it weren't for the hardships, he rolls his eyes. And that other line about things that don't kill you make you stronger, that one infuriates him.

The other day, Richard Speck was in the news again, the one who killed those eight nurses not too far from here. Anthony says, "So you're telling me the world needs that, that piece of shit, that speck? So we can appreciate...what?" Then he spit on the sidewalk, like he wanted to rinse his tongue.

41

Sometimes you want to scream. But you never do. Not because you disagree. But because you've known him your whole life and you know every pain, every grief he's ever felt. You know the source of his stubbornness and why he refuses to move on.

You try to remember what he was like before the fire. What everyone was like. Because every grief goes back to that. But it's like the fire destroyed your childhood. Not so much that it shattered innocence, though it did that, but it's as if you never existed before that. Because the fire defined everything. And still does. Not just you and Anthony but the whole neighborhood. And not just your neighborhood, but block after block. The whole city. Everything reeked of wet ash for days.

At least this is what you think you remember. If only you could ask. Anyone. Just to confirm. A simple question. How long did the smell last? But no one wants to talk about it. Even right after, no one wanted to talk about it. At least not to you. The two of you didn't know any better and kept your mouths shut. You do remember the coats, rescued from smoky cloakrooms and returned to parents, some of whom made their kids wear them for years because those big coats cost good money. But no amount of washing could remove the stench, and you want to scream, *Can't you smell that? Burn those damn coats.*

After his sister's funeral—nine years ago, you still can't believe she's gone—you and Anthony would sneak newspapers under your own winter coats, just so you could find out what happened. Who died? Who moved away?

December 1, 1958. The worst school fire in the history of Chicago, ninety-two children and three nuns dead, and no one said a word. At church, you would lean forward at every pause in the homily, thinking, now you'll find out. But no explanation ever came, only pleas to pray for the dearly departed. After a while, because it was too painful, the crowds thinned out at Our Lady of the Angels. Some started attending Holy Trinity instead. But many stopped going to church altogether. People moved away.

When they thought they were out of earshot, you overheard neighbors talking about the cause of the fire. How it started in the basement, near the boiler room. Some blamed the janitor, Mr. R, who could have kept the room neater, which meant safer, you suppose. But those who knew him always defended him. And because no charges were ever brought, he was quickly forgotten, and then he moved away, too.

Apparently, the police had a theory. A fairly specific theory. One that involved Anthony. At least that's what the two of you were able to piece together last week after sifting through the file folder Anthony had stolen. Inside it were school pictures of him and one of his school friends, Robert, along with their grades and disciplinary notices. Robert had a long record of unruly behavior, from fighting in school to setting fire to a cat in his backyard. Stuffed into this same folder were newspaper clippings about the fire, confidential reports, and most curiously, a timeline the police had created on where teachers and students were just prior to and after the fire. Robert's and Anthony's whereabouts were detailed, penciled arrows drawn from one to the other, and it all read as if a case was being made against them. Both of them were in charge of bringing down the wastebasket from their classrooms at the end of the day. They both would have been downstairs near the boiler at the very moment the fire started. You have to admit, it all seems convincing. Robert was always a troubled kid, angry and explosive—you never liked him—and he had the opportunity to start the fire. Provided the timeline was right. And Anthony was his friend. He could have helped in some way. Not that you believe that. Or he could have known about Robert's plan and said nothing? Which is understandable because who would believe that someone could do something so horrible?

You've had the folder for almost a week now. You've gone to the library to copy several of the pages. You're waiting for Sunday so that you can put the folder back where it belongs. Some things should stay buried. Though you're not sure this is why Anthony wants to return the pages. You're afraid he wants to look for more.

Every time the two of you read through the folder, you become quiet. The air around you thickens. Your voices become hushed, as if you'll disturb the dead otherwise. Which is quite possible for Anthony. Because he still sees her. She's still with him. His sister, Ellie.

6

❖

I smoked my first joint when I was fifteen, supplied by Perez after a 12-1 pounding by a South Side team of gorillas that seemed to know what I was throwing before I did. We were sitting on the bench in some park off Ashland Avenue. Everyone else had taken off. Perez and I were going to take the CTA home, and we were taking our time unlacing our cleats, trying to figure out what had hit us. Finally, Perez shrugged, sifted through his bag, pulled out this wrinkled, twisted cigarette, and handed it to me. Actually, he pushed it toward me, waiting for me to reach for it, but I sat there staring. Cars rolled by, the sun was high in the sky, and there we were, in the middle of a park full of people, with a joint in plain view. Though I'd never smoked one before, I knew what it was. Was curious, in fact. I leaned over, pinched the joint, and expertly concealed it in my palm, as if I'd done this hundreds of times, and waited. After he lit the joint and I'd taken a few drags, I thought, this could be the beginning of a long friendship, not with Perez but with *ganja*, feeling proud that I'd dredged up that word.

But two curious things happened. My sister, Ellie, didn't approve. Not that she ever said much to begin with. Yet, she was always there. Anytime I needed her. But suddenly she wasn't. I didn't connect this immediately to my smoking, maybe because the pot was causing me to care less about her disappearance. But during a moment of clarity, having gone days between lighting up, I realized. I sought out Perez and we got high so I could dull the ache of not seeing my sister. Anyone else could have pointed out the obvious flaws in this logic, the smoking only pushing her further away, but that's how I was thinking. After that, I quit. And waited. The longest three weeks of my life. I've never viewed myself as deranged or loony, though I probably should, but those three weeks of cold sweats in the morning, over what I might have lost, got me thinking that maybe I belonged in Dunning with all the other certified lunatics. When she finally returned, I realized the second curious thing. High, I no longer obsessed about my cursed leg. In fact, I barely gave it a thought, just as one might not think of an arm or a finger that was operating perfectly fine. I knew I faced a choice and was racked with guilt for even considering the pot over my sister—besides, why would she care, she was dead—but in the end, I needed my sister more.

Lately, here's what I keep thinking, which is idiotic. I keep thinking she can give me clues to how she died, like she's some phantom that exists outside my own skull. Though she's real enough.

"Do you remember anything?" I ask. "Anything at all?"

I'm in my bedroom.

"You really want me to remember? You really want me to relive those horrible moments?"

She looks placid, with her pasty smile and downcast eyes, as if she feels sorry for me. *You're pathetic*, I know she wants to say.

It's afternoon, but I've forgotten what day it is. I need to get a calendar in here, pin it up on my bedroom door, make plans.

"I found this folder."

"You *found* it?"

"Yes, I found it. But I should have left it alone. After all this time...it's like I swatted a hornet's nest. I should have...I'm worried."

"That people will think you had something to do with..."

Yeah, I'm worried what people will think. That I started the fire. Because you hear of old cases, how the arrest comes

46

later. I'm not sure what would be worse, going to jail, or people believing I killed all those children.

I gaze out my window that faces the street. The police did interview me right after. I'd been out of the classroom, helping to move boxes out of a truck. They wanted to know if I'd seen anything, if I'd been with the other boys near the truck the whole time. They wanted to know if I took down the wastebasket at the end of the day, like I usually did.

"So, you're worried...about yourself?"

"I wouldn't do well in jail."

"Why don't you tell them what you know?"

"I don't know anything."

She smiles.

I could use a joint, I think.

"You're going to have to let me go one day, you know."

I stare at my cast. Three more weeks.

"Why do you keep me around?"

Lately, she's been glaring at me. I struggle to my feet and balance on my good leg, reach for my crutches, and trudge down the stairs and out the door. She skips along behind me as I make my way to the corner store on the next block, where I plan to buy a sheet of candy buttons and sit on my front stoop and pry them off with my mouth, one by one. Ellie and Maryann and I did this more times than I can count, comparing the colors of our tongues.

"You should call up Perez. He leaves soon. He can bring you something. To help you relax."

It feels good to be moving. With each step, I lunge so swiftly that a breeze sweeps through my hair.

"It's not your fault. You were just a kid. We were all just kids."

I guess you could call what I do now running. And I know that if I keep up this pace I will fall. But I don't slow. In fact, I pump harder. I can barely hear her. I need to leave this neighborhood.

"Go easy on yourself, for cripes sake."

My chest burns, a welcome heat, but I'm winded. *How can a body get out of shape so fast?* I have to ease up.

"Easy."

"It wasn't my fault."

"That's what I'm trying to tell you."

But her voice is hollow.

I stop, fight to catch my breath, and turn. She's gone.

We were all just kids.

7

Freddy and I, we go long stretches in his Eldorado where we don't talk. It's early morning, overcast, a hint of fall in the air. He breathes in steam from his black coffee, chomps on his unlit cigar, taps the wheel, punches the preset stations on the radio, sings along to Dean Martin, while I stare at the apartments and houses that change dramatically every few blocks. From crisp awnings and ornate railings to porches that sag and windows boarded up with plywood.

Stir crazy, I called him last night to see if I could join him on his rounds. Not only could I join him, but he'd make sure I got paid. I could tally the numbers, he told me, whatever that means. I'll do anything, I told him. I can start saving. Get my own apartment.

"You want coffee, kid? We can stop."

I shake my head and look away, my throat welling up over this...this kindness. What the hell is wrong with me? Lately, I've been feeling like I'm the one who doesn't exist. Like I'm a ghost of myself, who continues to breathe and talk, but like I'm watching myself, too. Struggling to get through a day. Maybe everyone feels this way. And when someone can penetrate my ghostliness, I choke up for a second.

I feel safe next to Freddy. Like there's a swaddling of protection around us that feels vaguely familiar and right. And I can forget... me. I wonder how much of this has to do with his sweetly scented Caddy that cradles and glides, and how much has to do with Freddy's little assurances, the way he runs a comb through his jet-black hair, the other hand trailing for good measure, all without a trace of boasting.

The first few stops are behind asphalt trucks, plumes of reeking smoke from hot tar roiling above the pit. When the men see Freddy, they break out in shit-eating grins and extend their arms in greeting. Freddy makes a big show of avoiding their grimy hands, a game they play. They take one look at me, the cast on my leg, my wiry frame, this kid who hasn't worked a day in his life, and ignore me. My leg can bear weight now, so I'm walking but with crutches, which probably makes me appear more awkward than I already feel. I'd ignore me, too. Freddy carries a clipboard but doesn't write anything down. Instead, as he leaves, he and the men exchange insults about their manliness, grabbing their crotches now and then, a gesture I'm not sure I'll ever master.

Twice, out of the corner of my eye, I think I spot Lipschultz on the street, his big bald head shining like a beacon. A third time, I swear I see his white Chrysler LeBaron creeping behind us, though I still haven't ruled out that I'm mistaken. And I realize I can't escape him.

We drive to the liquor store Freddy owns on the South Side. As I push myself out of the car and scan the other storefronts, checking for LeBarons, I think of Perez and what he'd say. *Oh, man, we're gonna get killed.* I decide to rest my mind, vow not to judge. Though I must admit, this is not a street I'd walk down alone. Bars on windows. An old man with a grizzled beard sitting on the curb with a paper bag between his knees. My eyes are on high alert, but Freddy seems to know everyone, so I plod along close behind and smile stupidly. Freddy turns and says, "A bunch of *mulanyans*," which is crude Italian for eggplant, or black. Freddy, who is Irish, doesn't say this with any derision or sneering. Just stating a fact, as if that told the whole story. Once in the store, I loosen the grip on my crutches, but I've never felt so white.

He marches to the cash register and nudges aside a big woman whose nametag says Melba, who playfully resists. He pulls a manila envelope from the bottom drawer and taps it against his palm. The envelope looks wadded with bills. "Be right back, kid." He slips through the swinging doors at the far end of the store.

Melba glances in my direction, and her smile disappears. She looks through me.

I curl into my crutches, studying my shoe. A Converse high-top, just the right one, of course. It occurs to me that when I lose the cast, this shoe and the one at home, in the closet, will be worn unevenly. This is the kind of thing that drives Ellie crazy, though I probably won't give the shoes another thought after today.

I peek up at Melba and inch closer, thinking *mulanyan* is an accurate description for the richness of her skin. I'm envious. My olive skin looks pale. I feel pale. "That's something about Marshall, isn't it?" I call.

She turns to me, like she's surprised I'm still there.

"Say again," she says. Her tower of hair threatens to collapse.

"Marshall. Thurgood Marshall. It's really something, ain't it?"

"Who is Turgid Marshall?" I love how she draws out *Who*, like the name is a song. I want to let her know how pleased this makes me feel. *She* wants to return to scanning the store for thieves. I take in the smart floor plan, high shelves on the outside, low ones inside. She can see everything. But the store is empty.

"Thurgood," I say, thinking about returning to the Caddy. But I've gone this far. I'm determined now. I swing a step closer. "Thurgood Marshall. Johnson just appointed him. A few weeks ago. The first judge ever...to the Supreme Court...the first *black* judge ever." Then I blurt out what I want to swallow back as soon as I start. "I thought you'd be—"

"What? Thrilled? 'Cause a brother is a judge? You haul your crippled white ass in here and 'sume you know what I thinking?"

My vow not to judge has lasted fewer than five minutes.

"And what kind of chump name is Thurgood?"

51

My back stiffens. "His real name is Thoroughgood," I tell her, louder than I intend. "He shortened it." I tell myself to calm down but a kind of rage or outrage overtakes me. "He's the grandson of a slave, imagine that, and now he's on the Supreme Court and, yeah, you should be fucking thrilled. We should all be fucking thrilled."

"You send that uppity Thoroughgood here to help me with this goddamn register. Then I'll be thrilled." She presses one of the buttons, makes a show of it. The word *pint* appears on a tab in the window at the top. "Or is pushing one of these damn buttons beneath him now?"

"I forgot to tell you." Freddy's voice. "Melba will rip you a new one if you tangle with her."

"I was just toying with him, Mister Freddy. The boy's trying to give *me* a civics lesson."

Freddy belts out a laugh, which turns into a cough.

She hollers over the cough. "He was just about to bring up Brown versus the Board of Education in Topeka, I think. Isn't that right?" All her South Side sass has disappeared. A smile pokes out from one corner of her mouth.

"Melba here is a single mom working her way through law school at night. Might take her ten years, but—"

"Could take me twenty, with the lousy pay I get. You should be ashamed."

"Let's go, Antney. We got *work* to do." And this gets them both sniggering.

I feel like I've been in a Golden Gloves match, my face pummeled, my good leg wobbly.

A man glides in and settles himself before the shelf of whiskeys. Melba calls out the man's name, jokes with him, then turns to Freddy and winks. "You take care of yourself, Mister Freddy." Then, not loud enough for the other man to hear, she adds, "And take care of this boy, too. Tell him he can forgive himself for all that white guilt over slavery. He wasn't there. And, if he was, he woulda done something to gum up all that meanness. I believe that. I can see it in those big brown eyes of his."

I want to hug her, but I can't even look in her direction, just a quick glance before I trudge out. But she's already returned to her scanning.

Back in the car, Freddy can't wipe off his damn smile. He pulls a cigar from his shirt pocket and wedges it in the corner of his mouth.

"Melba toast. That's what you are," he says.

"Thanks for the heads-up."

"How else you gonna learn? Stick your hand in and...Bam!" He pulls at his face and shakes his head, bursting with glee. "You won't forget Melba, will you?"

He puts out his palm and waits for me to glance over. Then his fingers spring shut. "Bam! Like a mouse trap."

"More like a bear trap."

He laughs and, because it's not laced with malice, I laugh along.

She was right about my white guilt, I suppose, though I haven't given this a thought until now. Was I that transparent? She must have smelled it on me the second I walked into the store.

Now that she's brought it up, I'll add white guilt to the dark guilt that already weighs me down. Why not?

I have to rest my mind. I have to stop...

In government class, when she'd get bored, Miss G used to encourage tangents. In the middle of a lecture, she'd turn to the chalkboard and put up a quote and ask us what we thought. The one that comes to mind now is, "I think, therefore I am."

The guys in the back quietly transformed this into, "I fuck, therefore I am," which seemed a fair alternative.

My problem is that I *do* think. I overthink. Yet I still feel myself drifting away. Like I can't grab hold of anything. Or I'm afraid to. I think, therefore I am not.

8

❖

I walk out to the mound and have a yearning to kick up dirt
but I can't, not on one foot. I swing my crutch like a hammer
and punch a little dirt around. It's not the same. I climb the
mound to the rubber and turn toward home plate and lean, like
I'm looking for a sign.

Straightening up, I gaze at the sky, searching for an opening
in the clouds. "How about a sign?" I call out, startled by the
smallness of my voice against the vast field. *Why am I here?*

I'm not looking for reasons for my existence. My concerns
are more immediate. I want to know why I asked Freddy to drop
me off at my old high school. When the bell rings at 2:55 and
everyone clears, I'll trudge up two steep flights of stairs and find
Miss G's classroom. But then what?

Freddy offered to swing by again to pick me up after his last
stop, and I paused, realizing the importance of my answer. "No
need," I told him. And I must have done something with my
voice or my eyes—after spending the day with Freddy, this came
naturally—because he grinned and said, "Some broad, hey? Not
everything down there's crippled, hey, Antney?"

"Just meeting a friend," I told him.

While I wait, I toss a ball against the sandstone bricks of the
school. The ball is practically new, abandoned near the backstop.
I watch it bounce once and catch it with one hand, over and over
again, effortlessly, without a thought, and I'm filled with such

longing. Which hits me in flashes of pleasure and grief. When the bell rings, I roll the ball back toward the backstop.

Inside, the stairs are waxed and more treacherous than I remember.

Near the top, I hear a scratchy voice from below. Miss G is calling my name, her steps a raspy patter, hustling to catch up. But I can't stop because I'm in a rhythm, and to turn now would disorient me. Plus, I like the idea of being chased and soon overtaken. At the top, I turn and gaze down as she emerges into view. My chest is heaving, I'm gasping for breath, and when our eyes meet, I can tell this amuses her.

"You're pretty fast on those things," she says.

She has a book bag slung over one shoulder, a maroon gradebook in her other arm, notes clipped to the cover. Her hair needs combing. Her eyes are raw from a full day's work. One cheek looks redder than the other. But her smile is broad and, suddenly, I know why I'm here. No one else greets me this way.

Between breaths, and while taking in her tweed skirt and cupped white blouse, I answer, "Yeah-uh."

She raps on the cast. "Poor thing." She tugs on my arm, and we start heading for her classroom.

"Why the—?" I gesture to her skirt.

"Observation. By the principal. Thought I should look professional. For once." She glances at her watch. "And I have a post-ob in his office in an hour."

After some back and forth about cabin fever, my going back to work soon, her classes this year, we reach her room, where I take my old seat near the front. As she wipes the chalkboard, talking over her shoulder, it occurs to me that I've never seen her sit. Maybe during tests? Yes, because I'd steal peeks, half hoping she'd look up and catch me.

As I begin to find my breath, I feel heat at the back of my neck. It beads with sweat. "Sorry to drop in. I should have—"

"Stop."

"Long day?"

"Just running up and down stairs all day. I'm still the young teacher. Four different classrooms."

"Do you ever feel...you know...lost?"

She stops her erasing and steps toward her desk. She leans against the front of it, like she's ready to teach class. "What do you mean?"

I scan the charts on the bulletin boards behind her, as if searching for an answer.

She hops on the desk and I think I glimpse a flash of whiteness between her legs that I tell myself to forget about. As my teammates would say, *You wouldn't know what to do with that.* She folds her arms.

"I don't know...lost...like there was a direction or a goal once, and now the only thing left is a faint memory of that?"

"That's what you want? Some direction in your life?"

"I don't know what I want. I wouldn't mind being back in this desk every day."

She smiles and shakes her head. "You don't mean that."

"Maybe not. But there's something about being back here."

"Life always seems simpler looking back."

"Is that one of your lines, you know, when you get bored? One of the lines you write on the chalkboard?"

"I get bored?"

"You know, while teaching. And then we'd discuss the line."

"You think...those quotes were...for me? You thought those lines weren't planned?"

"They were?"

"That's far out. I love that you think that. I really, really do. But no, that's not one of my lines. Though maybe I'll use it. *Life's always simpler looking back.* And I'll give you credit. Put your name next to the quote. They'll wonder who this Anthony Lazzeri guy is."

"I wonder the same thing myself," I say, lightly, so she won't press, though I want her to. She picks up on my reluctance, of course.

"What do you wonder, Anthony? What's going on?"

I point to my cast, as if that will explain everything. But I can't find words. Bright voices from outside, two stories below, interrupt my thoughts. I can't make out what they're saying, but the give and take seems breezy. I listen for a while, grateful for these sounds that poke the silence.

"I feel like...like I'm in pieces." I knock on my cast, like she'd done earlier. "Literally."

"You'll get that off soon, no?"

"Which worries me."

"I don't get it."

"Me, either." I shrug and offer a sheepish grin.

She shoots me the squinted glare she reserves for the annoying student who won't give her a straight answer. Which hurts. And shames me into offering more. Though I don't. Not right away. Studying my leg, I talk about doctors' appointments and itching. She doesn't say a word. She doesn't look away. She wears you down with her silence, one of her teacher tricks.

"In case you haven't noticed," I finally say, "I'm a little self-destructive. It seems like everything I touch—" I happen to look up and see that this pierces her. "What?"

"Keep going."

"I didn't mean to upset you."

"You tell me you want to hurt yourself and you don't expect me to be upset? Well, newsflash, I'm upset."

I catch another blur of whiteness as she repositions herself, but I swear it's because of the movement of her legs and nothing else.

"For the record, I didn't say I want to hurt myself. I—"

"You point to your cast and tell me you're self-destructive. What am I supposed to make of that? Correct me if I'm wrong. Will you do that? But I think you're telling me that you threw yourself in front of...in front of tons of moving steel. Is that about accurate?"

"I wouldn't quite put it that way," I say, hoping to lighten her up. How did we get here?

The glare again. "So how would you put it?"

"A car. A moving car is how I'd put it."

"Anthony," she says, drawing it out, her face twisted in disapproval.

And this is what gets my throat welling up and the rims of my eyes warm. Not my admission, not her realization, but her pity, her disappointment. I take a few breaths to settle myself, to ease the ache in my throat, and I begin to tell her about my leg, stammering and stopping.

"I'm not explaining this well."

She hops off the desk. This time, curious, I do glance as she untwists her legs, my first intentional peek. Then she sits next to me.

I explain again, recounting the other times I hurt my leg. She doesn't say anything, though it's not a trick this time. She's baffled.

"I know a woman," she finally says, certainty rising up in her. "An Indian woman."

"From India?"

"From India. She works on...I don't know how to describe it. Oneness? Body image?"

I gaze in her eyes, blue pools of assurance. She could have said witch doctor, and I would have agreed. "Is that where you buy your pot?"

She shakes her head. "Incorrigible, that's what you are." She gets up and rips off a corner from a worksheet and comes back and writes down a phone number. Hers. She places it in my waiting palm. "Call me and we'll go see her."

I push the rubber tip of the crutch against the heel of her shoe, though what I really want is to grab her hand. "Thanks," I tell her.

When I get up to leave, she pulls my face close to hers and kisses me on the cheek. "Promise me," she says. "Promise me you won't hurt yourself."

I can't get any words out, not right away, but I nod and hug her and vow to stay out of trouble.

When I get outside, a white Chrysler LeBaron is parked in front of the school. Just as I make out the figure behind the wheel, the passenger door glides open, and I realize I won't be taking the bus home.

9

❖

My shrink calls what I do a coping mechanism. When I'm cornered, she says, I turn all philosophical. Which is why, when I make out the shape of the holster under Lipschultz's white shirt, I begin to ponder my existence on this planet. Twenty years is a good, long time. But, in the cosmic scheme of things, eighty years is as much of a blip as twenty. If I can have more, sure, I'll savor every second. Though I know I won't. But the lie is the truth now, with puffs of Lipschultz's rancid breath filling the car. I lean away from him, root down into the upholstery to take in its leathery scent, but it smells faintly of cotton balls soaked in iodine.

Brown clouds scud across the sky, but I can't decipher what this means or what type of clouds they are. Twelve years of schooling and not a single day on clouds.

I could have pretended I didn't see him, but that would have been like postponing the inevitable appointment to the doctor, who asks you to turn your head and cough while he holds your balls. Your balls are his, and you don't dare move.

Lipschultz finally speaks. "I need your help."

He drives northbound on Ashland at an old man speed, gripping the wheel at the proper ten and two. But traffic signals are only suggestions to him. When a crossroad clears, the red light doesn't hold him.

At Belmont, we turn left, farther from our neighborhood, and bump along for a good twenty minutes before he pulls into the cemetery at Cumberland. A cemetery! Fuck. I become Jean Paul Sartre and that Nietzsche guy, and all the other philosophers who ever lived, combined. Those are the only names I know, even though I took a whole class on the great thinkers of the twentieth century. I practice spelling them in my head and, while I do, I remember another one, René something, the one who wrote about thinking, probably because he had a girl's name and had to withdraw into that while the rest of his classmates teased the shit out of him. *I think*, he thought. Yeah, sure, you think. I imagine his parents saying, *Stop thinking and get a fucking job.* Which calms my nerves, thinking like this. About thinking.

We get out of the car and I look over my shoulder, calculating how long it would take to reach the bus stop outside the cemetery gates. But I follow Lipschultz because I'd be an easy target to run down. And who's going to question a cop?

He hands me a map. "I can't read these things anymore."

We find his wife's grave and, while he prays or whatever he does, I can't help noticing a plot nearby with a tarp covering what looks like a fresh opening. It wouldn't be too difficult for an ex-cop to wrestle a cripple into that hole just before closing time and kick some dirt over him.

Back in the car, we head toward home, then pass where we should turn. He fingers his holster now and then, like he wants to remind himself of something. He misses stop signs occasionally. Doesn't ignore them, just never sees them, and I find myself gripping the door handle whenever we approach one. Dusk begins to settle, and we reach the lake and merge onto an access road I've never noticed before at Navy Pier. Except for the gulls circling the trash cans near Bob's Barbequed Shrimp, open apparently from eleven o'clock in the morning to three o'clock in the afternoon, the end of the pier is deserted. Flags flap on the mooring buoys in the distance. Waves crash and recede, as they've been doing for a million years.

When he gets out, I linger inside the car and consider locking the doors. The flags become still for a moment before the wind picks up again. I'd rather he strangled me in the car than tossed me in the lake to drown. I finally tumble out but keep my distance from him and from the edge of the pier. *Cooler near the lake,* the weatherman always adds. This has never really registered before now. A sharp chill laces through me. I search for toeholds, a rope I can hang on to. There's a pay phone in front of Bob's, but who would I call and what would I say?

Lipschultz stands with his hands in his pockets, staring out at the water. Two boats in the distance, almost imperceptible, sail away from each other. When he pulls out his gun, I step closer to the car, but I'm too far away for the car to do me any good. All he has to do now is turn. Twenty years versus eighty. Not much difference. I think about rushing him, or my clumsy version of rushing, maybe tip him off the pier with the end of my crutch.

"Ever use one of these?" he says. The gun is an extension of his hand, like it was made to fit his palm. I've never seen a gun before, not like this, and I can't take my eyes from it. He gestures easily, like an expert smoker handling a cigarette.

I want to answer him, but I can't find my voice. I shake my head.

"Let me ask you something," he says, and turns. "Are you afraid of dying?"

Somewhere low my insides tighten. I shrug, still searching for my voice. When I find it, "Go fuck yourself," springs from my lips.

He smiles, but it's a vacant smile, like I remind him of someone else or another place. "Exactly," he says. "But I want to ask you something, Frank. Are you afraid of dying? Because there was a time when dying seemed like the worst thing that could happen to me."

Frank?

"Now, not being able to shit in the morning is all that matters, you know what I mean? I need your help with something. When I picked you up, there was this pressing concern I had, but for the life of me I can't think what it was. You get that sometimes? And now I finally remember what the fuck I've been trying to remember. A couple of weeks ago, someone was in my house. I kept telling myself I was crazy, no one came in, nothing was missing, but I just know it. I feel it. I think it happened on Sunday when I was at church, and I figured it was someone in the neighborhood, someone who knows me. And…I don't know how to say this… but my cop instinct tells me it was your son. Hold on now, don't get all defensive, I'd be the same way. Hear me out. I just want to scare him, maybe drive him out here and show him this gun to scare the shit out of him, just to let him know I know. Unless you want to handle it yourself. Though I can see why you wouldn't, after what that pussy sonofabitch put you through. I'd stay away, too. Far away."

"So, you just want to scare that little sonofabitch? Is that it?"

"Like I says, I can't prove it's Anthony…but it's him, all right."

"Yeah, like you said, the little fucker put me through hell." I don't dare move.

He turns to the water and takes aim at a bobbing buoy and fires a shot that's not nearly as loud as I would have guessed. "He did do that," he says. "Put you through hell."

"And what would you have done? If you were me?"

"I wouldn't have left, that's for sure."

"So, you think I left because of what Anthony did?"

He blinks, confused. "Want to take a shot?"

Because I don't want to upset him and because his arm is outstretched, waiting for me to reach, I grab the gun, hold it away from me and point it toward the darkening water.

"Go ahead. Take a shot."

I raise the gun, close one eye, and aim at nothing, my finger on the warm trigger. My hand shakes. "I've been thinking," I say. "What Anthony did. It wasn't so bad after all."

"Shut up and shoot," he barks. "Wasn't so bad. Wasn't so bad, my ass. You been smoking that hippy dope?"

I pull the trigger, startled by the force of the kickback. And surprised the gun is still in my hand. "Maybe he didn't do it."

"Like maybe he didn't break into my goddamn house?"

"Well, yeah."

"He did it, all right. That fire didn't start on its own."

Holy Mary. So that's why my father left? Because he thought I killed my sister? I raise the gun again, feel its heft, stare at the barrel, then gaze at Lipschultz. This is the crazy bastard who planted that seed in my dad's head. I'm pointing the barrel right at his heart. But I know there's not a chance I'm going to shoot him. Or at least I don't think there is. He puts out his palm and motions for me to return his gun. I don't know if I will. I don't know the next thing I'll do. For a moment, I savor the power I have and keep my aim steady, my hand a thing apart, a familiar feeling, but I know it's temporary. He reaches out, pushes the barrel away from his chest, and I relinquish the gun. I wonder how many people he's shot. One more won't make a bit of difference to him. I know he won't shoot Frank. But that sonofabitch, Anthony, who broke into his house, who has never given him his due respect? Bang. Pop. Because, right now, no one even knows where that little shit is and no one would know to look for him at the bottom of the lake.

10

⬧

I could be at the bottom of Lake Michigan right now," I tell her. My body is still chilled. My fingers tremble. I order my shoulders to relax but they don't obey.

Maryann drapes a comforter over me and joins me on the edge of her dorm room bunk bed. "You could have been sleeping with the fishes. Is that what you're saying?"

I smile, though it doesn't feel like a smile, and rub my palms together, trying to generate some warmth.

"Tell me again," she says. "What were you doing at school?"

I begin with Freddy instead and rush through my visit with Miss G and slow down at the cemetery and the pier. What I don't tell her is that I had the gun in my hand and no one in the world knew where we were, or that we were together, and that Lipschultz could have been the one at the bottom of the lake. Anything could have happened. What I don't tell her is that, while Lipschultz's flimsy hold on reality may have saved me this time, he's more dangerous than ever, and that if I could go back to the pier, feel the heft of the gun in my hand, I don't know what I'd do. That sonofabitch has left me with that doubt. What I'm capable of. I realize that my fist is balled tight and loosen it.

"I was—"

"You were what?" she asks.

"I was a little proud of my...my quick thinking."

She pulls up a chair and sits across from me now, leaning so she can see my face. But my eyes won't meet hers because I need to think, like I'm alone but not. I stare at the gray tiles, her thick blue socks.

"He was calling me Frank and I didn't want him to drive me home because, once we got back, I figured he'd begin to remember that Frank didn't live there anymore and this would confuse him. So, I told him to drop me off at the El stop on Fullerton. I didn't want him to know where I was going."

"You were afraid he'd find out where you were going?"

"Well, yeah, I didn't want him coming here. I told him I had to go to work. He winked when I said 'work' and then he put his hand up like he had a mug of beer in it and took a swig. 'Ha! Work,' he said, and we shared this…you know…this man to man moment." I glance at the stack of books on her desk. She should be studying.

"And you felt…?"

"I don't know. Like he was suddenly talking to *me* and insulting my dad at the same time…to get a rise out of me."

"You look…confused."

"I am. I'm confused as hell."

"And shaking." She covers my hands with hers. "Go on."

"I'm wondering if it was all one big act. To throw me off or something."

"You think he was faking?"

"He probably has this room bugged."

She looks around. "So, you think he might have the room bugged?"

"What the hell are you doing?"

"What *I'm* doing?"

"You're repeating everything I say." I reach over to the textbook lying at the end of her bed, which I realize I've been staring at. *Treatment Methods.*

"Fuck." I sigh.

"What?"

"You're not going to repeat 'fuck'? Or say, 'you seem upset'? I don't need another fucking therapist." I get up and head for the door.

"Wait. Please."

I pivot back to her on my crutches. "Is that why you're here? So you can study what's wrong with your freak of a pal, Anthony? So you can save his poor ass? Well, I don't need saving."

I turn again and reach for the door. Wait for her to stop me. *Please stop me*, I want to shout. I gaze down at my ratty cast. Of course I need to be saved.

I open the door and step out, wait for the latch to catch behind me. Then it does. I stand there. Feel the pulse in my breath. Down the hall, two girls laugh. They don't even glance in my direction. From the other end, footsteps echo in the stairwell. Someone calls a name I can't make out. I feel I'm missing out. I want to belong. Somewhere. I want to call Miss G and ask her for those college brochures. With my back to the door, I knock. Knock again. A third time.

"Maryann," I whisper. "Open the door."

She does finally. Then retreats to her chair. I hobble back inside and stand near the door. I'll have to earn each step toward her. *I was almost killed tonight*, I want to plead. As if that excuses my callousness. It's a ploy for pity is all it is, which I don't deserve. *I haven't been myself lately.* Also true, but still no excuse. *I could have...hurt someone tonight.* Which may or may not be true, but is disturbing, nonetheless.

"I miss you," I tell her. Surprised.

But she's somewhere else. She can't hear me.

I search for signs of fury. The pinched brow before she's ready to explode. I can handle rage. But her eyes are filled with hurt, with familiar wounds. When her lips begin to quiver, I tear into myself for being so stupid. *How do I always manage to take us here?* I think of all the checkpoints in the past five minutes where I could have veered to avoid this. I could have been more honest, for starters, about why I'd visited my old high school. The stupid selfish bastard that I am, I could have looked at her to see what *she* needed. But too late. Always too late.

Her crying opens something in me. Some crack of murky light. A boldness.

"I have to ask you something, Maryann. I've been thinking about this a lot and I've been needing to talk to someone." I take a step toward her, then retreat to her roommate's desk chair. "I know you hate when I tell you not to cry, so I'm not going to. You go ahead. I'll talk. Tell me to shut up when you can't stand to hear my voice anymore. Too late, I know. What I've been wondering is..." I pause because I begin to choke up, not over what I want to ask, but because I'm trying too damn hard to turn this into an ordinary moment between us, which dredges up a yearning for summer days when I would tumble out of my house in the morning and find her waiting for me on my front stoop.

"Do you...are you different when you're alone? Like you're a different person?"

Please, please...look at me, please. I'll settle for a glance. Not that I deserve one.

"What I mean is...not just this...but for example, are you meaner when you're alone? Like Nonna can be in the room, and my thoughts are all...they're all...tame. Then she'll take off for the store, and I'll be there by myself, and I'll look out the window and all this meanness is unleashed, which embarrasses me. As if I've been playing a role and, once she's gone, my real self takes over. The thing is, I don't know my part anymore. My real self seems...foreign to me. Like someone I don't know will be walking by the house, with two healthy legs, and I'll think, *Well, fuck you for striding around without a worry in your head about your legs.* I'm not really serious, I wouldn't ever say that to the person. I don't feel...anger, but there's a satisfaction I get, and then the mailman will come by and not leave any mail, and I'll think, *Well, fuck you, too.* Again, not really meaning anything, but still. Like I'm irritated with the world."

"Everyone does that," she says, her voice a squeak.

Relief engulfs me. "You? You do that?"

"Well, yeah. And fuck you, too."

We erupt in nervous laughter. I glance at her textbook on the floor, barely remembering tossing it there, and a realization hits me. She's not taking psych to save me, but to help herself. And now I begin to cry. I wipe hot tears, hoping she won't notice, but I can't stop. If I can stifle the sounds of my sobbing, that would be enough, because she won't look at me anyway, but I can't hide that either.

She doesn't move. Only her hands flutter, like she's wringing them. After all we've been through, crying shouldn't be something to hide. But we're both experts at keeping our pain at bay.

"I wish you could see her," I say, barely.

Though we rarely broach this, she knows exactly what I mean.

"I'd give anything if you could see her. If you could feel close to her."

"I do. I do feel close."

We're both sobbing freely now and I scoot over to her chair and sit at her feet and place my head in her lap, feeling her stroke my hair. "It'll be okay," we tell each other. "We'll be okay." Though I'm not sure we would believe this if we were apart from each other...alone.

11

After leaving Maryann, hopping on the El, and transferring to the Division Street bus, I crutch down my block, one painstaking sweep at a time, waiting to be ambushed by Lipschultz. A part of me is hoping for the ambush. Because there's more I need to find out. But only as Frank. Like, did he see me…did he see *Frank*…necking with a neighbor? How did I not think of asking that?

Mom will be asleep, she's used to me disappearing, but Nonna might be up, pacing like a jackal, so I slip into our gangway through the alley.

I slide my key in and ease open the door, but the sound of the crutch proves harder to muffle. Inside, I ready myself for the first step upstairs, then stumble, my knee hitting wood, and I crumple into a crawling position. I'm not hurt, not badly, but in the darkness, despair sweeps over me, which I chalk up to a long day. I'll allow myself a few seconds to wallow here, I decide. Out of nowhere, a memory assaults me. Sneaking up these same stairs, not long after the fire. Around midnight. Because I didn't want to come home. Worrying everyone. I can still feel the first slap at the side of the head. Then a flurry of slaps. The memory becomes a real thing, like it's happening now. Nonna can't stop herself. The slaps begin to sting, but I know that Nonna's callused hand feels nothing. I don't try to stop her, or even glance in her direction, because I know her fury is really aimed at my father.

With each blow, she's thinking, *Non diventare come mio figlio.* Don't become my son. Don't become Franco. After a while, I put up an arm over my ear but her aim is precise, at the side of my head, like she's going to drill some sense into me. I let her finish. Her small hand won't hurt me. She needs this.

When she's done, she walks away without a word, and the memory fades.

I climb the stairs to our apartment, to my bedroom, where time slows, where I can be myself. Where Ellie is waiting, as I knew she would be. Because it's night and because I need her. For years, Maryann has been telling me that I should tell my shrink about Ellie. She says it's like going to the doctor and not telling him you're spitting up blood. She has a point. I don't argue. But I still don't bring Ellie up in the sessions with the shrink. Maybe I'm afraid they'll lock me up, as they probably should. Which is ironic because Ellie would come right with me. Or would she? Is that what I'm afraid of? Mainly though, I keep Ellie to myself because I don't want to diminish anything, like I did while smoking pot. I don't want to be "cured." It's like gazing at a sunset along Lake Michigan. It's enough to see the beauty. Talking about the sunset only ruins it. I'll allow a gasp, a *Wow,* maybe. But, beyond that, I'll become ornery if I try to find words. So, no, I don't want to talk about Ellie.

"Ornery, huh?"

"I...I need this—"

"What? What were you going to say? You need this what?"

"This."

"There was a word you wanted to use."

"Sanctuary. Yeah. Big deal."

"So, this is like holy to you."

"Yes. Some people see Mary. I see you. But you're no saint, that's for sure. You're a pain in the ass lately."

"Pain in the ass?"

"Don't start the repeating. Maryann already put me through that."

71

"Maryann put you through that?"

"Stop. I mean it. Even Maryann doesn't understand. Not really. I can't blame her. My brain doesn't work like everyone else's. If I brought you up to my shrink, she'd call me delusional. But I'm not. I *know* you're not...I don't really believe. Oh, I don't know. If I *am* delusional, it's one goddamn comforting delusion."

"You need to find Dad. That's what's bugging you."

"Why'd you bring that up?"

"You know why. It's all that matters. You don't want him to think—"

"What if he does?"

"You need to tell him. Maybe that's why he...why he kept leaving."

"Like it's my fault."

"Call it what you like. Your fault. Not your fault. But he needs to understand—"

"That I'm not some psychopath?"

"Yes."

"Am I?"

"What do you think?"

"What do you think? What do you think? You're thinking I could've helped set the fire and then forgot, lost myself in some state? That's not my thing. I don't know...maybe it is. I've been through all this with the shrink. I don't forget my leg. It's just not there, not mine. And, with you, I don't fool myself into believing. You're what my shrink calls a *sanctuary* for me. But a source of anguish, too. Like you wouldn't believe."

"Because you think you might have been responsible?"

"No, that's a separate thing. Just the anguish of...of not having you."

"You do. You do have me. For as long as you need."

"But I don't kid myself. I know what's real. I think. How can you ever know?"

"But facing what's real is another matter."

"Facing the truth, or reality…or whatever, is overrated."

"That's a convenient conclusion."

"Thank you."

"You don't talk to yourself, do you? I mean, other than with me?"

"I have to think…I don't think so."

"But you don't lose yourself. That's not your thing."

"You're funny. I just have a bad memory."

"Another convenient truth."

"I guess I do."

"Do what?"

"Talk to myself. Under my breath. I have some of my best conversations under my breath."

"You're crazy, you know."

"Everyone talks to themselves. That's not a sign of anything. I know, I know, I have enough other symptoms."

"Just find Dad."

"Okay, I find him. Then what? It's not like I'm going to convince him to get back with Mom."

"That's not the point. You know that. He just needs to know. You need to know."

"Why he left."

"Why he left."

"And if he left because he thought I was this loser kid who played with matches…then what? I don't even know if I can convince him he's wrong. I don't know if I can convince myself. I just don't remember."

"Forgetting is not your thing, you said."

"But maybe it *was* my thing, back then. Maybe I—and I'm not trying to be funny here—maybe I forgot. Maybe I hit my head and blacked out. How would I know? Or maybe it's like—"

"What?"

"Lipschultz. Does he know what's happening to him, to

his brain? Does he know where he was tonight? Does he know who he was with?"

"That's the $64,000 question."

"I remember that show."

"Because forgetting is not your thing."

❖

Ellie stands guard all night, which means I don't sleep much. I keep waiting for lumbering footsteps, Lipschultz towering over me with his fingers around my neck. If he's lost who he is—in his mind he's law-abiding, *the* fucking watchman of order in the neighborhood—what will that unleash? Some oozing, twisted version of who he thinks he is. Bent on righting wrongs. Namely, me.

12

⬦

No, Frank ain't been in here," the bartender says to Freddy.
Puffing his barrel chest, Freddy turns to me. "Your
old man ain't been in here," he reports, as if I haven't been
standing right next to him.

Our third tavern. Each time our stay gets longer.

When he picked me up, he said, "It's going to be a slow day,
kid." I looked to see if he was joking, but he wasn't. And that's when
I began to drop hints about finding my dad.

He bellies up to the bar and points to the stool beside him. "How
long's it been?" he asks. "Since you seen him."

My eyes are already adjusting to the dim lighting. To the stale
smells of beer and the bleached dishrag slung over the bartender's
shoulder. I wonder if he's Stan of Stan's Tap, but his shuffle tells me no.

"I'm not sure," I say, though I know it's been fourteen months.

"Your mom didn't throw him out, did she?"

"I dunno."

I don't know, my mother would correct, though she has her own
way of twisting expressions, while my old man would boff me
lightly in the back of the head, pretending to agree. They'd never
all-out fight because he didn't have that in him, which riled my
mother. Her fury had no target and, when she tried to battle him,
he became exasperated and left. These days, the main sounds
in the apartment are Mom trying to be quiet, as if she doesn't
want to exist.

"Ever see him angry?" I ask. "My old man?"

He considers this, takes a swig from the wide mug, and shakes his head. "I mean, he'd get all pissed at himself when he couldn't hit the corner on an 0-2 count. Or at Tommy, if he was dicking around in the outfield, not paying attention."

Tommy is Freddy's younger brother by seven years.

"They still see each other? My dad and Tommy?"

"You'd think. They used to tear up the neighborhood."

"So what happened?"

Freddy gestures with his hand, as if the answer is obvious, but then catches himself and returns to his beer.

"Tell me," I say.

"Nothing. The usual."

But I could tell this was far from the truth, Freddy's gaze suddenly turning inward.

"What, he couldn't keep up with my dad's drinking?" And I'm thinking more of myself now. When people catch on that I don't smoke weed or have much interest in getting wasted—I won't say they shun me—but I'm some anomaly they can't figure out and they drift away, which they probably don't even notice. *I have my reasons*, I want to tell them.

"Yeah, I think that's it. Your dad alone could keep this place in business. And Tommy, you know." He stops himself again, reaches for his glass. His thick neck bends forward, like his head and hand are going to meet midway.

"That's not it...is it?"

"Sure it is. Tommy...he's got four kids. He's got no time to booze it up."

To emphasize the point, he takes a shot glass full of whiskey and drops it, glass and all, into his beer and waits a few beats before guzzling the whole thing.

"If I would have said, 'My dad hit on Tommy's wife, right?' you would have said that was it, you sonofabitch. I know you, Freddy. You can't bullshit me."

He lets out a wide grin. But doesn't say anything. Like he's doing me a favor by not telling me.

I don't get it out of him until three beers and another shot later and we're in the car. Ducking my questions has kept him thirsty, it seems. I insist on driving and, to my surprise, he doesn't fight me. Driving with the cast turns out to be surprisingly easy.

We have about an hour to kill before he has to check in with his supervisor, a questionable title, and I've never driven a Caddy before, so I savor the feel of the wheel in my hands, as if all I have to do is think about turning and the car obeys, gliding on air. I almost forget the pressing questions I have about my old man and his brother Tommy and dream instead about buying my own Cadillac Eldorado, black with a gold-inlaid steering wheel, which amuses me.

"What's funny?"

"I'm not giving this car back. This is me."

As we kid back and forth, and I try to tease the answer out of him, I realize something about Freddy that I suppose I've known all along. He needs my approval, though he'd insist he could give a rat's ass what anyone thinks. Some of this is tied up with my father, the star player, with his brief brush with fame, and I've seen this reaction many times with others, as if by associating with me—the son of the star—a sort of fame will rub off on them, too. Or at least they'll have a good story to pass on, about this guy they know who pitched in the majors, cutting me out of the story entirely. Freddy was there from the beginning, when my dad struggled to find his stride in high school, the older guy who was already working for the city and who encouraged my dad to follow his talent, who maybe feels he participated in his success. It's an illusion I know well. But the bigger reason Freddy wants my approval, I think, is because he knows how much I need him. Call it self-centered generosity. Maybe that's the only kind there is.

"So, my dad. Where we going to find him?"

He shrugs.

"Maybe Tommy…you know…would know. But, that's right, they haven't seen each other."

He shakes his head, tries to be deliberate about it, to show he can hold his liquor. But there's an unmistakable, drunken wobble to it. I know I have to bore ahead, before he starts to sober up, because I've seen that kind of sudden jolt, always more show than real sobering but still stubbornly resistant. *I ain't saying no more*, he'll bellow, if I wait.

"I can understand why Tommy and my dad don't talk. No big shocker there. My old man can be a sonofabitch sometimes. I don't blame Tommy. Not one bit."

"It wasn't that. Your dad's an OK guy." He tries to wag a finger to emphasize this, then becomes momentarily enthralled by the finger.

"He's a prick, that's what he is," I say. "A real prick. To drop your best friend like that."

"That's not the way it was. Not that way at all."

"Just because he's my father doesn't mean you have to protect him. He's nothing but a major-league prick and you know it."

"He didn't drop Tommy. It just…happened. After—"

Without realizing, I ease my foot off the accelerator, which gets Freddy looking out his window to see why the car's slowing. Shit. I press down again, back to where we were, ignoring the itch rising inside my damn cast.

"It just happened?" I ask.

"You know…after the fire. Things were different between them. Because my brother, Tommy—" He's lost in his drunkenness now. His voice becomes pinched into a curdled cry. "Tommy, he didn't lose anyone in that fire, you know. His kids—three of them were in school that day—they all made it out fine. And he never knew what to say to your old man after that. There was nothing he could say to… I think he felt like he needed to apologize every time he saw Frank and it became too damn much. Neither one of them could make sense of…

Why this kid and not that one? But, no, Frank ain't no prick. But my brother, he had his moments, let me tell you."

I'm grateful that he goes on about his brother.

My leg is itching fiercely now. Desperate, I search for a hanger I can pry apart to slip inside my cast so I can scratch this spectacular itch, but the only thing in the backseat is this morning's paper. I pull to the curb and stick a finger inside but it doesn't reach anywhere near the source of my turmoil. And I realize that this is no coincidence, this itch. For nearly two months, I've been hobbling around, giving little thought to my left leg. Because it's wrapped in a cast, deadened and useless, which seems right. My shrink would be proud that I'm making this connection, how my leg suddenly comes to life, now, after hearing about my dad, what *he* had to endure. I've never given much thought to him in this regard, as if the fire affected only me. *I lost a sister.* Those words never fail to jar me. But it never fully occurred to me that he'd lost a daughter. His baby. If I were alone, I'd beat myself up and wallow over my stupid selfishness. Or at least the stupid side of it, because I can acknowledge selfishness, which defines me, maybe all of us, though I'm not about to become philosophical. But stupid, yes. How could I have glossed over his pain? Because he rarely showed his anguish...his despair. Whatever the hell he was feeling, dulled by constant lubrication, a low-grade buzz keeping his racking sobs at bay. At least when he was around me. Because, as absurd as this sounds, we'd never talked about what happened at Our Lady of the Angels school on that cold December day...just minutes before being dismissed so we could run home, where we kids would have settled around our console televisions with our hot cocoas to watch Garfield Goose on Channel 9 and listen to the sounds in the kitchen increase in intensity as dinner neared. No one ever talked to us about what happened that day at school, but we did return to the after-school routines. We relied on these routines, even if they were infused with a clattering silence now. I may have even given some thought to another idea back then—that, collectively, we were all sitting in our living rooms, safe and warm, *survivors*, though I wouldn't have used that word, but there would have been this bond between us, which I still feel. Which I will always feel.

My old man had his own routines, I guess, that didn't include me. Or my mother. Or Nonna. Right now, he's probably sitting in some neighborhood bar, watching the end of the ballgame, wondering why those guys and not him, forgetting his part in his short career. Then again, he was never one to drown in self-pity. He didn't believe he deserved the pity, whatever its source. Still, it had to cross his mind now and then, how close he'd come. And then the next thought, to temper his regret, because regret always led to this. How close Ellie had been to getting out of the school that day. His little girl.

I glance again at the paper. *The Daily News.* A foolish idea begins to take hold, but I can't shake it, which is no surprise. Suddenly, I know where I want to go before quitting time.

13

✧

After a week of hopping from bar to bar, all the ones Royko writes about in his column—Blue Sky Lounge, Twilight Inn, and this place, Cullerton Tap—hoping to run into him, I'm starting to feel comfortable on a stool. I finally understand the allure, the brown light pushing away the harsh brightness outside, whether it's sunlight or streetlights. I understand why my old man felt so comfortable in these places. Even the names are intoxicating.

When I finally find him, this is the clever line I come up with, "I could be your legman."

He glares down his beak nose, through black-rimmed glasses, regards my cast, and smirks. The smirk is the same one he wears in the photograph at the top of his *Daily News* column. The same plain tie, though it's loosened.

"I'm serious."

"I already have a legman, kid." His voice is craggy, reed thin, and full of sediment. I'm pretty sure he's not even forty, but he seems ancient.

"I'd do it for free."

This makes him pause. He wipes a thumb down his frosted glass, his fingers gripping the handle of the mug. I'm interrupting his drinking. He's taken one long swig of his beer, and now he has to listen to this gangly gimp kid go on about work, which ended for him hours ago.

"Call the office. Free or not free, I got nothing to do with hiring, kid."

"You have a card or something. With a number on it?"

He shakes his head and seems amused for the first time. "Some legman you'll make."

I slink to the other end of the bar and join Freddy, who's nursing his last beer.

"Who you talking to, Antney?"

"No one."

"No one?"

"Mike Royko."

His brows shoot up. "Mikey's here?"

"You know Royko? You never said squat—"

He slides off his stool and lumbers up to Royko, who seems glad to see him but turns sour again soon after. One of those engraved faces content with misery. He and Nonna would get along well.

After a while, Freddy calls me over. I wave him off, anxious for him to be more insistent, which I know he will be. Finally, I give in.

"This is Antney," Freddy announces.

"My legman."

They ignore me and get around to talking about sixteen-inch softball, which gives me the opportunity to pipe in about baseball—had he ever heard of Frank Lazzeri? Detroit Tigers, sixteen innings pitched, 1.34 ERA—but I remain silent and stare at my right hand, imagining different grips on the ball. Eventually, I decide on a different route. There are plenty of pauses, Freddy plastered, and Royko content with the silence, probably thinking about the column he has to write tomorrow. Or trying not to think about it.

"Did you know Jack Lawson?" I ask.

"Before my time."

"But you've heard of him?"

"Sure."

Jack Lawson was one of the first longtime editors at the *Daily News*.

Freddy joins in. "His grandfadder."

Royko regards me, as if sizing me up, impressed but wary, too. Who knows what kind of reputation my grandfather left behind? Though I'd never met him, the stories I heard made him out to be severe.

"And his old man is Frank Lazzeri," Freddy adds.

Royko shrugs, with the corners of his mouth lowering. The name doesn't register. But he does ask, "Any relation to Tony Lazzeri?" Of the Yankees.

"Distant cousins." Which was probably true. I looked it up one time. Our families come from the same small village.

"I hate the Yankees," he says. A slow smile broadens because he knew I was trying to impress him.

The next day I take the Grand Avenue bus downtown to his office, and Royko acts as if he's never seen me before. But I can tell it's an act and that this is how it's going to be between us. I search beyond his contempt for some wry twist, but he needs to save all his cleverness for his columns.

He gets a nod from a woman with olive-rimmed glasses, pinched at the corners, which make her look catlike.

"Here," he says. "You can sit here. Write down 182 ideas for columns. Hand them to Gracey when you're done."

Why not 200? I want to ask, but he's gone. He slips into his office, where I can glimpse him pacing. He ambles out now and then, stopping at the burping water cooler and the coffee pot, taking in the rows of desks, the clacking typewriters, not as loud as I imagined, but not once does he glance in my direction. He makes small talk with a few of the secretaries, looking like a boy trying to avoid his homework.

He's thinking I'll come up with ten ideas and whimper away, never to show my face again. But I've been reading his column almost from the beginning, after Ms. G brought in his story about some alderman, who claimed residency in the city but who lived in the suburbs, so I know what gets him going. I brought the column to my dad, which instantly began his routine of turning to Royko on page three before flipping to the sports section.

Forty-one of my ideas are about Mayor Daley. Human interest stories. When it snows, do the streets in Bridgeport get plowed first? What kind of mileage does the honorable mayor's limo get, and why can't he be hauled around in a compact? I'm not even sure he has a limo, but I type fast, taken with this electric typewriter that responds almost too quickly. I know how to type, a new graduation requirement at Wells, but I use two fingers because this is what I imagine Royko doing. When I get up to peek, pretending to look down at the street three floors below, I hear the faint hum of classical music wafting from a radio in his office, but Royko has his nose buried in that day's newspaper.

After a while, the Daley ideas start to sound the same, and I question if maybe I've already read them in Royko's columns. *Nothing new here*, I hear him growl. Ideas #42 through 53 are about city workers—precinct captains, Streets and San workers—the hours they log in compared to the work that actually gets done, which seems like a betrayal to Freddy, though he would understand my desperation. And it's not like Royko's going to take any of my ideas seriously. I squeeze in what I really want to add, #54: a hard-luck story about a former Major League pitcher who got released after a promising start. Whatever happened to that guy? I try to add a Cubs angle, think about turning the search into the trivia contests he loves to publish, to get the man's attention, but it seems forced.

At 3:35, I type up Idea #182: *Kennedy should have lost in 1960.* If he looks at any of these, I figure he'll look at the last one, to make sure I made it to the end, so it has to be a good one.

The Kennedy name alone will fix his attention. Just as I pull the paper from the roller, with what I imagine as the flair of a seasoned reporter, Royko marches up and tears it from me.

"You should have been done with this three hours ago," he says, and disappears into his office.

Am I supposed to follow?

I sit and wait and begin to suspect he's testing me. To see what I'll do now, without an assignment. I roll in another piece of paper and start a new list. Idea #1: Too many guns on the street, as in former cops brandishing their weapons on city piers, though I leave this last part out. Loose guns always get Royko riled.

An hour later, he springs out of his office wearing a softball jersey and baseball pants with his caramel-brown dress shoes. I expect a nod, a wink, but he makes his way toward the elevators without a word to anyone.

Do I come back tomorrow?

I do. And the day after that. Typing exactly 182 ideas each time, trying to come up with ideas for stories that will somehow end up being about my dad. But nothing clever comes to mind.

I call Maryann for help and finally catch her in her room between classes. But she can't give me a single idea. Or she won't. I can hear in the silence between her words that she thinks I'm wasting my time. Even if Royko does write something about my dad, she's probably thinking—because I've thought the same thing myself—my old man is not going to suddenly be found. And if he's found, then what? Nothing will change. We can't rewrite history. We can't undo flames, just as Royko, in writing about Kennedy, can't undo a bullet. To make peace maybe? Is that what I want? But that will never happen. Some events are too twisted and horrible.

"I'm not even sure what I'm doing here," I tell her.

A brief silence.

"Well, what do you want most?" she finally asks.

She won't hurry me. This is what I love about Maryann. I'm able to think. What I want is this—*to feel like a son again*. That's what I want, what I miss most. But I don't say anything.

We exchange awkward goodbyes and she promises to stop home soon, though I know she won't, as sincere as she is.

It's already four o'clock, so I try Freddy, who clocks out at noon on Fridays.

"Royko's got no soft spot for the Kennedys," he informs me. "Spoiled, good-looking rich kids, that's all they are to him. He took the JFK thing hard, like the rest of us, but…you know."

I imagine Royko glancing at my first list and tossing it in the trash.

I let Freddy go on for a while, then hang up and try a different tack. I keep the Kennedy angle, but I focus on all the people who believe they were responsible for getting him elected in Illinois. Because I learned, after sifting through *Daily News* archives in the basement earlier in the morning, that Kennedy took Illinois by only 8,858 votes, that he campaigned hard in our state for two weeks before the election. A few schools were let out early so students could wave at his motorcade of two cars, which stopped in several Republican strongholds outside Chicago. Royko could interview the teachers who let their students out. *They* got Kennedy elected, they probably think. Students went home that night and told their parents about shaking hands with John F. Kennedy, who was going to make a difference in their lives. Or Royko could interview the mayors of those towns, who set up podiums and loudspeakers, or better yet, interview the custodians who wired the speakers and the microphones and who stood reluctant, waiting for the speech to end so they could unplug wires and sweep streets, only to be caught up in the senator's easy Massachusetts cadence and homespun rhetoric, which sounded both ancient and new.

After three days of watching Royko pace and light up a cigarette and stare out a window, not really there, his eyes gazing out at nothing, I'm starting to feel that I know how he thinks. What will get me in his door is not my stupid persistence, because anyone can be stubborn, and not work ethic or dependability or all that other bullshit, and not even the ghost of my grandfather, maybe least of all that, with its whiff of nepotism, but what'll get me in is *one* useful idea on my list. If he can spend one less lousy day scratching for a damn topic to lighten his daily grind, I'm in.

Maryann

※

In my *Religions of the World* class, Professor Ramachandran told us to write "I am _____," then to fill in the blank over and over again for fifteen minutes without stopping or pausing, repeating answers if we had to. We were to become habituated to *I*, he informed us afterward, place *I* on a lower plane for once in our lives. He discussed purity and *arupa*, a kind of striving toward the infinite. Then he had us stretch and bend and twist ourselves into the lotus position so we could meditate and further shed ourselves.

But the writing and the meditating had the opposite effect on me. I couldn't lose myself as he wanted us to do because there wasn't much there to lose. For the past nine years, I'd dedicated myself—I don't think that's too strong a word—to helping Anthony get through another day. Even when the days became routine, my helping became routine, too. Like working on homework together at Nonna's kitchen table. Anthony always finishing before me, not because he was more diligent but less so. Then putting my homework aside and listening to him complain about his coach or his father or school or the changeup he couldn't master.

Sitting there meditating, though, I realized something that maybe I'd known all along, that my devotion—now I'm sounding all saintly, but that word is accurate, too—toward helping Anthony really served *me*. I didn't have to deal with my own grief and loss, and I didn't have to worry as much about all the cruel cuts from the other boys about my weight, though that proved impossible because, for a while, that's the only thing I could think about. But, at least with Anthony, I could put that weight aside—the weight on my shoulders, I mean. Anthony would enjoy the pun. Even my jokes I see through his eyes.

After class, I felt a fullness of *I* that made me a little drunk. The irony is that I wanted to hop on the El and the Division Street bus and rush home to tell Anthony about my discovery. Which I did that weekend. Or tried to. I got home on Friday night and, after throwing a load of laundry in the washer and having dinner with Mom and Dad that did *not* consist of thick gravy slathered over unidentifiable meat, I bounced up to his second-floor landing and knocked on Anthony's back door. No one answered. His mother, I knew, was working the midnight shift now and stayed with her sister on weekdays.

I meandered down the block. Kicking at dry leaves. Not knowing what I'd say to Anthony when I saw him. I wouldn't need to say anything, really. I just wanted to test if I'd still feel this newness around him or if I'd shrink back into a shadow. Would I casually mention that a couple of boys were interested in me, and that I thought I might be interested in one of them? Maybe next time. Baby steps.

"Maryann."

Startled, I peered up. Mr. Lipschultz with a carton of Lucky Strikes cradled in his arm. The paper bag didn't quite reach the top of the carton.

"Hello there." I hadn't been able to utter *Mr. Lipschultz*, not since being in his house, like he'd hear the lie in his name.

"Looking for your little boyfriend?"

That smile. Those twinkling eyes. Harmless, I'd always thought. What I wanted to think. But standing lookout inside his house, dreading the sight of that great hulking frame turning the corner, I felt the menace behind his kindly expressions. Or maybe it was the smell of the house, or the creased wear of the file folders stuffed in his closet, full of desperation, that turned me sour. If I hadn't been in that house, I might not have believed the story about the pier and the gun.

"How have you been?" I asked, staring at the cigarettes, thinking of a graceful exit. *You probably want to get home and start in on those. I'll let you go.* I imagined acrid smoke coming from those broad nostrils.

"I haven't seen him around lately. He been hiding?"

"He *is* a good hider." I began to wave bye, to push off. Anyone else would have taken the cue and turned away, but that big mass didn't budge.

A wildness crossed his eyes, or maybe I imagined this. Maybe it was just the steadiness of his gaze.

"When you see him, tell him I need his help. I need someone to watch my house. Just another eye, you know. Because I think someone may have broken in." He paused, not shifting his gaze. "You wouldn't know anything about that, would you?"

"How would I?"

He stepped toward me. "Say it. Say my name and tell me you don't know anything about that."

He grabbed my wrist, his fingers so big that I barely felt them, but they held me tight. I felt their power, how they could crush. I wanted to twist away but stood my ground and waited because I knew he'd grip tighter, like the Chinese handcuffs Anthony and Ellie and I once played with. Anthony was always the impatient one, Ellie and I slowly pulling our fingers apart so we wouldn't get trapped.

I stood my ground and matched his gaze, straining to hide my trembling. I willed myself not to move, to breathe, to lose my sense of *I*. To lose the connection to my arm, which was beginning to feel as if it didn't belong to me. I caught a whiff of whiskey curl up through his cologne and the stale scent of cigarette, none of which I found unpleasant. Because standing there, toe to toe, on a sidewalk square in the middle of a block I'd run down thousands of times, I suddenly saw the old man through Anthony's eyes. And, with that, for the briefest of moments, everything else fell into place. I realized what it was like to want to detach yourself from an unwanted limb. And gratitude filled me. In my desperation to remain still, I may have smiled. He grimaced, not used to such indifference. Or maybe he just forgot who I was, why he was holding my wrist. I imagined him grabbing my neck now to stop my smiling and I closed my eyes, and Ellie flashed before me, just as Anthony always described her, as a little girl, not just my memory of her but really there. Showing me how to be still, how to be whole.

14

❖

She's in my room. In my bedroom. Maryann. That's what keeps pressing on my mind, like a brilliant pellet of light against a scorched sky. I try to attend to her worry, to the rigid lines crisscrossing her forehead, her steady gaze, as if she's afraid we'll both disappear if she looks away. *Blink*, I want to shout. *Glance out the window or something.* She's shaking. Or was. I can still see the trembling in her eyes, if that's possible. Despite all this— which concerns me, it really does—I keep coming back to, *she's in my room.* Maybe because I prefer not to think about Lipschultz and the threat in his glare or his vice grip on her wrist or the strange wave of gratitude I feel toward the old bastard because he drove her here. That, I keep to myself.

"What should we do?" I ask. And, of course, I mean about our senile old neighbor, who lost it on the street, because no way *Officer* Lipschultz is going to threaten someone in public like that. But, with Maryann sitting at the foot of my bed, her knee pressing against my good leg, the question implies more immediate concerns. Mine. Besides, we could both use the comfort. She's wearing a Loyola Ramblers sweatshirt that's a size too big, but the swelling of her breasts beneath that fabric dizzies me.

She shrugs and relaxes her gaze finally, glances over my shoulder toward the window. It's more than a glance, it's a pointing with her eyes, so I creep there to pull down the crooked shade. I pause at the window so I can take her in, because the room doesn't seem like my room anymore, with Maryann in it. Reminders of my stupid younger self are everywhere—the trophies, the old clipped box scores pinned to corkboard, a Major League baseball from my dad on a cheap stand.

"You still have your key," I say.

From her pocket, she pulls out a pink strand of woven plastic all the girls were making many years ago in eighth grade, on the end of which is a copy of my house key.

"What did you tell your parents? That you were going to hide in my room till I got back?"

"I told them I was going back to school. That I had an early meeting in the morning. I had to pass your house and double back."

I see the duffel bag next to my dresser. "Are you?"

"Am I what?"

"Going back tonight."

She glances at the closed door and shakes her head in confusion.

I sit next to her again but don't dare touch her. I don't want to drive her away.

This time, *she* asks what we should do, and I think I hear suggestion in her voice, but I know it's just me and my jittery hopes. Then she links her fingers with mine and slides closer and pulls on my arm and dips her head onto my shoulder. I wrap around her, trying to dull my ache, because maybe this is all she wants, this warmth, and at first, yes, this is what we both want, which surprises me, but then she starts to breathe in my neck, and I can tell by her breathing and by the way she squeezes my hand—that unmistakable signal that she wants more—and I can't believe I'm here, that this is going to happen, so I move slowly, we both move slowly, because it's been so long, and I don't even begin to think about why and instead lose myself in her warm curves and wait for her to pull at my shirt and, when she does, we begin to claw at each other, abandoning our slow touches until we're on the bare floor, gasping and thrusting at each other with this savage desperation, trying to forget everything but this moment, this surge, this thrust, fighting for breath and giving in to one last sweet push, one last deep embrace, then collapsing onto each other, already savoring this warmth, this touching, our bodies weakened and open and done. And then we sleep.

❖

As soon as I wake, I know what the dream means. I get up to go to the bathroom, and Ellie is sitting in the hallway, waiting to hear about it. Beyond her, Mom's door is open, which means she came home to shower and left again for an overtime shift. I can smell the lilac scent of her pink lotion.

I close my bedroom door after me. Though Maryann is asleep, I whisper anyway. "A dragon was chasing me. In the dream. All over the city. We were passing streets and tall buildings, skyscrapers, but not. They were black, smoldering. But the dragon...he couldn't...get any fire to come out of him, just this smoke. And, when I realized he didn't have fire, I slowed down and faced him. He was harmless."

"It's Mr. Lipschultz."

"Yes."

"But you don't know he's harmless."

I slip into the bathroom because I can't voice this next part. And I know she won't follow. She's right. I don't know. But what I meant was that his old suspicions are harmless, the ones about my old man and Maryann's mom. I don't expect anyone else to follow the twisted logic but, if he's losing his mind, his suspicions don't count. They'll die with him. As long as there's no one else in this world who believes what he believes, then the belief doesn't exist. A convenient conclusion, but it feels right. And I can dismiss him. I pee and come back out.

"What I mean is...his beliefs—about me and the fire—are harmless now. If his memory is failing him, then he's harmless.

He'll never link anything together…not that there's anything to link. If he's losing his memory, his suspicions die with him."

Her eyes roll. She is skeptical. She disappears into her room, which we've left untouched since the fire, whose door is always nearly closed but never shut.

I go downstairs. I'll shovel some food on a plate and bring back enough for both me and Maryann, and Nonna won't know the difference. She'll be happy for my appetite. But, when I get down there, all I find is a jar of homemade strawberry jam and bread. I slice the bread and spread the jam and cut an orange into wedges and line the plate with them.

When I get back to my room, Maryann is dressed and sitting on the edge of the bed, as if she's waiting for a doctor. She glances at me and offers the barest of smiles, which I return, to hide my disappointment. Because I expected to slip back under the covers, where she would reach behind her and pull at me to move closer. Later, we would laugh as we devoured our plain breakfast. I offer her the plate, which she takes without hesitation, and we eat in silence. I want to ask if what we did last night was safe but, I realize, as I think of the question, that I don't care if it was, a part of me hoping last night was not. I've heard of people believing that a baby will solve all their problems, which always struck me as pathetic, but not at this moment.

I search for something ordinary to say. I point to the plate and finally manage, "I'm a good cook, huh?" I say it brightly, letting Maryann know that last night won't change anything between us, and she nods, relieved. I want to believe the same, that the two of us will always feel safe together, as if separate from the world, but the thought rattles around, hollow in my head.

15

⟡

As I knock at his door, I'm armed with these—
Your head is bigger than your ass.
Hey, whiskey breath.
You big stinking pile of alligator shit.

I could use Perez. Insults are his second tongue. I imagine his hands moving and his body bending to some beat in his head. *You candy-ass piece of no-good...*something like that.

But I do have this in reserve—
Your two boys, who never come to see you, they're waiting for you to die.
As the door creaks open though, I'm left with this—
Thanks for terrifying Maryann, which drove her to my bedroom. Thank you.

But when he looks at me with those watery eyes and his bulbous nose, this is what I say...I say, "I hear someone broke into your house. I want to help you find the cocksucker."

I don't realize until I say it that I sound like my father. *Call me Frank, you old bastard. Call me Frank.*

In his hand are two thick slices of bread that he holds like a sandwich, but there's nothing inside. He doesn't say anything. With great effort, he moves past me. All his old cop swagger is gone. He takes his place on the lawn chair at the top of the stairs, his perch. He's dressed for the day but not in his usual rakish style. A plain gray sweatshirt over navy pants and dark mismatched socks, which is the reason I notice.

He clears his throat. This is the first thing he'll say today. "You getting that ratty cast off soon? I'm tired of looking at it."

"Have you seen my dad around?"

He shakes his head and puts his bread down and presses a hand to his shirt pocket for a cigarette and remembers there's no pocket. "Sonofabitch," he mutters.

"Can I bum a cigarette?" I ask. "I'm thinking of starting. Maryann said you had a whole carton yesterday. She told me you were looking for me. Were you looking for me? Because I'm right here. What did you want? Do you remember?"

He takes in a laboring breath and lets it out slowly, as if there's a lifetime of regret in that drawn out groan. In the groan are all the police reports he's filed against low-life scumbags he could never rid the streets of and, when he came home, he made sure that his neighborhood, at least, was clean. But he had punks like me roaming around. And, when he turned inside, his own family wouldn't bow to his prick ways. Oh, everyone fell in line all right, but to what end?

The backs of his hands are papery and dry. I wonder if he studies those hands, if he marvels at the slow change in them each year, how those hands have betrayed him.

"You and me together," I say. "We're going to find the cocksucker who broke in."

He stands, and I back away, thinking he might take me by the neck. He slips inside and returns with a pack of Lucky Strikes and plops back into his chair. He taps the pack against his palm and a single cigarette magically slips out. He extends his arm and I take the cigarette and watch him light up. Watching someone light a cigarette always gives me pause. He pulls the matchstick from the book of matches and drags it expertly across the striker, toward him, and brings it up to the cigarette hanging loosely from his lips and cups his hands and bends his head and squints while the first puff curls up in gray wisps, and in a single sharp swipe through the air, he douses the matchstick and lets it twirl and fall to his feet. I take the matches and tug at one, but in my effort to match the grace of his fluid motion, I don't pull hard enough. Humiliated, I stop there and let the cigarette dangle from my mouth unlit. I'm hopeless.

"You think you can help me find my dad? You still have your... friends, right? Your buddies on the force? You think they might..."

He does something with his head. Rears it back a bit. He wants this to be negligible, and ordinarily it would be, if he were standing and rocking on the balls of his feet at patrol readiness, but he's not himself. But I can see that my plea for help, for his cop help, has pierced through the grogginess that he'd probably like to chalk up to the time of day. Eight-fucking-o'clock in the morning.

A few minutes before, I'd walked Maryann to the bus stop and I didn't know I'd be standing there until I climbed the steps and knocked.

"When's the last time you talked with your old man?"

"Months."

He nods and takes a deep puff. Contentment lines his face. He asks again, "When was the last time you talked with your old man?"

"I just told—" Patience. "Months." I peer at the matchbook in my hand, deciding. "When was the last time *you* saw my old man?"

His attention shifts from the ember at the end of his cigarette to some vague spot near the street, the smoke obscuring his view now and then. He points. "That's where you fell. Damnedest thing. I was sitting here. Just watching. I looked up and down the block. When I looked back, you were down. I didn't think anything of it. I figured you'd get up any second. And your dad... was your dad there that day? Let me think. No, I don't think so. When was the last time you saw him?"

"I'm not sure. Can you help me find him?"

"Where is he?"

"I don't know. That's why I need…he said he saw you, not too long ago. Didn't you two go down to Navy Pier together?"

This doesn't faze him. He's not even curious.

"Listen," I say. "I need to tell you something. I need you to pay attention. I know what you think. I know you think I had something to do with the fire. And what I need to know is…I need to know if you ever told my dad what you thought. Did you plant any ideas in his head…did you let him know you thought…"

A smile creeps in at the corner of his lips, and he sits up taller in his chair. The old arrogance seeps in. I can see it in the rolling of his shoulders, the way he leans forward, his elbow resting on his knee. And I know I've slipped. He's never told me about his suspicions. In his mind, the only way I'd know is if I'd broken into his house.

The smile disappears. In its place is a steely gaze. Does the old bastard remember more than he lets on?

I back down the stairs. "You sonofabitch," I say.

16

❖

With open palm, the woman points to the floor and invites me to sit on a piece of carpet that looks to me like it can fly. The paisley maroon and gold threads are dizzying and, for a second, my eyes blur.

I glance at Miss G, who nods in assurance, and I feel like a boy. Miss G sits, too, on her own small throw rug, and the three of us, each sitting cross-legged, form a triangle in the front room of this bungalow on the northwest side of Chicago. Outside the picture window, a streetlight begins to flicker. The days are getting shorter.

"Your cast came off today," the woman says.

She wears what I think is called a sari, bright and textured and perfumed with a musky scent that reminds me of Mass. Her skin is mahogany brown, unblemished. Her name has many syllables and begins with a V, but I can't remember the rest.

"And now you are worried. Because now you have to deal with the truth. You are not sure of anything anymore. For months, the cast has seemed *right*. But now it is gone. And you are not sure. . .what will happen."

She speaks plainly, barely moving, her delicate hands poised in her lap. I feel hopeful. The red dot in the middle of her forehead speaks of history and healing.

"Close your eyes. Please. I want you to go back to a time when you felt completely safe and protected. When you felt a wholeness flowering inside you. A time when the days stretched ahead of you unhurried like unbroken sky."

I ponder how many times she's delivered this unbroken sky speech, but soon I'm drawn in by the sweetness of her voice. I feel cradled by her gentle encouragement.

I'm back in my first-grade classroom with Sister Bernadette, who bends over my chair to show me how to grip my thick yellow pencil, cloaking my shoulder with her long flowing habit. She smells like candle wax and furniture polish.

I'm told to leave that safe place now and to focus on my breathing, in and out, like nothing else exists. When she senses that I'm drifting, as if she's in my head, she gently directs me back to the rise and fall of my chest.

When I open my eyes, ten minutes later maybe, Miss G is gone. I'm filled with a flash of panic, which passes just as quickly but leaves me red-faced for feeling so abandoned.

"Tell me about your leg," she says. The way she says *leg*, to rhyme with *peg* but not quite, tells me she's worked hard to master this foreign tongue.

She's spot on about the cast feeling right. Which still surprises me. You'd think a cast would shout, *Look at this useless piece of flesh and bone.* You'd think a cast would draw *more* attention to my cursed leg. But for three months I haven't had to think about my leg much at all.

"I'm crazy. That's all you need to know."

She nods, then disappears and returns with tea.

"I do not know what *crazy* means."

"Take a picture, that's what it means."

"In India, many things would be, in your eyes, crazy."

"My crazy doesn't have borders. I'm crazy crazy."

"How long?"

"How long have I wanted to…"

"Yes, how long have you wanted to separate yourself from your leg?"

I sip from the minty tea and glance at my healed leg and then beyond her to the stereo console. Turn on some Who, I want to tell her.

"I'm not sure."

"As a child?"

"Yes."

"And this…wish…it has gotten worse?"

"Maybe."

"Are there triggers?"

"I'm not sure."

"Do you have other…thoughts?"

"Other?" I feel heat at the back of my neck.

"Do you hear voices? Imagine things that do not exist?"

"How would I know?" I sound more defensive than I mean to.

"Know?"

"If I'm imagining, how would I know the difference?"

"Well, you know you have two legs, yes? Yet you imagine that one is less…real. I am trying to establish if this is an isolated…I want to discover the nature of—"

"My craziness."

"Labels are irrelevant, are they not?"

"If we're being hypothetical, sure. But we're talking about me, so I'd say the labels are pretty important."

"If this is so, why then choose 'crazy' for yourself? Why not a different label?"

"My buddies might be able to offer a few."

"Have I been rude to you?"

"What do you mean?"

"I have been nothing but sincere in my curiosity but, at every turn, you make light—"

"It's an American thing."

She nods, leans away from me.

"Sorry. I don't mean to be rude."

"You may be rude or whatever else you like. I am not insulted. I am only trying to understand. We can dance around, as is your tendency, but I am afraid I will not be able to help if I do not understand. And we do not have time—"

"But the dancing around, doesn't that tell you something? That I use humor to...downplay—so I don't *have* to be serious because serious scares the shit out of me because, you know, I've had enough serious for a lifetime."

"You have been in therapy, I see."

"Yes, and that's what my dime, or my mom's dime, has gotten me, that bullshit dime-store bullshit."

"Anger is good. And I suspected the serious. But I do not care to search for the truth like worms in the dirt. I simply want to know what you know. Not to judge. Or belittle. Nothing you say will shock me. And I can see that you are already thinking of several humorous rebuttals, something that would shock anyone, a reference to some anatomical anomaly, thirteen toes maybe, and I thank you for your restraint." She raises her teacup to her lips but doesn't sip. The gesture and the steam are enough. "There are deeper truths, of course, to which you have less access, but you can probe those during your time at...at the dime store. I simply want to explore more immediate relief."

"So that I don't hurt myself."

She nods and brings her palms together as if in prayer. She offers an inward smile, a kind of truce, but her eyes are unwavering. A truck rumbles by.

I wonder about the depth of concern one can have for a stranger—another American thing?—but I'm touched nonetheless. I explain that I don't want to hurt myself but that my leg seems like a foreign visitor sometimes. I don't mention that I want to hear her pronounce *leg* again.

"Not that I have anything against foreigners," I add.

A genuine grin breaks out. "Unless they take refuge in your body."

Her kidding feels like a breakthrough.

"I just want..."

"What do you want?"

"I want two things. I want to know *why*, for one. Why I do... why I am the way I am."

She bunches up her lips, as if wondering what to offer in the way of explanation. "I don't know," she says. "But I have a theory."

She waits. Some things are better left unsaid. That's the intent of her pause. I give her some subtle sign of assent, a widening of my eyes maybe.

"Allocation," she says.

"Oh, allocation. Of course. That's what I thought." I catch myself. "Sorry. Go ahead."

"What I mean is that perhaps no part of your brain was ever properly assigned to your left leg, at least not in the usual way. Perhaps due to the tiniest of strokes...most likely at birth, given the early onset of your symptoms. Did you have a normal birth?"

I'm startled. How could she know this?

"I had to spend two weeks in the hospital."

"I see." She places her delicate hand near her temple, as if this will explain everything. She moves her hand higher and points to her head. "This lobe here helps us understand our own bodies. If yours was damaged in the slightest, this could explain why your leg feels like a foreigner. But, if that particular portion of gray matter was later healed, but had nothing to do, it would look to invent other tasks to perform."

"Which is why you asked if I imagined...things that don't exist."

I expect her to say, *Precisely.* To flash her approval. And I feel pathetic for needing that approval. But she remains placid, inviting me to speak about the things I imagine.

She senses my reluctance but waits, then finally breaks her gaze and says, "The second thing. What is the second thing you want?"

This I can talk about.

"I want to stop...thinking. I want to walk from your front door to this spot on the floor without...it's like when you become aware of blinking and that's all you can think about, which drives you crazy, but you know it won't last. But with my leg, I know it will."

She rises in one swift motion and slips behind the half wall that separates the front room from the tiny dining room. But she's gone only seconds. In her hand is a long rectangular mirror, the kind you see in shoe stores. She sits again, close to me, the mirror propped in front of her and resting on its long side. She has me bend back my cursed left leg, like in a sprinter's stretch.

"What do you see in the mirror?"

"My leg. My good leg."

"Anything else? Any other part of your body? Can you see your other leg?"

"A little."

She moves the mirror. "And now?"

"It's gone."

"You cannot see your left leg at all?"

"No."

"Good. I want you to pretend now," she says. "You are good at pretending, yes? Keep your eyes fixed on your good leg in the mirror. Allow your body to relax. Focus again on your breathing. In and out. Deep, healing breaths. Now pretend that what you are seeing is not, in fact, a reflection, but your other leg. This is an illusion, of course. You are familiar with illusion. But it is a convincing invention, yes? Give yourself over to this. No harm will come. Let your eyes rest now. Close them, yes. Good. Gently roll your shoulders…your neck. When you open your eyes again, you will glance in the mirror, a casual glance. And you will be surprised, I think, by what you see."

She directs me back to my breathing, but I think of Ellie instead, vivid as always. *Any triggers?* I'm not sure, which makes me feel stupid. At first, I saw her only in the middle of the night when my body was exhausted but I couldn't sleep, a kind of hell I wouldn't wish on anyone. With maybe an exception or two. But now? I know when I will see her. I have some control. But a pattern?

"In just a moment you will open your eyes. But be forewarned—"

I don't hear the rest because I'm thinking about the word *forewarned*, how you don't need to say *fore* because of course it's fore. It wouldn't be much of a warning if it came after. And I know why

I'm thinking this way, to downplay, to deflect, and maybe this is progress, my catching myself like this. I'm not sure. I'm not sure of anything anymore.

She tells me to open my eyes and, when I do, I feel nothing. Which strikes me as unusual. To sit there and gaze without thought, without hurry. Ellie was good at this. Hugging her knees. Her eyes not quite glazed over but not focused either. A kind of cleansing, it seemed, though I'm not sure if this is a new thought. Before long, I'm—I want to be precise here—I'm *swaddled* in sadness. Because, yes, I'm an infant again, whole, with two strong legs that belong, at least momentarily, to *me*. Two legs. Mine.

I feel I should spring up and rush outside and shout to the sky, that beautiful unbroken sky, but I know that, as soon as I move, the illusion will disappear. But, mostly, from this innocent, childlike view, I see the years of heartache *ahead* that flash before me like electrical pulses—not just the shattered bones and plaster casts and the gimpy struts, but the rest, too—my grandfather's sudden passing, which finally broke my old man, what was left of him. I see blue flames lapping up the walls of the school; waking in the hospital the next day, trying to piece together what little I remembered; Mom pacing the house in a fog, that nurse's uniform her only anchor; Ellie, always Ellie, who will forever be trapped in that runty little frame of hers, with her own damaged leg.

What now? Is this a milestone moment? Do I walk around with a stupid mirror? Do I dare blink? Will any relief I ever feel be tinged with this sad pull? Is the trade-off worth it? It's not like I strut around beaming with cheer anyway. I should take this. Take this and run. Literally. Run.

❖

Outside, Miss G leans against the door of her '64 Rambler. It's a pewter four-door box, perfect for an old man. Yet, because it's hers, the car seems less square. The streetlight catches the collar of her blousy white top beneath her blue sweater. I want to tell her that the curve of her waist is lovely because it is and because she would like the word *lovely*.

"Thanks for ditching me."

"I'm here."

We climb in. A fresh trace of pot lingers in the closed air. What else is there to do while waiting for your crazy friend? If that's what we are. Friends.

"A mirror," I say, more to myself. "A freaking mirror."

"This has never happened before?"

"I guess I don't really look in mirrors. Which seems impossible. I'm sure I do. All the time. But it's not the kind of thing you remember. It's not the kind of thing—"

We sit in silence for a while, taking in the sweet leafy aroma. Then, something breaks inside me and I begin to speak without thinking without pause without worrying what she'll think.

"She asked me what I wanted to do with my life. What I've always wanted. And I told her that I just wanted to walk. Pretty modest goal, right? And that's when she got the mirror, and when she could see I felt lifted or uplifted or whatever it is she saw, she asked me if this is what I've wanted all along. And I told her, 'Yes, this is it.' But then she pressed. 'What else?' she asked. And I said, 'That's it.' But then all these other things came to mind that have always been there, but it's like I never gave them a chance to rise up or ripen or whatever, a part of me never even knew these thoughts were there, I guess. But what I told her was that I wanted one day to know love. And she asked me what that would look like. And I didn't realize, until she asked, was how little I want and how much it would mean. I want a house. I don't know why, I can't explain it, but I look at houses and my knees feel weak thinking about them. I want to be inside and protected by all the bricks or shingles—but it's not just the house—it's imagining sitting in a chair under a lamp reading the second edition of the newspaper, studying the box scores. I don't know if I ever told you this, but sometimes I wake up in the morning and pretend my life is a box score, and I rank the things I did the day before. How many home runs did I have yesterday? How many triples? Strikeouts? And I don't mean like what you usually think of when you say, 'getting to first base.' That's not what I mean at all. Well, sometimes. But, usually what I mean is, how close did I come to shedding my old self and becoming someone better, someone who deserves to have a house and to, like, know love? If I'm feeling sorry for myself or acting petty, I might have three or four strikeouts that day, which is fairly typical when I'm dwelling on my own family, which wasn't exactly domestic bliss, which is why maybe I want more for myself. Sometimes I give myself four walks because I wandered around in a daydream all day. Do you do that sometimes? Wander around not really talking with anyone and not thinking much of anything? Just getting by. Anyway, I just want to be with someone. That's not asking for much, I don't think. I don't even know what I'm saying anymore. It's like that mirror has unleashed something in me, and I want to go back in there. Look, even from here, peeking inside at the lamplight in the big picture window does something to me. It reminds me of this other life I want to lead. Do you get that? That longing?"

She reaches for my hand and pulls on it so that I'll nudge toward her, and in the front seat of her old Rambler, we kiss, and I realize that I've imagined this moment, the coldness of her lips mingling with the warmth of her tongue, and I inhale her peppermint scent and warm skin, which seems new yet familiar. I allow my hand to run along her lovely waist, but that's all I allow on this cold night in the front seat of her car under bright, frosty streetlights. And, for now, this is enough.

Maryann

✳

This is what I imagine. Anthony begging Royko to write a column about his dad. Not the brightest idea for a story. Because who wants to read about an old ballplayer who messed up before he barely began? I guess some people might like that kind of story. We all mess up. We're all a little self-destructive. But I think most people would read about Frank Lazzeri and not feel too sorry because how many people get the chances he got?

Anyway, what got me imagining was the newspaper. Which I don't see much. But someone had left it open to Royko's column and placed it on my bed this morning. The story wasn't about a washed-up ballplayer. The story was about the fire.

Here's what happened. I know it. Anthony writes down all these topics, and Royko shoots them down. He hardly reads them. But then he comes across the one about the fire—of course Anthony would get around to that—and Royko's eyes light up. Because even though it's nine years later, the story is still huge. Just mention the name of the school to anyone connected, just say *Our Lady of the Angels*, and people tear up. The nine-year anniversary is coming up. That was the gist of the story. How far we've come. With new alarm systems inside the school and fire drills. Why Royko didn't wait until year ten makes sense to me because everyone will be writing about the fire then. To write about the fire *nine* years later shows that each one weighs as much as the other.

For me, every day is an anniversary. The memories don't fade. Even that morning, which was identical to a thousand others, but the one I keep coming back to. I ache for the brightness of that early sun. What I wouldn't give to have that again? *What I wouldn't give.* This has become a refrain for me. And the answer is always the same. I'd give anything.

We stood to recite the singsong Pledge of Allegiance, our hands warm against our hearts. We sank into our polished desks, heads bowed and hands folded to say the Our Father and a Hail Mary. Sister Josephine turned a new page on the calendar. December 1st. Christmas suddenly in sight.

On the bottom of a worksheet on fractions were extra boxes for practice. I filled in my Christmas list in code. PB stood for purple bicycle, RAD meant Raggedy Ann doll. And on and on. When I got home I planned to show the code to my dad, who would make a big show of cracking it. He was usually reserved and serious but, when we worked together to solve some puzzle, he became a different person, allowing himself to be more playful and affectionate. I carefully tore the bottom of the worksheet and folded it and tucked it deep in the pocket of my uniform. Even this tiny rush of anticipation, tinged now with sadness and regret, I ache for. Because I never showed my coded list to anyone.

I remember turning to the window, hoping for snow, imagining running home for lunch, my hot breaths rising cloudlike in the frosty air. Sister Josephine interrupted my daydreaming with a ruler's rap on her desk and a stern glare, followed by her usual gentle grin. I loved Sister Josephine, I yearned to please her, and I welcomed any kind of attention from her.

We worked on handwriting and spelling then. I could never remember how to spell *embarrass.* Or *withdrawal.* Sister pulled down a map of faraway places to help us understand our place in the world, and I felt small, but not unimportant. Ellie and I ran home for lunch, where our moms had chicken noodle soup waiting for us because we'd both been sick with the flu and a fever over Thanksgiving break. The soup likely came from Anthony's grandma.

After lunch, everyone seemed tired. Social Studies always sent a fog through the room. The rest of the afternoon is a blur, until the end of the day.

I asked Sister Josephine if I could go the lavatory. I didn't really have to go, but I was tired and bored, and I couldn't stand to sit there another minute, even though we would be getting out in only twenty minutes. We were supposed to be filling in the names of countries on a world map, getting a head start on our homework, but I was staring at the clock. The huge second hand was sweeping toward 2:40. By the time I got back from the lavatory, it'd be almost time to line up to go home.

As I marched from Sister's desk to the door, I glanced back at Ellie, who knew what I was doing and smiled. We would giggle about this later, I thought. And then she did this thing with her eyes. They slid toward Jimmy Passolini, who she knew I liked. *Take him with you*, she was saying. *Walk together. Hold hands.* Just looking at her eyes, I could hear her scratchy voice. I had to turn away to keep from giggling and attracting Sister Josephine's attention. I hadn't told Ellie yet. I hadn't told her I was starting to like her brother, instead. I didn't know if I could. In a few seconds, I would pass his room and peek in.

But the doorknob was warm. I was afraid my fever might be flaring up again. When I opened the door, a rush of smoke poured into the room. I turned to Sister. A glimmer of accusation crossed her face. *What did you do?* She rushed past me and closed the door and pulled me back into the room. But we'd both seen the blackness in the hall.

"Children. Rosaries."

She gathered us around her desk, all forty-six of us. We knew we weren't allowed to leave the room without the alarm sounding. And besides, all that smoke. We wouldn't be walking through that.

"Pray, children."

She started on the Our Father, her words more deliberate than usual, which I didn't think possible but, before she could finish, the high window above the door burst and dark smoke filled the room. And still no alarm. Ellie and I were shoulder to shoulder, clutching each other's arms. The room grew darker. Everyone rushed to the windows, screaming for help. I followed, gasping for air. But there were too many kids. I fell to my knees. "Ellie," I called. I couldn't recall letting go of her arm. "Ellie." I thought she was behind me.

I crawled, not knowing where to go. But I could breathe better down near the floor.

Soon, kids began jumping from windows. We were two floors up. Were people catching them? Where were the firemen? The white walls changed to a gray-pink. In seconds, the room turned hotter. The smoke was oily thick. And now, finally, came the alarm. I didn't see the blaze, but the hem of my skirt caught fire, and I stamped it out. I needed to get to that window. I pushed myself past one body after another and reached the window and realized that Jimmy was boosting everyone to the high ledge. I placed my foot in his waiting locked grip and reached the sill and took one long look outside. There were bodies down there. Some were moving. Some were not. A man came running toward the school. He stopped just below me. He looked up and put his arms out and pleaded with me to jump. I took one last look into the blackened room. Someone's long hair had caught fire. The girl raced to the other window and, without hesitation, leapt. Just below me, inside, others were clawing, waiting for me to move. Beginning to push. Far below outside, the man still had his arms out. I didn't think he could catch me. I looked back to the room. Ellie appeared. Her face smudged. The blaze roared now. She reached up and took my hands. She knew what I needed. She always knew. She pushed.

I wish I could tell you what Ellie was thinking at that moment. She wasn't any more religious than the rest of us. Nor any more courageous. I won't deny the panic in her eyes, though I've tried.

I've tried to remember her as placid. But she wasn't quite that. She was my best friend. That's what she said to me with that push. That she would be with me always.

I sailed. The cold air felt good. And the man, he didn't quite catch me like you might picture. But he softened my fall and moved me to the side and waited for more kids. But no one else jumped from that window. One second they were there. And then the window turned black.

I don't remember how I got home that day. Just that it was dark and cold. Someone had draped a coat over my shoulders and wrapped a scarf around my head. My next memory was standing by the front picture window of our house, gazing out. The streetlights had come on. I studied the circle of reflected light on the asphalt, the way it splashed softly from the center, the way it had done yesterday and the way it would do the next day. I glanced in the direction of the school. I needed to go back. I needed for someone to take me back there.

Mom and Dad rushed in and out of the house. Tears streaked Mom's cheeks. Each time they passed they had to touch me. But I must have given the impression that I was okay—the numbness of shock must look that way—because they left for long stretches.

I wanted to bolt out to find Anthony, but something in my parents' haste told me I shouldn't. I heard them talking about searching hospitals, calling the police. The police had a list of names. I didn't understand any of this.

When I think back, I become angry that my parents left me alone. But this is a new feeling. Necessary, the doctors tell me, if I'm going to get better. I think I prefer numb. Besides, how could anyone have known what to do then?

I heard the screen door creak open, which surprised me because I hadn't seen anyone on the stairs. I didn't turn. My glazed eyes were fixed on that light. I remember hoping it was Ellie at the door, bursting in to tell me that there'd be no school tomorrow. Or Anthony, not saying much at all, just nodding and looking at the floor, his shoulders slumped because he thought he was too damn tall, and asking if I was okay.

Even when the figure on the stairs slipped inside I didn't turn. Because I could see it wasn't my mom and it wasn't Ellie and I feared that when I broke my gaze, everything would change forever. But I could prevent that doom by not looking. The dark figure of Nonna shuffled toward me. She pulled me by the hand and guided me to the kitchen, where I sat and followed her labored movements from the cupboard to the refrigerator to the stove. She shook her head and whispered tortured prayers. I didn't know then that her grief was inconsolable. I could think only about myself, and her kindness, how she was determined to place something warm in front of me, how she knew I needed this. Not once did I give thought to what she needed, how she'd lost a husband the year before and had been mourning and shriveling away ever since.

He was a butcher in the neighborhood, with broad shoulders and oversized hands. He came home bloodied each night, and I steered wide of him. But there was a gentleness in his eyes that I never recognized until his wake, where I studied the photographs displayed in the funeral parlor chapel.

Her husband had taught her about loss, had prepared her as well as he could for what would come next. But neither one of them could have imagined this.

Ten minutes could have passed or an hour but, before long, a bowl of brothy soup on a saucer appeared. Nonna sat close to me, stroking the back of my hair. I bent over so that the steam would surround me. With trembling hand, I picked up the spoon and stirred, taking in the salty warmth. I turned to her. The year since her husband's wake had been hard on her. The creases around her mouth had stiffened into a grimace. *This* was all she had left, this nurturing with her food. I handed her the spoon and let my eyes blur and waited for her to feed me.

17

$\diamondsuit$

I thought the mirror would be like the pot, that my capacity to imagine would diminish. But that didn't happen. The mirror didn't take Ellie. Not yet.

It took weeks of practicing on the floor before I could begin to understand what I was feeling. And another week to come up with words to describe that. The mirror sent me into this detached grief time, when everything around me shimmered with the intensity of *now*. During long hikes through the neighborhood, I'd glance down. No other sidewalk square glistened like the one before me. I lifted my eyes and the light splattering through the leafy branches opened something in me. I knew others in the world were moving at their usual brisk paces but, for me, time was glacial. Grief time without the grief. Or mostly. Or like prayer without the prayers. All because of a mirror, which I had to swipe from the Hush Puppies on Chicago Avenue. When the bow-tied shoe salesman marched back to retrieve a size 10½ penny loafer, which cracked me up, him believing I would wear such a thing, I left a crisp five next to the register and booked out of there with the mirror under my arm.

And wholeness. That washed over me, too. Though I didn't want to examine that. I didn't want or need to understand because to know would undermine the changes I felt.

I looked people in the eye now. I never realized I hadn't. Maybe not ever. I wanted to go back to everyone I'd ever known and apologize for staring at their shoes, for missing so much.

Today, December 1st, 1967, the ninth anniversary, I had breakfast with Nonna. Or I ate, I should say. Sunnyside eggs. Cold. I brewed coffee and asked her to sit. I couldn't recall the last time I'd seen her sitting in her kitchen. But she wouldn't and stood with her back to me at the sink. I didn't bring up all the questions I suddenly had, with my newfound clarity, because I didn't want to make her sad, which was stupid because I was trying to protect her from a sadness she already owned. Though she probably buried that to protect everyone else. She needed that illusion—that she could hold the family together—despite all the evidence that she was failing. There wasn't much difference between any of us, I decided. We all walked around trancelike, believing our own delusions.

What I wanted to ask was, *How do you get up in the morning? How do you go on, with your husband gone, your sweet granddaughter taken so young, your derelict son missing in action, his wife rarely home, your twenty-year-old grandson with his cursed leg barely looking at you? Who are you cooking and cleaning for?* Years ago, she had a second freezer delivered to the basement so she could store her homemade pasta and sauces and bread, while she ate like a bird, withering into shadow. After I brought up a few safe subjects—the size of last summer's beefsteak tomatoes from the backyard, whether we would have to endure another blizzard this winter—I asked her about Nonno, whether he ever regretted coming to America.

She scoffed. Or I imagined this, because she hadn't turned.

"No, really. I want to know."

She spoke to her open hands, occasionally turning, her broken English broken further by Italian, not because she couldn't think of the words, but because this was how her mind worked. My Italian is marginal, but what I pieced together was this: *When you come to new country, you no can afford look back. Young people, they no look any place.*

"But you and Nonno..."

The conversation felt familiar, like we'd talked about this before. She threw up her arms and shrugged. *No choice.*

I wanted to believe I'd inherited her fierceness, that I'd do anything to provide for my family.

I gazed out the window and could take in both the ash tree that shaded her garden in summer and Nonna's hazy reflection, as if she were in both places but whole, which had more to do with my recent obsession with mirrors than with her, but the image seemed fitting. As frail as she appeared, there was nothing flimsy about Nonna, and I wondered again if any of that iron will was in me, but I suspected not.

So, this was why we heard so few stories of the old country. Not because of shame or regret as I'd always imagined—betrayal and estrangement and retaliation over land disputes and late night avenging—but because to look over one's shoulder at what came before would spell disaster. Added to that, I'm sure, were all the superstitions Nonna harbored. She couldn't pass a threshold without crossing herself. She whispered incantations over every pinch of pepper and salt. Attached to her rosary was what looked like a red chili pepper but what she called a horn to ward off evil. Tucked away on a high shelf in the kitchen was a vial of dirt from Italy that she fingered sometimes for good health. And forget about turning on an electric fan, which would send you straight to the doctor.

"What about now? Do you want to go back now?" I immediately regretted the question because I heard the implication, that there was nothing to keep her here, that she was cooking for no one.

She seemed to catch full well my meaning. A heaviness descended on her. I imagined her gaze turning inward.

"I stay," she said.

She stiffened her back.

"I belong."

Then she shrank again, curled back into her hunched frame.

18

⬧

I lay on my bed and looked out at the bright sky. If I avoided
glancing at the doorway, I could sink into the silence and sort
out what I needed to do.

"You've been ignoring me."

"I feel like I've been ignoring myself."

"Your leg is better?"

I didn't answer. I was in no mood for this.

But she was insistent. "How are Mom and Dad?"

I crossed my pale left leg over my right and examined the river
of veins, then swept my gaze upward to my thigh and touched
the old dividing line between good and cursed. While the cursed
part still felt like a distant cousin, I could tolerate it.

"Hello-uh."

I turned on my side, my back to the door.

"What happened to Mr. Lipschultz?"

After he died, but before the police tape went up, just three
days ago...though it seems a lifetime...I went back inside his house.
I waited until it was almost night but not so dark that I'd have to
use a flashlight that someone on the street might spot. His sons
had already poked through a few times, one time with a realty
sign that the youngest son, George, carried over his shoulder.
I imagined the big white stake as a baseball bat, probably not
unlike the piece of lumber he used when he played with my dad
in high school. But the Lipschultz brothers, they always came

early, before work, ransacking what they could carry—the TV, the console stereo, the clock radio on their father's nightstand. The gun, too, I guessed. Or guns. I kept looking for the boxes at the back of his closet to be hauled out, but they apparently weren't worth anything to them. I never had replaced the file I took.

Maryann was in the hospital by then. She wouldn't be barging in on me. Otherwise, I could only be spotted by someone in the alley. A light snow had been falling all day and the wind had picked up and anyone stepping out to empty their trash would be shielding their faces, not looking around for an intruder into a dead man's house. At least this is what I kept telling myself. In the days leading up to my visit, I also noticed how neighbors, as they passed, would glance briefly at the house, some of them shaking their heads, then quickly turn away. They wouldn't even notice any movement inside and, if they did, the ghostly fluttering would cause them to scurry away faster.

I'd stuffed my coat pockets with rubber kitchen gloves, two dish towels, a wad of napkins that the commercials said wouldn't rip, rubbing alcohol, and pliers. I didn't need the pliers, but they made me feel safe and ready.

I moved more swiftly than the first time I'd broken in with my crutches, but that's not the way it felt. I felt clumsy and deliberate, certain many times that I'd glimpsed the old man's big head, which turned out to be a lamp or a clock or an object that didn't even resemble a head, like the wooden-peg coatrack near the front door. Worse, as I began to wipe clean all the surfaces I may have touched, I started thinking.

I dabbed one of the towels with alcohol and the other with clear water from the bathroom sink and polished the handle of the toilet and faucet and the doorknobs. Some of my thoughts had the urgency of fire. What if someone does peer inside and sees me? What if the cops do investigate and find that fingerprints had been wiped off? Maybe it would be better just to smear them all together with a dry towel. Which turned out to be a useful idea and caused me to move quicker. But another thought seized me, gripped me by the throat. I was walking toward the bedroom closet, the diminishing light causing my eyes to strain, the stench of old man and whiskey, and a disinfectant to hide that, hitting me full on, and I stopped and quietly crumpled to the floor. The wind howled and I wanted to be back in the warmth of my own room. *What if I see him?* What if I see the old bastard? What if he becomes as vivid to me as Ellie? A steady presence in my life. Through the dread and the howling of the wind and the heaviness I felt in my legs, I began to shake with nervous laughter. I tried to restrain the laugh, to stifle the sound, but I became convulsive with it, doubled over, because I thought that if I started to see that big head and those animal brows at every turn I'd have to become a pothead, the biggest pothead in the city. I'd become the authority on pot in Chicago. Other potheads around the country would come to visit, and we'd all understand each other without speaking a word. But they would have no idea. By then, I would have forgotten, too.

My eyes were tearing and I didn't know whether to laugh or cry, but the dread returned soon enough. A dripping gray dread that clouded over me, no matter how much I would rub myself out of existence in that house. Were there other clues they might find? Did my shoes leave impressions? Did my coat drop microscopic fibers? After all, if they decided to investigate, this was a cop. One of their own. They'd take their time, use every means possible. I should have wrapped myself in plastic bags, one giant condom. A big prick who should have never swatted the hornet's nest, that was Mr. Lipschultz, who always had to force your hand. It was his fault he was dead.

"So, did you kill him?"

Leave me alone. Though I didn't say it out loud. At the pier is where I should have finished him off.

Maryann

※

The hospital felt like a convent, cloistered and safe and suffocating. The only thing I learned in my brief stay there was how to hide my meds because, after a day, I knew I didn't want to end up shuffling around like my tunnel-eyed roommates, all pasty ghosts whose mouths moved without sound. Oh, sure, there were the occasional screams and the moaning at night, signs of life at least, but during the day, my fellow loonies remained mute, which only amplified everything else, their thick socks padding along linoleum, their heavy sighs. I swear I could hear the whisper of their fingers against their hospital-issued cotton gowns.

Mom and Dad presumed their little girl could use some rest. I came home from school one weekend and lay on the couch under a quilt and wouldn't move and wouldn't speak—couldn't speak. At least that's how it felt. Which seemed familiar. Even if they'd shown me then where I'd end up for eleven days, I don't know if I could have mustered more than a word or two of protest. They summoned Dr. Craig, whose specialties were coughs and colds and the occasional ankle twist, who worried, as he took my temperature on our couch, that I'd had a nervous breakdown, which I soon realized is a catchall term that means nothing but that gives doctors a weighty diagnosis on which to hang their hat as they retreat to their offices. *If this is a nervous breakdown*, I wanted to scream, *then I've been broken for nine flipping years.*

At the hospital, I shortened my stay by learning to smile, even when it pained me to move. But, if the doctors had known what awaited me in the neighborhood, they would have kept me a while longer.

I'm usually good at reading Anthony. He's like a paperback you stick in your back pocket. He and his problems fit back there comfortably and you know what he needs to hear, but sometimes there's no getting through. I didn't run into him the first day I got back, not even the second, which was unusual. By then I'd heard, and I wondered why he hadn't broken down my door. When I finally saw him—because my mom and dad thought it would be a good idea for me to walk, to take in some fresh air, clear my thoughts, find a routine—he looked like one of the chronics at the hospital, the bottoms of his eyes rimmed purple, his fingers jittery, as if he needed a long-sought cigarette, though Anthony didn't smoke much.

The afternoon sky loomed low and gray. There was a chill in the air, jacket weather, yet Anthony stood there in his tight white t-shirt, his arms folded. He was letting his hair grow out, like one of those San Francisco hippies. Squinting mindlessly through a cloud of cigarette smoke would have suited him well.

"Talk to me," I said, as I walked by him.

He fell in step with me.

My parents were right. Being outside slapped me awake. I stepped on every shriveled leaf. I inhaled the crisp fall air and the soapy scent from Anthony's t-shirt that his mother must have hung outside to dry.

"It's ironic, isn't it?" he said.

"What is?"

"You being at Dunning. When it's me who's crazy."

"I guess it's official. We're both crazy."

"Thanks for not talking me out of my being crazy."

"You're welcome. Why didn't you come see me?"

"I'm not sure," he said. "I wanted to."

"Did you go to the wake?"

He shook his head.

"The only ones I've ever been to," I said, "were for—" I had to stop myself. "For your grandfather."

"Me, too. Talk about crazy."

I knew what he meant. After the fire, he meant. How we were kept away from all the Masses for the dead. "Yeah, but looking back, maybe it wasn't such a crazy thing. I'm not sure we would have been okay...going to all those wakes."

"You're right," he said. "Look how okay we turned out because we didn't go."

We reached the end of the block and I turned the corner and he followed. We passed brick two-flats and sided bungalows and pale cottages set back from the street.

"It's weird," I said. "Whenever I peeked outside my bedroom window at his house, I was always a little cautious, because it's so close. But I never even realized I did that until I got home and found out he was dead. The funny thing is, you can't really see much when you look out. But I was always thinking he'd be looking out from his blinds or walking through his gangway—not like he was peeping in or anything—but I was afraid he'd be passing my window at the same time I looked out."

"I know. It's like I hold my breath when I pass his house, the old bastard. And then I realize I don't have to."

"Is it terrible that we feel..."

"What?"

"Relief."

"Can we talk about something else?"

Talk about something else? *For years you've been crowing about the old bastard,* I wanted to shout, *and now you want to talk about something else?*

"You seem...different," he said.

"I was going to say the same thing."

After I pressed a little, he told me about the mirror he stole and how he didn't feel so fractured. It sounded to me like he'd joined a cult, but I tried to hold back judgment. I wanted to ask about Ellie, if the mirror had pushed her away any, but she's not an easy subject to bring up. Around Anthony, there are plenty of mines to avoid.

And then, as if reading my mind, he asked, "How'd you…you know…get in there? What pushed you over?"

I wanted to tell him. But there are some things I've never told anyone, not even Anthony. Especially him. Because to give voice to what I saw before I floated down from that fiery sill all those years ago feels like sin to me. And to tell Anthony would be torture for him. Let him hold on to his fantasy that she's still here.

What pushed me? *I kept seeing her eyes*, I wanted to say. *Your sister's eyes*. But instead of serenity in those deep brown pools, I saw pleading. *Take me with you*. Why didn't we just jump together? Why didn't I pull her up? Because I had to admit, finally, that with her weak leg, it would have taken too long. We would have both died in that fire. I chose me over her. That's what sent me reeling.

"I guess I was depressed," I said. Which wasn't untrue. "Like there was a blanket over me."

Out of the corner of my eye, I could see a little nod. "And the blanket is kind of light but it still buries you because…"

I took his hand, which was cold, then reached under his arm with both hands to warm him. "A better question," I said, "is how I got out."

"How'd you get out?"

I told him about hiding pills and saying what the doctors wanted to hear. "And I made a decision."

"A decision?"

"Yes."

"Well, let's hear."

I wasn't sure I could explain. It was a private decision I'd made at a group meeting at the hospital. I'm not even sure what they were talking about, but there was a woman there with a screechy voice that I wanted to strangle.

"Don't you hate it when…You remember that Peccoraro girl?

Lisa Peccoraro. She was in my grade. She used to come over sometimes. The big glasses."

"I think so," he said.

"I remember being so happy when she moved away after fourth grade because I couldn't stand her anymore, because all she did was complain."

"So, you made a decision to find her and apologize?"

"No. Shut up and listen. I realized something at the hospital. I realized I was her. Not her exactly, so shut up, but *like* her. I realized that most of my day is filled with feeling sorry for myself. I'm as big a whiner as Lisa Peccoraro, but I'm just more quiet about it. I'm a secret whiner. Think about it. You get up in the morning for school—well, not you because you're pathetic— but say you have to get up earlier than you want…you feel sorry for yourself, right? You get a tiny cut on your finger and it's all you can think about. You're waiting at a vending machine for the paper cup to come down, which is like a little miracle, the way it falls from the chute, but it lands upside down and soda splashes on your shoes. And…fuck!"

He laughed, like he was imagining the sticky mess.

"These are just the small things," I said. "You and me, we have bigger things to feel sorry about."

I couldn't quite get to what I wanted to say. But he waited for more. Anthony was good at waiting.

"I'm not sure I'm explaining myself…"

"Try."

"It's like your mirror. It sounds like voodoo to me, but I can tell you're…I don't know…better somehow."

"No, I get it. But what's your decision?"

"No more 'Poor Me.' That's what I decided."

I glanced up at him as he tried to rein in a smile.

"I know, I know. It sounds impossible, and I'm not sure if this— this feeling or commitment, or whatever, is going to last even a week, but just thinking that thought—*no more feeling sorry for myself*—and

125

the change is immediate. Like I can breathe again. I can't explain it. I've been...numb for so long. And I'm tired of...I'm tired of myself, of feeling this way."

He smiled full out now. "I have to say, you're sounding a little like me."

"You're a bad influence, I know."

"Your...theory. It sounds familiar. Like something we've talked about before."

"I would have remembered," I said.

"Or something I thought about."

I glared at him. "Like I can read your mind? Maybe. Sometimes it feels like we share a brain. Which is a scary thought."

"So, basically, we're all pathetic whiners but we don't tell anyone because then no one would want to have anything to do with us."

"I wasn't focusing on that part of it, but sure—"

"I wasn't finished," he said.

"You weren't?"

"Actually, I was. But I get it. I do. All that 'Poor Me' business makes you...like...possessed."

"Good word."

"And you start to believe your own bullshit about yourself."

Maybe we did share a brain.

Before we knew it, we were across from the school, rebuilt and bland and unrecognizable. Shiny bricks and shiny windows, like something from the future. Inside were sprinklers and alarms, and no fire would ever blaze there again. I tried to figure out where the window would have been where I'd jumped, but thankfully I couldn't, that's how different the school looked.

We stopped for a minute but didn't say anything. What the hell was there to say? Blocks away, traffic thrummed on Division Street. Birds chirped away with their stupid chatter. *It's December,* I wanted to shout. *Give it a rest.*

I thought of something to say, finally, but held back. *Once we start moving,* I thought. But what I wanted to say would lead back to

Mr. Lipschultz, and I didn't want to agitate Anthony. Or was this more self-pity? Was it that I didn't want to upset Anthony because of how shitty this would make *me* feel? I had to be constantly on guard, it seemed. But since I was through with "Poor Me," I pressed ahead, big toe in cold water. I pulled on his arm to get us moving again, and Anthony stumbled over his feet, as if he'd just learned to walk again, which reminded me of other times.

I missed his graceful strides on the mound, the way he'd rear back and gather up this…this force, this funnel of fury, but then he'd stop for the briefest of moments, like this was a game of freeze tag, his body tight and coiled and ready, and when he started moving again, the rest was pure and true, his leg and torso and arm unwinding and the ball sailing torpedo-like toward the catcher's floppy mitt. It made me envious. That little puff of dust that floated from Perez's mitt made me envious. Not for baseball or pitching, but for something I could do that would be so freeing, where I wouldn't have to think.

"In the paper the other day…what Royko wrote…was that one of your…your suggestions? Because it sounded like, I imagined that you…"

He didn't answer or nod, and I took this as, "Yes."

I knew we were both thinking about the end of the article where Royko wrote that, to this day, the cause of the fire remains unknown.

"Did he ask you?"

He knew what I meant, but he was going to make me voice it.

"Did he ask you about…the cause?"

"Not in so many words."

"And what did you say?"

Our shadows bounced along the sidewalk squares ahead of us. I wanted to point this out to him.

"I told him that it was still under investigation, as far as I knew. I think I might have smirked or something, I felt something twist in my face when I said it because I wanted to say that *I* was still under investigation. By this old bastard cop in our neighborhood, who wouldn't let it go. He—"

"Sorry. I know you don't want to talk about that. But now it's over. You don't have to worry about that again. He was a frustrated old man with nothing else to do with his time than to hatch up crazy theories."

But Mr. Lipschultz's death, and my attempt at putting his death into perspective, did nothing to ease the worry lining Anthony's face. There was something he wasn't telling me. He wanted to, but I knew he wouldn't. Not then.

When we neared our houses, I let go of his arm and we slowed our pace, not wanting to say goodbye quite yet. But this thing unsaid had come between us and left us with little else to say.

"See ya," we said, at the same time. And we slipped into our houses.

A week later, I understood. A week later, yellow police tape lined Mr. Lipschultz's house.

19

❖

Freddy had me plowing snow and salting side streets and patching potholes that couldn't wait till spring. My territory was the east side from Madison to North Avenue. On days when there was nothing to do, I'd ride with him to keep him company, on the clock, of course, and earning overtime if we stopped for a few beers because in the winter you had to be ready, he said, and being ready, on call, was work, wasn't it, though we never got any calls. He always left the number of the tavern where we could be reached. I asked him one time, "What if they trace the number back to a bar?" He thought this was the funniest thing he'd ever heard.

He decided on the Billy Goat Tavern on lower Michigan because he hadn't been there in a while and he hoped to run into a few of his cronies from Streets and San, while I was hoping we'd gotten there too early for them so we could talk. It was just past two o'clock. Since I was with Freddy, the bartender, Sam, didn't card me, and I downed the first one and nursed a second because I wanted to be both loose and clear, a state I couldn't achieve in the Caddy.

The Billy Goat was one of those places that couldn't decide if it was a cheeseburger joint or a bar, but the combination of sizzling grease and yeasty booze struck me as just about perfect. The food was terrible and the booze made you forget that fact. At a far table was a mother with her three young children picking at fries and dipping them into ketchup. At the end of the boomerang-shaped white bar were two men exchanging quarter shots. And Sam, whose famous Uncle Billy put a curse on the Cubs because they wouldn't let him bring his goat to a game one afternoon, poured drinks and flipped burgers and never stopped talking and never took a day off. He was compact and solid and never wore anything but a starched white short-sleeved shirt, white work pants, a white apron, and a white paper diner hat with a red band running around the upper rim. He was either what you might call charming or a royal pain in the ass. This is what I observed and committed to memory and observed again, instead of talking to Freddy, who was content to luxuriate in his sudsy draft.

He sat on the stool next to me, curled around his mug, his brilliantined hair gleaming. When he lifted the mug, his pinkie flared, a detail I'd never taken in before.

"So you have your own liquor store and drop your dough at taverns."

He sneered.

I think he enjoyed having me around—not just someone to keep him company, but *me*—though every once in a while, like now, I could see this wheel spinning in his head and locking on what a pathetic loser I was and how I was more like a wife than a drinking buddy. *I was kidding*, I wanted to plead, but I'd waited too long. Mid-glare would have been the time. But this would pass. With Freddy, everything passed in the span of a few sips.

Earlier, in the car, we'd been talking about the war, and I remembered a detail I couldn't dredge up then, and now I turned to Freddy. I opened my mouth but stopped myself before another misstep. I was about to mention all the anti-war protests I'd been reading about. Dr. Spock was arrested not too long ago. This was a name he'd know. But, with his son serving, he needed to believe this was a just war. Under ordinary circumstances, I'd throw out these little grenades anyway and watch him pounce on them, mainly for my own amusement, though he seemed to enjoy enlightening me on the world according to Freddy. Talk of protests, though, would have only ticked him off and pushed him further from where I wanted to go. I needed his help.

Maybe I'd mention Perez. I'd sent a letter to him the day before, addressed it to a base camp in Norfolk, Virginia. Though, for all I knew, Perez was already marching through rice paddies with his infantry unit and shooting at an enemy he had no quarrel with. In the letter, I told him I'd been drafted by the Chicago White Sox but that I refused to sign unless they drafted him as well and that he'd better get home soon so that we wouldn't miss training camp. I attached a few box scores I knew he'd like to see, along with the league leaders in home runs and RBIs and the rest. I told him that I watch the war on TV and, whenever I see some news guy like Dan Rather reporting in fatigues from a battlefield, I never focus on him but behind him at the soldiers, searching for my friend. I left out what I really wanted to say, what I needed to tell someone. But there was no one to tell. Not Maryann. Not Miss G. Not even Ellie. Maybe Freddy.

I said nothing for a while, let him settle in.

He did a double take toward one of the tables. Sitting alone, cradling a mug, was a rumpled guy I hadn't noticed with a big, square head and thick eyebrows.

Freddy pushed himself off his stool. "Come here a sec," he told me.

We slid over to the table.

"How you been, Chief?" he asked the man, whose eyes slowly focused, like he'd been roused from a dream. Freddy took his beefy hand and shook it, but got little in return. "It's been a long time, Jack. This here's Antney. Frank Lazzeri's kid. You remember Frank, right? Antney, you're looking at one helluva fireman."

"Not anymore."

"Living off that fat pension, huh? Well, you earned it."

Jack waved this off, his gaze still foggy.

"No joke. Nothing could stop this guy..."

The more praise Freddy lavished, the more withdrawn the man became. But Freddy wasn't giving up.

"Jack...hey, Jack. Take a look at Antney here," he said, too loud. "Antney, he was in the fire. At Our Lady. You...you pulled him out. And look at him now."

I stood there with a dumb smile.

The old fireman studied me, a glint of recognition crossing his face, Freddy's clumsy lie fitting easily into his almost decade-old memory. "What do you know," he said, then turned into himself. "'Course the damn ladders, we needed another couple of feet, they didn't reach the windows, it was awful, those kids jumping, we couldn't catch them all. 'Course when the alarm came down, dispatch relayed the wrong address, we rushed to the rectory instead of the school, too much damn time passed."

As he spoke, it was clear that no time had passed for him.

"So I pulled you out of there, you say?"

He shook his head, unable to take in this information, as if he could only think about the ones he didn't save. "'Course those ladders were too short. Another couple of feet, that's all we needed. And dispatch. You know where they sent us? Too much damn time had passed."

We let him go on for a while before heading back to our stools.

"Sorry about that," Freddy said. "You with all your questions. I thought... Anyway, thanks for playing along."

I swallowed the last of the beer, warm and bitter, not a single question rising up. I glanced back at old Jack. His lips moved, forming silent words of regret. I felt like I understood each one.

"You ever play softball with Royko?" I asked.

He shook his head. "Naa. He was always too serious." Which meant that Freddy wasn't as good as Royko.

"Weren't you going down to his office for a while?" he asked.

"He didn't pay me as well as you do."

"You didn't make a penny, did you?"

I laughed.

"Sometimes you just have to pay your dues," he said. "Maybe, in time, he would have taken care of you."

"I thought of that. But he barely talked to me. He walked around miserable all the time."

"That's because he was working. He needed to get that column out. Every goddamn day a new column."

I helped him with that, I wanted to shout. He used one of my ideas. He wanted to know what it was like being a student at Our Lady of the Angels in the middle of all that panic. I told him I was just a kid and that my memories were spotty, but I told him what I knew. I became research for him, though not a very good source at that. And, after, he barely talked to me again. Never thanked me. I imagined Maryann—who, by the way, was ignoring me because if she saw me she'd have to ask if I did it, if it was me who finished off the old man—I imagined her telling me to stop the "Poor Me" routine. I tried, I did, and she was right. The effect was instantaneous. But my sorry self always returned. Maybe that's why Royko never talked to me. He could sense the self-pity dripping from me.

Was regret the same as self-pity? Because sitting there, tapping the counter top, I couldn't begin to squelch regret. If I hadn't pursued Royko and he hadn't written that article, Lipschultz wouldn't have ratcheted up his stupid investigation, and he'd still be alive. Later tonight, feeling good, I would call up Miss G and ask her to meet me downtown and we'd take in a movie—I heard *The Graduate* was pretty good—and I'd give her an update on my leg, and then who knows? I imagined Maryann shaking her head, amazed but not surprised that I could still be thinking about carnal concerns at a time like this.

I picked up my glass and swiveled my stool toward Freddy, not enough so he'd notice, and cleared my throat. "I heard Royko talking one day. In his office. About softball. He loves talking about sixteen-inch softball. He said cops usually had the best teams because all those guys grew up in Chicago."

A simple remark like that usually got Freddy going, but he just nodded.

"Ever play on a cop team?"

Nothing. Not even a little eye roll. Instead of the usual cigar, he pulled a cigarette from his pack of Chesterfields and let it dangle from the side of his mouth and struck a match and watched it flare up before bringing match and cigarette together, all with deliberate precision that said he was going to savor this cigarette because he'd made a deal with himself that he could smoke only two at this bar...or any bar. Why I relished watching this little ritual I couldn't explain.

"What's on your mind, Antney?"

"Whattya mean?"

"All day with something on your mind. Out with it already. You mixed up in something? What's her name? Is she pregnant? There's nothing you can tell me we can't fix."

I grinned. A pregnancy was the worst he could imagine.

I told him about the police tape going up at a neighbor's house. A former cop.

He straightened up and turned to me and grinned in acknowledgment. "Schulzy. Yeah, I heard."

"You knew him? You knew Mr. Lipschultz? Is there anyone you don't know?"

He pointed to himself. "Precinct captain. For his precinct. Yours. Ah, you don't know shit. I'd see him every...wait, what're you saying, Antney? You know something? You seen someone prowling around?"

What happened to those three beers you just pounded down, I wanted to ask.

"No...no...no, I didn't see anything."

He leaned back into the bar and glanced furtively over his

shoulder to make sure no one else had come in. "Poison. That's what they're saying. Probably an accident. Because he was—" He pointed to his head and put on an exaggerated frown. "He was, you know, losing it. But they needed to make sure. And I guess that's what they're doing now. Making sure."

"Holy shit," I said, hoping to sound convincing.

"Let me get this straight." He scanned the bar again. "You didn't see anyting. You don't know anyting. So what's eating you?"

I came out with it faster than I expected because it was the truth more or less. "Well, like you said, he was losing it. And he...I don't know...he had it in for me. Always did. I'm not exactly sure why. I think he thought...he thought there was something I could have done maybe to stop the fire. Because the kid they were looking at for starting it, he was...you know...we used to hang around together. Not exactly a buddy...but..."

"And you know this how?"

"Know what how?"

"That they suspected your buddy."

Because I saw the file, I almost said. "Mr. Lipschultz didn't keep it a secret. He was practically in my face with it. Like he enjoyed it."

"And so you're worried that—"

"I'm being paranoid, I know. But...I saw the police tape go up. And one guy after another was going in there with his little briefcase. I figured, yeah, he was probably killed. And if they start asking around, it's no secret he had it in for me and—"

"You've been watching too much *Mannix*, Antney. That's your problem."

"You think you can find out?"

"Find out what?"

"What they're looking at."

"Or who they're looking at?"

"Like you said, the old guy was losing it. I can see him trying to poison himself, not enough to kill him maybe, but to make him really sick so he could pin it on me. That's how crazy he was."

"Whoa. Whoa. *He's* the crazy one? You're talking… The dirt ain't even cold yet, and you're…"

He guzzled the last of his beer.

"If you can just check," I pleaded. "You didn't know the old bastard like I did." My words sounded more biting than I'd intended.

"You got nothing to worry about, Antney. But, if it'll make you feel better, I will. I'll check. If your name comes up, I'll tell them you were a crossing guard when you were a kid."

He scratched his head and took a long drag from his cigarette, as if deciding something. Then, from his jacket, he pulled out a slip of paper, placed the paper on the bar, and pushed it toward me. "I wasn't sure I was going to say anyting," he said.

On the paper, torn from a bereavement pamphlet, was a phone number. "What's this?"

"A phone number."

"I can see it's a phone number."

"At the wake. I saw your old man."

I backed off the stool and stood on two strong legs. I towered over him now. I snatched the paper, glossy and creased, studied the familiar handwriting, then glared at Freddy.

"You were at the wake? You went to Mr. Lipschultz's wake. And my old man was there? When the fuck were you going to tell me?"

"I'm telling you now. Why so shocked? The son, George, he played ball with your old man. They used to run around together."

"I know." My mind raced, but I felt numb at the same time.

"And you. Why'd you go?"

"I love going to wakes. Nothing like a good wake."

I checked my pocket for change for a phone call. What the hell was I doing the night of the wake? Nonna had left dinner for me on the stove. That's all I remembered. "Did he ask about me? Did my dad want to know—"

"Look, there's the phone number." He pointed to the phone booth in the corner and flipped a dime in the air. I moved and the dime fell miraculously on my waiting palm. A shiny surprise. "Call."

I stumbled to the booth without thinking and picked up the phone and dropped the dime in the slot and listened to it throw some switch inside and saw my fingers find the holes in the rotary dial and heard the seven satisfying swishes back and forth, a sound that never failed to please me. And soon, miles away, a voice on the other end that had been human but then twisted and condensed into some kind of electrical code and then untwisted to became human again on my end would set off a series of tripwires in my ear, the eardrum vibrating and tiny bones rumbling and the nerves sizzling, nothing less than a miracle, and I would hear the familiar voice of my old man in my head. That was the hope at least.

20

❖

Francesco Antonio Lazzeri would never become the butcher his father wanted him to be. Which wasn't always a certainty. As a boy, he didn't mind helping at the shop. At the end of the day, he swept away the straw that had been strewn across the floor in front and then mopped the tiles and, when they dried, he laid down new straw for the next day. In the back, he carried vats of bloody fat and bone to the walk-in cooler, never asking how those parts would be used, though he knew they would be. He laundered aprons that appeared clean at a glance but always carried the faded smears of slaughter. He hosed the concrete floor beneath the cutting table, one square foot at a time, and watched the pink water gather and swirl into the drain, then he'd repeat the process until the water turned clear, which seemed like it never would.

This is one of the few stories my father ever told me about growing up. What remained unspoken, but what I came to understand, is that no matter how hard he worked, he could never please his father. And, with each passing year, he would defy everything his father ever wanted for him.

This is what I thought about as I approached my old man that Saturday. Blood and guts and defiance. He waited at a bus stop near his place in Humboldt Park. I didn't bother to ask why we couldn't meet at his apartment, but I was relieved in a way, too, because I didn't want to examine his new life and this other place he preferred over his own home. And, besides, he wouldn't have told me the truth about why we couldn't meet there, though I had a few guesses. I imagined torn window shades and lumpy couches charred with cigarette burns and the smell of squalor.

His shoulders were hunched inside his gray parka, the afternoon sun slanting toward him.

"Hey, Pop." He hated when I called him that.

He'd been watching for me from the other direction, the wrong direction, and I startled him. "Anthony," he said. A broad smile crept through his frozen stubble and he put an arm around my shoulder, and we walked like that for a while, his arm resting there until it wasn't. "So good to see you."

You could have called, asshole. You could have seen me anytime you wanted, asshole. But the weight of his arm on my shoulder pushed those thoughts aside.

"There's a little place here, around the corner. Leena's. We can sit. Diddja eat yet?"

I didn't answer, not for any particular reason other than, with my old man, you didn't need to answer. He was always a pace or two ahead, or behind, of any conversation, and he might have forgotten he'd asked.

We got to a small diner and removed our coats and sat across from each other in a booth near the window, and I was reminded of how people were drawn to him. The waitress had trailed us and helped him with his coat sleeve. She took his jacket and set it on a high hook in the aisle without a glance at me. He didn't need to tell anyone he'd been a Major League pitcher because he looked the part so well. His strides were confident and unhurried, his frame long and sturdy, unlike my gangly lankiness. And he had a good face. Always a three-day beard, which seems impossible. Warm, dark eyes. A solid chin that didn't draw your attention. Likewise the nose, but slightly broadened, which left an impression, that unlikely pairing of the Roman nose and those long legs. Tufts of hair crept up from the collar of his mud-colored flannel shirt.

And those hands. The way his fingers used to grip a ball made my legs weak.

"So, you saw Freddy," I said. *And what about Mom? Did you see her? Was I the only one not at this wake?*

I caught a whiff of his cologne, dry and musky and achingly familiar.

He signaled for the waitress to bring him coffee, though she was already headed in our direction with a simmering pot. For Frank. Anything for Frank. She began to turn away but doubled back when I looked up at her. She held out the pot and gazed at me with questioning eyes. I wanted the coffee but I told her no, put off that she'd ignored me. As she scurried away, I realized I hadn't turned my cup right side up. That I failed at these little exchanges, and then felt slighted for no reason other than my own stupid fumbling, made me sink into the cushion of our booth.

I pulled at a loose thread on my end of the red vinyl tablecloth.

"Was Mom at the wake?"

"No."

"But Nonna was there."

This made him squirm. He barely nodded.

"She knew you'd be there," I said.

"I never miss a good wake."

"That's what Freddy said."

"Maybe that's where I got it. He has a way of rubbing off."

"Like a disease."

"Exactly."

"Why'd you go?" I asked. I wanted to add, *How'd you find out?* The news of death had its own mysterious life that I would never understand, like a coffee cup that would remain forever upside down. Maryann would have liked that little leap, from obituary to tabletop, though she would have punched me and told me to stop the Poor Me nonsense already.

He ran a hand through his thick hair, chopped short, wavy and sculpted. "Why'd I go? For George, I guess. We used to... you know." His hand turned in a circle.

I could tell this wasn't all. If Nonna had gone there to see her son, maybe he'd had the same impulse. He could see his mother and he wouldn't need to apologize for leaving us. A wake was neutral ground.

I realized we didn't have much to say to each other...no, that *he* didn't have much to say to *me*. I was the one who'd called. I was the one who had to keep this going. He was the child, suddenly, and I was the parent who'd dragged him here against his clear wishes. Why couldn't everyone else, including that waitress, see him as I did?

But, being with him, he was hard to hate. He seemed defenseless, his hand trembling slightly when he reached for his cup. Maybe that's what drew people to him, that combination of confidence in movement, like a sleek horse, and meekness in temperament, as if he'd been beaten. If I hadn't been sitting across from him, he would've pulled out a travel bottle and spiked the coffee. It was past noon. Why not? I breathed in, to pick up the scent of liquor on him, but couldn't detect anything.

If we weren't going to catch up, I should bore in. Then I thought I would test out my child-parent assumption and wait him out. I turned over my cup and made sure it clinked as I did, something to break the silence.

Even though it was Saturday, I wore my work pants and boots and thermal brown coat, scuffed at the elbows, to show him I was making it in the world, that I didn't need him. The decision had seemed forced earlier that morning, as I trudged to the bus stop, but now seemed fitting as he cowered like a boy.

"How's work?" he finally asked.

I told him what I did, and about me and Freddy at the taverns, and I could tell he was going to make a joke of this, about how he should put in an application, but his drinking was a sore point between us, even though we'd never exchanged a word on the subject. My mother supplied all the words. That he never raised a hand to her or to me was about the best thing I could say for him.

Without thinking, I mentioned running into Royko and working at his office before a brief jolt of panic seized me. The column. About the fire. The fire was another thing we didn't talk about. He read Royko every morning, but he must not have been thinking about that column right then because a contented smile spread to his cheeks as he imagined me sitting at a desk outside Royko's office. I got caught up in the smile and the ease at which the words spilled from my mouth—when had I become such a yakker?—and, before I knew it, I blurted out, "So are you coming home? For Christmas?"

I was grateful suddenly for diners' voices and calls from the kitchen and plates rattling and the movement of cars outside our window, which took on new fascination for us, and that blessed waitress who wouldn't let Frank's cup dip below half and who continued to ignore mine.

"I'll have some," I said. "Coffee."

If I asked her to take a peek at Frank Lazzeri there, I don't think she would have seen the squirming. There was no visible change. Yet I felt it in my bones. My eyes shifted from the cars to the waitress's retreating steps to my father's chin, that didn't quiver, to his eyes that seemed cloaked now. My question about coming home still floated between us.

He sipped from his cup and began to reach to his shirt pocket for a cigarette but thought better of it.

I'd been discovering that, when you stopped feeling sorry for yourself, you didn't feel as much pity for anyone else, either, which seemed like a problem to me. I'd have to ask Maryann about this. But I did feel something, like I wanted to save the sonofabitch. But I waited.

He brought his folded hands to his chin and leaned on the table, the weight of the world on his shoulders, a move I'd seen many times, usually after my mom dropped the job ads under his nose, a gesture so meticulously gentle it was murderous.

His hands came apart, then together again. He glanced at me but decided the pie menu would be more enticing. He shook his head, as if deciding against the pie. "I can't go back to that flat," he said finally, his eyes flashing to mine, then back to the menu. "Nothing to do with you."

He was a terrible liar, the lie always tacked on to some truth and trailing off. Why even try?

But I didn't start any fire! I wanted to shout. *The old bastard who planted that idea in your head is cold and dead. Bury his poison with him.* A poor choice of words, which made me grateful I hadn't said any of it out loud.

"I know you've had it rough," he said. "But you're better off without—"

"Don't be feeding me any of that 'better off without you' bullshit."

It's true, I'm sure he wanted to protest. But he was better at folding his hands to his chin.

I wanted to plead, *Come home. Shut up and come home.* I wanted to tell him something that would tie us together, make him *want* to come home. I could tell him about my leg. He would finally understand the injuries. I could tell him about Ellie. No, that I'd never do. I could tell him about Lipschultz. I needed to tell him about Lipschultz. That, without question, would bring him home. Or would it drive him farther away?

"First of all," I said, "how the fuck does anyone know what's better for someone else?"

"You're right."

"Stop agreeing with me."

"I know."

"Stop." I heard my mother's voice in mine, the exasperation. She'd begin to shout, but how do you keep that up with someone who's agreeing with you?

"You've been through a lot," he tried again.

"You don't know my life. You don't know what…I've seen. Second of all, I'm twenty fucking years old."

The waitress suddenly appeared. "Ready to order?"

"Give us a minute," I said. She waited a good long beat, then filled my cup and glided away.

In my head, I furiously tallied what he didn't know about my life. Like waking up in the hospital and smelling ash. Like lunging in front of and swerving away from a moving car. Or talking with poor Ellie. Waiting for cops to bust into our apartment any day now. And the current running beneath all this? The pressure of being Frank Lazzeri's son—expected to carry on his gifts and to avoid the curses—which, when it came down to it, meant the drinking. My old man didn't know any of this. He didn't know anything about me. All this ran through my head, but what came out was, "You don't know what it's like to lose a sister."

He winced and his hand flinched, as if for hard drink, pure reflex. When had I become so heartless? And why? What good would come from wounding him like this?

"I imagine," he began. But he trailed off.

The faraway look in his eyes got my throat swelling, but I didn't want to give up my fury yet.

"Stop feeling sorry for yourself," I said. "I know you lost her, too. Your little girl. I'm not forgetting that. Not for a second am I forgetting that. What that must have been like for you. But…I've been through a lot, too. You said it yourself. But not once have you ever asked. What it's like…for me."

"That's why—"

"Why what?"

"You're better off—"

I had to resist calling him every mother-fucking street name I knew. I drew in a deep breath. "Let me decide," I said. "What's better. And…"

My eyes began to well up. He gave me a few seconds to catch myself.

"And what?" he asked.

"You do a lousy job deciding what's best for *yourself*." I wanted this to sound harsh and biting, another cruel hit, but I knew I'd missed my mark. My damn voice cracked.

One side of his mouth curled up because he was comfortable with *this* sentiment. *He was a loser.* This was his motto. He was a fuck-up and admitting this was his only defense.

I was grateful for the half smile. But it only confirmed what he knew to be the truth about himself and I realized we hadn't gotten anywhere. This was all he'd remember. That he was a loser, that he didn't deserve better. I'd been tearing him down, which only built him up. *Shit.*

But then he leaned toward me, his face close, and he said, "So tell me."

"What?" I said, knowing perfectly well what he meant.

He folded his arms across his chest and waited.

I couldn't do it. I couldn't tell him what I'd shamed him into asking. What it was like for me to lose a sister. Because I didn't know where to begin.

Other thoughts crept up that I had to battle. *You didn't even come to the hospital. You didn't see my cast. For eight weeks, I had a cast and not a call, not a card, nothing.*

Finally, after a long, slow sip of coffee, I breathed and searched for calm. I willed myself to forget everything and pushed aside all my gripes, which were pointless. I said, "Show me how to throw an off-speed slider."

He balled up a wad of napkins. I thought he would make an actual ball appear, like this was some magic trick. He cocked his wrist, ready to explain. But he shook his head after a while. "You know...I can't even remember. Not exactly."

"You're one royal fuck-up," I said.

"The goddamn king," he said.

We ordered BLTs and gazed at the flow of cars, the sound of their engines and the occasional horn muffled by the thick glass of the diner. In that anticipation of waiting for our food, my mouth watering, I peered toward the swinging doors that led to the kitchen and turned back to my old man and finally said, "I need you to know something. I need you to know…I didn't start that fire."

21

❖

Once the idea crossed my mind, how could I not follow him? Just to see. And I'd get to play detective for a few minutes. How could I resist that? And, with my old man, I didn't exactly need to be Dick Tracy.

He walked fifty yards ahead of me, half a football field.

Talking about the fire—or finding ways not to talk about it—had thrown him off his stride. He stumbled ahead, probably thinking about his promise to keep in touch, which he wouldn't keep. I could see the lie in his eyes, distant and flat. For a second, the corner of one eye had twitched as he tried to convince himself, but he couldn't even do that.

Walking now, he kept his head down, his hands in his pockets, and not once did he look back or in any other direction. He turned left onto a side street and left again into an apartment complex that didn't look as shabby as I'd imagined. Brown brick. Four stories. Two wings. At least six flats in each wing. I stood across the street and waited for movement at one of the windows, something to indicate that someone had just gotten home and needed to adjust blinds or let in a rush of cold air. My mother would scold him constantly for this. She was always chilled. But I didn't spot anything. His apartment faced the back, maybe.

I counted to a hundred. In case he pissed first and then went to the window. Nothing. I studied the apartment buildings on either side of his and couldn't detect much difference. On the other side of the street, where I stood, bungalows lined the block. Their owners peered out of their expansive picture windows each day and were greeted by this mass grid of apartments.

A truck rumbled by. After it passed, I gazed again at my father's building and noticed that one of the windows on the top floor was now opened a crack. I imagined him inside, going to the fridge and pulling out a cold can of Pabst, which was oddly satisfying to me. I would tuck this away in my mind's eye as I made my way to the bus stop. But, as I turned to leave, I noticed a hand at the window and then the window slamming down again to keep in the warmth.

❖

When I got home, after sidestepping Nonna and bouncing past Ellie on the stairs, I burrowed myself in my room. I wondered if everyone in my life was a phantom. Because they all looked at me with stone eyes, barely registering my existence, walking out of my life without a word. How could I know? Or maybe I was the one who didn't exist. Maybe I was part of someone else's huge head trip. I suddenly understood every head song I'd ever heard. If Perez was here, I'd tell him I needed to score some heavy shit. He'd bust a gut on the floor laughing because he'd never heard me use *score* this way, and I wasn't sure now if I'd used it correctly. I didn't know anything. I felt the guilt of feeling sorry for myself because it was Perez who was weighed down like the marching dead. Here I was with an entire apartment to myself, or so it seemed, with a record player in my room and instant meals downstairs.

I hesitated to phone Maryann. She was home now. She was always home. She'd taken the semester off and planned to start again in January. A new beginning. And she didn't need me bringing her down. But I did anyway. I called. And, as I waited for her to come over, I gazed down at the street. The police tape around Mr. Lipschultz's house was gone. Which meant they'd moved on to phase two of their investigation. Or so I imagined.

Maryann got stopped by Nonna, she told me, who supplied her with two biscotti, necessary nourishment for the long climb up the back stairs. She handed me one of the biscotti, which tasted like Mrs. Mazzolini's—many years ago, she and Nonna would bake together—and sat at the foot of my bed in her puffy blue jacket. She'd done something with her hair, though I couldn't say what. It was parted down the middle—was that it?—which made her look less like the girl I'd always known.

I sat on the chair next to my dresser, which held my record player. Out of the corner of my eye, I saw the turntable spinning 45 rpm without a record. Before I called, I'd been trying to decide between "In the Midnight Hour" and "A Whiter Shade of Pale."

We savored Nonna's little treat, studying the last bites before finishing it off.

"Your grandmother…she takes care of you."

"She does. This tastes like Mrs. Mazzolini's…"

Suddenly restless, she stood up and toyed with the zipper of her jacket, teasing me, it seemed, though I was likely wrong.

"I need an Italian grandmother," she said.

"Everyone does." I studied the treat. "I could make these, you know."

But I had other things on my mind. My fingers trembled. I wanted her to take off that jacket. I wanted her to take everything off, and for the two of us to slide beneath the cold sheets and lie there in each other's arms without words while the rest of the world sank away and all thought receded to white. The bedroom door needed to be pulled shut, though. How to get there without signaling my desires? Or maybe that's exactly what I needed to do.

"Shut the door," she said.

"What?"

"The door. Shut it."

There was a finality in her voice I found both reassuring—*Just tell me what to do*—and terrifying. I suspected doom.

"Come here," she said.

She took my face in her hands and kissed me hard and, as I reached for her, she nudged me away. "Sit down," she said.

I knelt and played with the zipper on her jacket.

"No! Over there. In your chair. Sit."

"You've made it a little hard to concentrate."

"I know. I know that. And we're going to finish what I started. 'Cause I know what you want. And I know you won't be able to think of anything else if you're wondering if it's going to happen. So we'll get that out of the way. It's going to happen, okay. But we're going to talk first. I've been doing a lot of thinking and I need to say some things and hear some things. Okay?"

I crawled back to the chair, my heart in my throat. "Go ahead," I squeaked.

"Those nine days in the hospital. They really got to me. I realized how easily any one of us can slide into that dark hole of…of brokenness, and I decided I wouldn't let that happen to me and I decided that when I got out I would face things head on, I wouldn't shy away from—"

"You mean, like me. Like I'm good at."

"Yeah, like you. You're an expert at not facing things. But there's no time. We're all here for such a short time. You'd think we would've learned that by now, you and me. But we didn't. I'm starting to. I want to. What I need is for you to be completely straight with me. No holding back. Look at me. Start there. Look at me."

"Okay, okay, I'm looking. What do you want to know?"

"Start with the leg."

"It's better."

"But?"

I shrugged.

"Look at me."

"This would be easier if I were on the bed with you and we were holding each other."

She wrapped the jacket tighter around herself.

"Sorry," I said. "The leg? The leg is better, but I still wonder sometimes where my body ends and where the world begins. I can't always tell what's real and what's not."

"It's all real," she said. "Even if it's an illusion. Because you have to deal with it. The dealing with it is real. You're real."

"You definitely need to become a therapist, because I'm feeling better already."

She broke her gaze and shook her head in dismay.

"Sorry." The last thing I wanted to do was upset her. What the hell was wrong with me? "I guess what I mean is that I feel sometimes like I'm playing a role, one that I don't particularly like. I know I can't change the play. That's out of my control. But I want to play a different part. You know what I mean?"

"Maybe."

"I mean, there's so much happening out there. People fighting wars, people protesting against war. I feel like something big is happening, and we're sitting here on Avers Avenue doing what?"

"Where do you want to go?"

"I was thinking...what's stopping me from going to, say, California? What's holding me here? But, now that my leg is better, they'll probably draft my ass, anyway. So, maybe Canada, because I can't picture myself sleeping in some foxhole. But at least I'd be away from here."

She let her arms fall. Underneath the jacket was a crisp blue blouse with buttons. The top buttons near her breasts were tight. I imagined fumbling slowly with each one.

She didn't mind my peeking. She knew what she was doing.

"Here it is, Anthony...I'm going to ask you a question. I don't want a joke back. I don't want a shrug. Just tell me. You talk about leaving here. Is there something here you're trying to...escape?"

She'd eliminated my main arsenals. Now what? The truth? I would try one last tactic. "And if I asked *you* a question, you would be completely straight with me, too? I mean, whenever we get around to talking about...school, the fire, what you remember...

you…I don't know, you…you look like someone kicked you in the gut. But you…I don't know…you fight it. If I asked you about that, would you tell me?"

She bunched her lips and her entire body moved in a kind of slow nod. "I would. But only if you truly wanted to hear."

Of course I didn't. I couldn't bear that. And she knew this. And had me.

She tapped her foot, waiting. When she realized what she was doing, she stopped.

If I wasn't upfront with her, she'd zip up that jacket and I'd never undo those buttons. She wasn't exactly a genius but that's what it felt like.

"What am I escaping?" What direction could I go? I planned on telling her about my old man, but that wouldn't be enough.

"Let me help you, Anthony. Let me ask you this, do you know anything about what happened to Mr. Lipschultz?"

I nodded, my mouth twisting.

"Did you have anything to do with what happened?"

I wouldn't look at her. No matter how much she insisted, I wouldn't gaze into those eyes. I wrung my hands and imagined all the hand wringing my old man had done over the years. And, finally, I said, "Yes."

She pushed herself from the bed and began pacing, peering out the window each time, as if expecting a squad car to pull up.

"Tell me," she said. She sat on the floor and pulled me down with her, our faces close. She smelled like strawberry shampoo. "Tell me."

I stumbled and started and told her every detail about that night, which I have since tried to erase without success.

"My God. What did you do?" That's all she could say. Over and over. And this. "Poisoned! My God! You're sure? You have to…*we* have to get away from here."

She paced again, stopping at the window each time, peering out, trying to collect herself, her breathing labored. Finally, she rejoined me on the floor.

"I can't believe it," she kept repeating. A thought suddenly occurred to her. "And you don't see *him* now, do you?"

"No."

"Thank God. Thank God for that."

I was afraid to tell her that I hadn't seen Ellie again until weeks later. I didn't want to utter this aloud. It was bad enough that I'd had the thought.

"Listen," she said. She pulled a joint out of one pocket and matches out of the other. "I've been doing a lot of thinking." She held the joint in one palm and the matches in the other, as if weighing them. She knew the weight of what she was suggesting and waited to see if I would take them from her.

I did. I rolled the joint between my thumb and finger, inspecting it, then placed it on the floor with the matches on top of it.

"I don't know," I said.

"It's time to move on, Anthony. For the longest time, I was envious. And I almost convinced myself that I'd be able to see her, too. But I don't have that in me...what you have. Which is a gift. And a curse, too. But you need to let that go now. And besides..."

She didn't finish. With all her talk of not holding back, she couldn't bring herself to say it aloud, either. But I knew what she meant. This pot would serve as a kind of guarantee that I wouldn't be haunted by *him*.

"You're trapped. Don't you see that? If you don't do this, if you don't let her go, you'll never leave this apartment. Even if you go to Canada, or California, or wherever."

I'd been thinking the same thing. I'd been thinking of going back to see the mirror lady, telling her about Ellie, to see if she had a mirror for that. And Miss G would be waiting in the car again. Maybe I'd tell her everything, too, because sometimes she seemed to know me better than I did myself.

I lit the joint. One joint wouldn't change anything. We both knew that. I could always stop. But the first shallow drag still seemed colossal. I passed the wrinkled cig to her, and she drew it in deeply, as if encouraging me to do the same, and I could tell she'd learned a few things at college.

I didn't feel anything. Maybe a bit of tiredness. But I could see the mellow soon overtake Maryann.

"What else?" she asked. "What else is weighing on you?"

I told her about having lunch with my dad and following him, which should have sounded inconsequential, after talking about poison, but not to me. If it made me seem like a hardened bastard, at least I wasn't holding back.

"I was about to walk away, march to the bus stop, but for some reason I went to the door and looked for his name. And that's when I saw it. I found his name all right. Frank Lazzeri. But it didn't just say Frank. Below his name was my mom's name. Just as big as his. Not like it was tacked on or anything."

"Oh, my God."

"I know."

"When I walked in here, you looked like you'd been run down by a truck or something. My God."

"So they *both* needed to get away from me."

"Maybe that's what it feels like, but you don't know that. You don't know the whole story. There must be—"

"What?"

"I don't know."

She stood and took my hand and guided me to the bed, where we sat and held hands and finally turned to each other.

"I want to be clear about something, Anthony. Are you listening? Look at me."

"I'm looking."

"I'm feeling a little shaken right now. A lot shaken. But I want you to know that what I'm going to say has nothing to do with that. I've been thinking about this for a while, and I want to make sure I get this out."

"What?"

"I love you. I've always loved you. And I will always love you. I will always be here for you. But what we're about to do—" She broke her gaze, looking awkward suddenly, struck shy by what she wanted to say. "What we're about to do—" She stole a glance at the bed. "We will never do this again. Never. We both have to move on."

Tears began to fall, some of them mine.

There was more she had to say, but she realized that what she'd said was enough.

I was about to ask if she still wanted to do this, but she reached for the back of my head and pulled it to her chest, probably so I wouldn't see her shaking her head. Amid salty tears and tentative grasps, we lay together without hurry, taking in each brush of an arm, each entanglement of a leg, gently peeling each other's clothes off, then touching and breathing and thrusting toward each other with a fury reserved for two people in love whose tomorrow is stolen. Then we collapsed onto each other and slept, a sweet weightless dozing. Later, after wiping the grogginess from our eyes, we clutched and pawed again, and through more tears, of resignation this time, we made unhurried love a second time.

22

❖

I woke with Maryann gone but still fragrant on me. I burrowed my head beneath the sheet and breathed in, trying to bring back what I could from the night before. Her dark scent mingled with the acrid leaves we'd smoked, and I could picture her curves and feel the softness of her tongue on my neck, and I began to harden and weep because I knew what we'd done would never happen again. I burrowed deeper, aching to preserve every touch, every moan. I let my hand crawl low because the image of Maryann pulsed clear in my mind, she was there next to me, and I pretended my hand was hers. But I stopped because another image began to intrude, not unlike the image that had startled me awake weeks before. It began as a pinpoint of blackness, and I knew I wouldn't be able to stop its damn worming its way through. I tried. I pulled my hand up and tried. But I felt like I might suffocate and snapped the sheet back and opened my eyes to drain away the Polaroid in my mind of Lipschultz lying dead on his kitchen floor. How much weed would I need to smoke to erase that? And I wouldn't resort to anything stronger. Not this time. I gripped my chest, as if this would stop the hammering.

I'm an expert at sidestepping, at evading, at changing the subject, at not showing my hand, at not saying a goddamn thing—an expert—and yet I'd told Maryann everything. Because to hold back would have meant not getting in her pants, to put it crudely, which I don't mind, but what we'd done together was holy and pure…and yeah, dirty, but beyond comprehension…a kind of primitive renewal. Besides, I needed to tell someone all those things. I needed purging. Though I must have failed at this because my heart was only now easing its pounding.

The nightmare had begun, I'd told Maryann, three Saturdays earlier. I woke that morning and Mr. Lipschultz was in my face, telling me how I'd rot in jail. His face wasn't real, but it wasn't a dream, either. I was unmistakably awake. Though I couldn't shake him. I could almost smell the rot of his breath. And this went on for I don't know how long. Terrified, I rifled through my dresser and found Perez's gift inside the deck of cards and placed it under my tongue. Soon, "Purple Haze" became more than a song. It felt like I'd *written* the song. The opening riff pulsed through me, over and over again, seeping through my arms and my one good leg. I became the song. I couldn't recall much more about the trip, other than hobbling in and out of the apartment because I had to *move*. Which must have exhausted me because, much later, I found myself back in bed again, waking up a second time, as if from a nap. The sky was darkening. I thought I smelled bread. But, when I went downstairs, there was no bread. There wasn't even much of an aroma, just a faint trace from maybe the day before.

I searched the usual places for bread in Nonna's kitchen but came up empty. I shrugged and started making myself a bologna sandwich with stupid Wonder Bread, and I wouldn't have given any of this another thought if I hadn't glanced out the kitchen door. Nonna was coming out of Lipschultz's house. She trudged down his stairs and slapped her hands together, as if to remove any excess flour, but they were clean. The slapping was about finality. *That's done*, said those hands.

Her screen creaked opened and then sprang shut. In one graceful sweep, she slammed the wooden door and turned the lock and swept her hands together again, up and down, then wiped them one final time on her dusty apron.

Our eyes met, and there was surprise in hers.

You hungry? she said with her eyes. She took in the insulting limp slices of my sandwich. *I make some a thing.*

*The bread…*I wanted to ask…*where's the bread?* But I felt like I'd caught her in something and didn't want to corner her. I would give her an out. But that aroma. I breathed in deeply. It was unmistakable. I couldn't think of much else now. And she knew.

Nonna, she's a master at evasion, too. She marched past me to the refrigerator and began to fill her cutting board with onions and garlic and chopped away without another word.

You took the bread to Mr. Lipschultz? All of it? Not a single loaf for us? But I didn't say anything. I didn't know what to say. I went back to my room and listened to side B of *Revolver* and came back down at dinnertime. She'd already left for church. Sundays were for Mass, Saturdays for confession. I found a plate of cold chicken and buttered peas, and a salad with vinegar and oil and oregano. But no bread. As I ate, I scanned the counter and the top of the oven for a loaf.

Another faint odor began to assault me, something stale and bitter that I hadn't noticed before. I leaned into my meal to block the scent, then finished and straightened up and looked at the savory oil left on the plate. I almost reached for a slice of bread. This was Nonna's kitchen, and reaching for bread from the wire basket in the middle of the table was a natural reflex, though her baking had become less and less frequent over the years. But the basket was empty. And, tonight, my plate would not be wiped clean. I was a little devastated.

I caught another whiff of the intruding odor. And as I swirled the juices on my plate with my fork, the source of the odor began to dawn on me. Rat poison. I'd worked with the stuff at Streets and San. Months ago, I'd brought home a couple of boxes for Nonna. I carried my plate to the sink and searched the usual corners where Nonna and I would spoon it out, mostly on the back porch. But I didn't see anything.

I checked under the sink. An open box was there, the usual spoon beside it. I crouched down to tamp down the flap, to stem the smell. And that's when I saw it. On the side of the box, slashing the picture of a beady-eyed rat, was a single streak of white. I knew the poison was gray. The poison was gray, wasn't it? I picked up the box and peeked inside, to make sure. Oh, please God, let it be white inside, let it be an old box from last winter, maybe the stuff calcifies and turns white.

I ran a finger through the middle of the streak and stared at my finger and was tempted to taste it but didn't, of course, but that's what it was, unmistakably, a fresh streak of flour. Holy mother of God.

I put the box back exactly where it had been and washed my hands several times and wiped them on my pants as I paced frantically from one end of the apartment to the other. Even when my hands were dry, I kept wiping them. That was the only thing that kept me from passing out. This mad pacing and the frantic wiping of my hands.

I knew I had to get out of there. I couldn't face Nonna. But I became transfixed by my pacing. I couldn't stop.

A car door slammed. I raced to the window to see if it was Lipschultz leaving his house. And if it were? Would I rush to him and shake him and plead with him not to eat the bread? But it was just Mrs. Weed. Probably driving off to get some supplies.

I checked under the sink again, to make sure I'd placed the box back where I'd found it, then left the apartment and continued my pacing farther and farther down the street. I glanced over my shoulder to see if anyone was following.

Should I knock on his door? And say what? Nonna wants the bread back? He probably downed the entire loaf already. She probably brought over a stick of butter, too. Who could resist a few slices of fresh bread? I was too late. But I could warn him, at least. Send him to the emergency room. And, hours later, a paddy wagon would be picking up poor old Nonna. *What were you thinking, Nonna?*

And then another bright thought I couldn't hold down. *He'll be dead. The old bastard will be dead.* And my worries about a squad car pulling up in front of my house to cuff me would be over. But this was a fleeting thought.

I couldn't move fast enough, so I began to run. I ran for what seemed like an hour. So fast that all I could think about was the sucking in of my breath, these deep gasps that strained for relief. And when I finally stopped, my left leg throbbed. I'd pushed it too hard, and my old compulsion to crush the damned leg returned. I deserved this punishment.

I thought of calling Freddy, who could make a few calls, maybe. Make things right. I didn't know how, but for a few blocks I held out hope. It would be a hard call to make, I knew. In the end, I didn't call, a regret I'll have to live with. And Freddy would have told me, "Relax, kid."

So I did nothing.

I waited.

I didn't even try to sleep.

The next morning, the winter sun burst through my window and stirred me awake. I must have dozed off for a few minutes. I was sitting up in my bed.

In a couple of hours, Lipschultz would leave for church. I returned to my pacing, lingering at the window, startled by the slightest movement or noise.

A sickening dread overtook me as I saw the usual entourage of neighbors leaving their houses for nine o'clock Mass, but not Lipschultz. The other ushers would have to cover for him. And one of them would surely call his house after Mass. Or maybe I could do that, pretend I was calling from the church. And, by the way, I could suggest, get yourself to the emergency room if you're not feeling well.

I realized I didn't have his phone number. Why would I? What reason would I ever have to call the old bastard? But I wasn't about to call information now and go on record.

Instead, I bundled myself up and limped over to his house and knocked on the front door. Because I had nothing to hide. He didn't answer. I knocked harder, peeked through the window. I went around back and peered through the lace curtains his wife had picked out years ago, and sprawled there on the floor was old Lipschultz. I knew I had to back off from that window and casually saunter home, before someone spotted me, but I couldn't tear myself away. I felt sorry for the old guy.

But I did, finally. And slunk home.

Nonna was at church. Right now, she'd be turning her head, counting the ushers. Searching for that big dome.

Out of desperation, an inkling of a plan began to form. By noon, I knew what I had to do, but I also knew that I'd have to wait until dark. I couldn't risk being seen. The wait for the sun to fall was torturous. I sat by my window, praying that no one would appear at his front door to find out why he'd missed Mass. Maybe praying is the wrong word because I didn't dare bring God into this.

Torturous, too, was reaching for the key on the high sill and trying to still my hand as I inserted the key into the slot in the door. The more swiftly I tried to move, the more gnarled and shaky my fingers became.

There was already a slight stench. I didn't know if I could do this. A night light from the hall was shining. I wouldn't need the flashlight I'd brought.

I thought I should check his pulse, but his body hadn't moved. And I'd need to remove Nonna's garden glove to touch him. I couldn't do it.

I took the box of rat poison out of my pocket. I'd already wiped it clean of prints. I removed it from the plastic bag and knelt down by the body—it wasn't even Lipschultz anymore, it was a body, which made it easier in some ways, but I thought I might pass out, and wouldn't that be a nice headline? *Gimp Found Beside Poisoned Cop!*—and I heaved in a settling breath because I had to finish what I'd started. I took his hand, his pulseless hand with those huge sausage fingers, all bluish gray, and placed his thumb and fingers around the box, pressing his prints on the cardboard. Then I gently placed his hand back onto the floor.

I rummaged through a few drawers before finding a spoon, then stirred two teaspoons of poison into a half-filled coffee cup on the counter. I dipped the spoon back in the box, careful not to smudge his prints, then placed the box next to the jar of Coffee-mate on the counter. That was it. That was the story. The old man had gotten confused. He'd accidentally poisoned himself. I already started believing this. It didn't seem all that farfetched, given all the vileness he spewed his whole life, or what I knew of his life.

I turned to leave but froze when I remembered. *Where was the damn bread?* I tore open the fridge, the light assaulting me for three solid thrums of my heart. I tried the garbage, picking through banana peels and cigarette butts. In a panic, I marched to his room for a glimpse at the nightstand. Nothing. I had to get out of that house. I had to get out, now. But I couldn't go empty handed. Back in the kitchen, I nudged his hulking middle with my foot, thinking the bread had gotten lodged beneath him. No sign. Some sound came out of me, a pathetic whimper. He'd eaten the whole thing, I decided. That was the only explanation. Then I glanced at the counter. In plain sight was a familiar loaf. Half a loaf. Roughly torn, as if he couldn't wait to devour it. I ripped apart the remaining half and stuffed everything in my pockets, along with every crumb.

As I left, random lines from prayers rose up reflexively and taunted me. The nuns had taught me well. I knew I wouldn't be heard, but I prayed anyway, asking God to spare me from damnation and prison and Maryann's scorn. Because, even then, I knew I'd tell her. I got no answer, other than a bracing December gust of wind, sharp and unforgiving.

23

✦

D ays later, from upstairs, I heard unfamiliar footsteps in
Nonna's kitchen. My first thought, which chilled me but
that I couldn't dismiss, was that old Lipschultz was lurking
around down there, brewing up some special potion for me. Even
if this wasn't real, even if this was only my guilty imagination—
well, that would have been worse—I had to investigate.

With light treads, I made my way downstairs and heard an
unmistakable real presence. Then a shadow crossing the kitchen.
Mrs. Mazzolini was at the door, about to leave.

"You scared me," I called out, hoping I'd do the same to her,
which I did.

She cried out something in Italian, then calmed herself and
said, "Soup. I leave soup. Minestrone. I know you like."

"Thanks. Thank you. *Grazie.*"

She reached for the doorknob, but turned back suddenly and
sat me down. Before long, a bowl of steaming soup was placed
in front of me, along with three thick pieces of her homemade
bread, the sight of which seized my heart for a second. I pushed
aside the bread and leaned over the warm bowl.

"Eat. Enjoy. I go."

"Wait," I said. "I want to ask you. Why do you…every day
you wear the same…always black. I never asked you…"

I knew the answer perfectly well. I wanted to hear it. Her
voice alone was comforting.

She pulled down the sides of her sweater, pursed her mouth to hide a swell of anguish. I thought she might sit, but she leaned into the table, her slight frame not budging it in the least.

"Your sister. You miss, no?" She heaved a sigh, as if she might cry. "Well, I miss, too. So many children I miss. Even if I don't know name, I miss. Every day. Every night. I pray." She smiled at me. "I pray for you, too."

"I need it."

She rolled her eyes and nodded at the same time, a gesture that spoke of Italian hillsides. *Of course*, she was saying. *Anthony Lazzeri needed help.* The most obvious thing she'd heard all day.

She pinched my shoulder and left, the sweet scent of anise trailing behind her.

Nonna appeared soon after, and I told her about the soup and Mrs. Mazzolini's prayers and recalled how the two of them used to cook together. Then, finally, I got around to what had been weighing on me.

"Why'd you stay, Nonna? You stayed the whole time. At the wake. Mr. Lipschultz's wake. Why?"

She stood at the sink, her back to me, while I leaned against a countertop.

"Is why they have," she said.

"Is why they have what?"

"Wake."

"I don't understand."

"They make wake, so people they know."

"Know what?"

"If breathe. If they keep...*morte*. 'Cause some a time, long time ago..."

"They have wakes to make sure the person is dead? Is that what you're saying?"

She shrugged *of course*, the corners of her mouth curling into a mock scowl. "Is true."

"You weren't sure he was dead?"

"I want…make sure he…sonomabitch no come by my kitch no more."

As if she were suddenly alone, a fury of whispers burst from her lips, mostly unintelligible. So she thought. *Sonomabitch. By my kitchen. Talk talk. Mio nipote e prigione. Ha.*

Prison! Her grandson in prison!

I felt something give beneath me and gripped the counter. I glanced down at my cursed left leg. Lately, whenever I was dealt a blow, my damn leg collapsed first, the rest of my body following its cue. I wouldn't allow Nonna to see me crumple, so I trudged to a chair and sank into the table. This was the old bastard's parting gift to me. Planting this poison in Nonna's head. That I had killed my sister. She would never believe this, but that the thought crossed her mind was torture enough. What she had believed was that Lipschultz was about to arrest her grandson. That would have been his play. He bore down hard on her and told her that jail was coming. In a matter of days. Unless I went to him and told him everything. Then he would make all of this disappear. She could help. She could talk to me. Ask me to do the right thing. The exchange would have gone something like that. Because he regarded Nonna, in her old country ways, as simple. He would be able to manipulate her, he thought, and she would bow to him.

But the thought of her grandson, Anthony Lazzeri, in jail, flipped some switch inside her. *What would he eat in jail?* Her reasoning might not have gone much deeper than this. She would do anything to stop this. Her solution probably seemed fitting to her. Poison for poison.

"What did he say? When he came here?"

She didn't answer. She'd said enough words for one day.

I watched the second hand of the starburst clock on the wall sweep one complete revolution.

"You can go to jail, you know."

I waited for her back to stiffen with the recognition that I knew what she'd done. But I saw nothing.

I hadn't told her…I wouldn't tell her…that I was ready to go to jail for her. I was probably an accessory, wasn't I? Jail was where I'd go anyway. No use both of us getting locked up.

She rapped the pan down on the dish rack and started in on a baking sheet. "You crazy," she said. "Nobody go to jail." She pffffted and whispered again. *I no go. He sonomabitch.*

I could barely look at her, but I couldn't look away. What she'd done. What she'd caused me to do to protect her. I wouldn't have believed she had this in her. No one would believe it. Maybe her mind was slipping, too. Maybe she didn't fully comprehend what she'd done, as if some sleepwalking self had taken over. But her movements at the sink, those fingers dipping into water and emerging to attack the baking sheet, not an effort wasted, were more fluid than I'd seen in years, as if she'd finally been called upon to act. She wasn't just some dark shadow lurking around a kitchen cooking for no one. Her family needed her.

❖

I went upstairs and tried Maryann at school. No answer. I called Freddy. His wife said he was out. He probably hadn't come home from work yet. Thursdays were late ones for bellying up to the bar. I'd been pressing him about the cops and what they were up to. He didn't know anything. But I hadn't talked with him for a few days. I called Miss G. She said I should come to school the next day after work. She sounded lighter than usual, a mysterious lilt in her voice, as if she'd decided on something. I imagined Friday afternoon cocktails and a light dinner and driving around in her car and stopping to neck until she couldn't stand it anymore, then turning the ignition and heading toward her apartment. I didn't picture more. I wanted to savor the anticipation. I needed this distraction.

She was pushing files into a tall silver cabinet when I ambled in, the last of the slush from the newly fallen snow melting from the toes of my work boots. I noticed because there was someone else in the room, a long-haired girl with her back to me, stapling papers to the bulletin board, and gazing at my shoes was always my first option when I didn't know where to look. The girl had on a chocolate-brown top that puffed out at the sleeves and faded jeans with loose threads at the bottom. There was the hint of red in her long hair.

"Anthony, you made it. Good. This is Alexandra."

Alexandra. I'd never met an Alexandra. She turned and waved with her fingers. The front of the top was cut into a vee and loosely laced with a thin cord. Something about the swell of her breasts seemed unusual, and I realized she wasn't wearing anything under all that brown. She turned back to her stapling, and I turned to Miss G to avoid staring...to avoid being spotted staring, that is.

"Hiya," I said.

"Hiya. Come in. Take off your jacket. Sit. We were just... Alexandra was helping me out. She's been helping."

She talked while she filed and, whenever she turned to the cabinet, I stole a glance at the back of that brown blouse, looking for signs of a strap. Thank God for public education, where girls didn't have to wear uniforms.

"Alexandra, that's good for now. How about sorting these cards?"

I remembered the cards. They were part of a simulation game on the Civil War. Miss G tossed them on her desk, across from a small desk where I sat, and picked up a few papers and held them separate from a few other pink carbon copies and finally stopped her flurry. "I'll be right back. I need to get these to..." She trailed off and left, leaving in her wake the scent of all that paper and carbon and the faint trace of black markers.

Sitting across from Alexandra, I realized now why Miss G had asked me to stop by. Rather than orchestrating some awkward staging of letting me down easy, which she knew I'd find insulting—she was flattered by my interest, she'd insist, cared about me, cared so much in fact that she'd allowed that to interfere with her judgment, but there *was* the age difference, not exactly insurmountable, but still, and we had been teacher-student and now she didn't know what we were, though she would certainly spare me any mention of an old boyfriend back in the picture or that she couldn't imagine being with a Streets and San worker or that we didn't have that much in common or that she'd decided that yes, she was finally moving to California, for real this time—instead, she'd introduce me to Alexandra, who was also confused about college but firm in her ideas about what she *didn't* want to do—work in a factory like her parents, work behind a desk sharpening pencils, work solely for money—though she was timid in expressing these ideas because they were her ideas and she didn't want to impose them on anyone else, and I found out much of this because she felt immediately comfortable with me, the result of Miss G talking about me, which I would have liked to hear, and because I looked her in the eye, a conscious decision that kept my gaze from roaming elsewhere, and because after a while I wanted to know and listened, and in this way, I forgot about myself for a while.

She was that girl in class you never noticed. And, when you did, you felt stupid. Because she'd been there the whole time, this strong, quiet, beautiful girl with the freckles and green eyes that seemed impossible, who might seem a little awkward at first because she was used to being invisible, which was why she may have worn the sun-yellow cotton headband in her brown hair today, not that she wanted to draw attention to herself, but she liked the way it framed her face and because no one would notice anyway, and so this was a small thing she did for herself.

"She must have gotten lost, huh?" I said.

"Must've."

"So Miss G was talking about me? What did she say? I'm afraid to hear."

The cards had been sorted, and she looked around for some other task to occupy her hands. "Not much. Mostly about college. Because I told her I wasn't sure. And she talked about, you know, how maybe the two of us should talk because we're both unsure."

"Like maybe we would cancel each other out, and then we'd both know what we wanted."

She laughed politely at my weak joke, out of mercy. A good sign, I thought, feeling more and more grateful for Miss G's kindness, who had visited me in the hospital and brought me to the mirror lady and offered me a tablespoon of tenderness in the car, maybe had gone too far with that and now needed to retreat, and who had now led me here, to Alexandra, who I was certain had her own closet full of burdens and regrets but who was wholly unfamiliar with mine. And, because of that, there was a kind of purity in our talking, each unaware of the other's past. I wanted to preserve this, prolong the innocence between us. Because I knew, in time, if we became friends, if we went out, that I would taint her. My sorrows would become hers, and I wasn't sure I wanted to do that to someone.

"Alexandra. I never met an Alexandra. I'm not sure what to think of it."

"You're not sure what to think of it?"

I'd been thinking about her name and gotten caught up in these private thoughts and knew I should retreat, but I was feeling comfortable, as if I were with Maryann, the thought of whom caused an ache in my chest. And I'd been discovering that talking helped to ease that ache.

"You know, some names are harsh. Like Ralph. Ralph Kramden. Remember that show? Jackie Gleason. And some names, they're soft. Like Lisa. So I'm not sure about Alexandra. What to think." I paused to give her a chance to run out of the room. "But I like it," I added, a beat too late. She didn't flinch at least, as if she'd had doubts about her name, too.

"I'm named after my grandfather. Alexander. So, yeah, it's a little...different."

"I like it. And to have that connection with your grandfather."

"I never met him."

"Still."

"You're right. I do feel...I don't know...this kind of a bond with him that I can't explain."

Until that moment, I couldn't quite put my finger on what I saw in those green eyes. They were distant, like she was searching for something she was afraid she'd never find.

"Miss G, she says you have a friend over in Vietnam."

I nodded, not sure what to add.

"My brother's there."

I shook my head. *Sorry.*

"On the news, every night now, they tell you how many U.S. soldiers were killed." She paused, as if trying to recall the latest report. "Every time I hear, I stop. I try to prepare myself for the knock on the door or the telegram or however they do it. Which is maybe my way of...it's the only way I can think about it. Like I won't be able to deal with that sadness all at once if it comes, so I swallow it in small doses."

"It's hard to let go of someone."

"And then, after my dread passes and I can breathe again, I get really ticked off. How many Vietnamese were killed? Why don't they report that, too? Their lives mean something too, right? If maybe we think about it this way, maybe that's how this fighting is finally going to come to some end. And then a commercial will come on and then the Monkees. Can you believe that? We're in the middle of a war and they're still making episodes of the Monkees. And this is the worst part—I watch it, I watch the show. I can't tear myself away."

She seemed embarrassed for having gone on like this but didn't want to draw attention to that and so simply stopped. I listened for Miss G's footsteps.

"So, what are you doing? After you're done here?" I asked.

She scanned the room, pretending to tally all the stapling and sorting that needed to get done, but her eyes turned cold as she weighed an answer. She wasn't used to this dance. She slipped off her headband and pulled her hair back and slipped the headband on again, touched it along the sides to get it right, all of which excited me because, one, she was playing with her hair, and two, for a moment I wasn't there. She'd turned inward, lost in possibility. *Do I tell this jerk—who doesn't know what to make of my name—to disappear, or do I give him a chance?*

So, I waited, because to say anything now would cloud the intent of the question, which, in the growing silence, became more packed with meaning.

She made another pass around the room with her eyes and said, "I'm not doing anything, I guess."

"Me either," I said.

24

❖

When the weather broke, I'd hitchhike to California. Not tell anyone. Because there was nothing to hold me in Chicago. That thought, and the image of me climbing into the cab of a truck and listening to the hissing of the trucker's CB as we rumbled east, put me in a dream state as I hustled to the bus stop for work that early Monday morning. And, because of my daydreaming, I didn't see the car pull up a few paces ahead of me and didn't fully register the passenger window sliding down until I heard my name called.

Who the hell? It wasn't Freddy, not in a Thunderbird. I approached the car and leaned down and squinted. I raised my hand to visor my eyes. Holy hell. Lipschultz. That big face. The same fat face. The cheeky jowls. Those steady eyes that locked onto you. I removed a glove and touched the car to make sure it was real. Freezer cold.

"You remember me, right?"

I nodded, panic rising up my spine like a slow flare.

"George," he said. "Next door."

The old bastard's son. The old bastard reincarnated. With the same gravelly voice. Those troglodyte lips.

My first thought was, *Don't knock on Nonna's door. Don't eat the bread. Torture me instead. I deserve it.* I turned to look toward my apartment. We were far enough away not to be spotted by my fugitive grandmother. Maybe I'd take her with me to California. What a pair we'd make with our thumbs out.

I dared to meet his eyes again. He waved me inside. A delicate gesture. Even with those thick fingers, he didn't possess the heavy-handedness of his father.

Oh, no. Not again. I've taken this ride before.

But I climbed in. I didn't have a choice. I couldn't let him see me being evasive.

The window slid up, sealing us in.

"Where you headed?" A whisper of whiskey on his breath.

"Bus stop. Work. You don't have to."

"It's an icebox out there, pal. I saw you walking."

And just happened to be driving by.

"How's your old man?" he asked.

"He's okay." He let the silence build, waiting for me. "Sorry about your father. The neighborhood…isn't going to be…the same."

"Everybody will be able to breathe now," he said. He glanced at me and flashed a confidential half smile, but I wasn't biting. I stared ahead, my head turned slightly toward him so I could gauge his intent.

He asked me where I worked and insisted on driving me there. The least he could do for an old neighbor.

Then he'd know not only where I lived but where I punched in. He could find me anytime he wanted.

He undid the middle two buttons of his black overcoat. A fresh wave of smoked cigarettes was unleashed and settled into the already stale smoke smell wafting from the upholstery. "Mind if I ask you a few questions?" he said.

I shrugged because I didn't know if I had a voice.

"Did you notice anything different? With my dad?"

He had to use "dad"? Not "father" or the casual "my old man" but fucking "dad"—like he wanted me to know how close they were and how hurt he was by the old man's croaking, so I would break down into some weepy confession. Well, I didn't intend to crack that easily. *Dad!* The nerve of the bastard.

"What do you mean? I'm not sure what you mean."

Too much. *I'm not sure what you mean?* The question would have been enough. I was sounding nervous. Maybe because I was.

"Did he come out of the house? Did you see him walking?"

"Sure. All the time. He was walking all the time. If the weather was…you know. He sat on the porch a lot. If the weather…was… okay."

A little tap on the steering wheel, as if he was tallying my missteps.

"Did you talk to him?"

"Sure. Sometimes…sometimes we talked."

"Did he seem like his old self?"

Was he an asshole to the end? Did he still intimidate and threaten? Sure.

"I guess."

"He didn't seem like he was losing it?"

Play it cool. Not yet. "Uhhm. I didn't see him *that* often."

"Right. That's just it. If you don't see someone too much, you can see the change. You know what I mean."

And you, you sonofabitch? You'd come by every night? You need me to weigh in when you're the expert at not seeing him?

"He'd call me Frank once in a while. That's about it. Is that what you mean?" Too much. Too fucking much.

He pursed his lips, a smugness crossing his face. "And you just thought of that? Right now you thought of that?"

"What do you mean?"

"I asked if he seemed like his old self." A hardness crept into his voice and into the muscles of his jaw. "And you said, 'I guess.'"

On second thought, stop by Nonna's house after you drop me off, you cocksucking son-of-a-whore. Have some bread. I stuffed my fists into the pockets of my jacket. This I didn't need. *Everyone will be able to breathe now.* Not everyone. Not yet.

"I guess," I said. I was thirteen again, sullen and distant. Did this asshole have kids of his own? Had he witnessed this act at home?

"Hell of a thing to forget. My dad confusing you with someone else."

"I didn't forget. I just didn't...think of it. When you asked."

I'd already told him where I worked. No use jumping out at the next stop.

"My dad," he said, "he didn't like you, did he?"

We were old pals, him and me. "I don't know. I really...don't know."

Out of the corner of my eye, I saw the grin. "I thought you might say, 'I guess.'" The grin broadened into a cruel smile.

I tried to hide a deep, heaving breath. I wouldn't give him the satisfaction of hearing me sigh. He had nothing, I told myself. Otherwise, he wouldn't beat around like this.

"So you didn't see anyone creeping around his house? Maybe by the back door?"

The key. Had I wiped my prints off the key?

"No. I wish I could help you." *I wish I could help you.* "I didn't see anything." Don't ask don't ask...don't ask. "Why? Did someone—"

"Did someone what?"

"Nothing. I'm just wondering why you're asking."

"Look, you and I both know my old man was losing it. And we both know he had it in for you. You can tell me. Did something happen between the two of you?" He lowered his voice, trying to infuse it with kindness. "And, whatever you tell me, it stays here. Between the two of us. Did he say something to you to set you off?"

I thought, *You are not your father. I spent more time with him in the last ten years than you did. And I learned a few things. And you learned nothing. That good cop bullshit won't get you anywhere. You need the old bastard here with you for that to work.*

I turned and eyed him squarely. "Me and your old man, we were pals."

He nodded, all the kindness draining out of him. Like his dad, he couldn't stand punks who didn't bow to his threats. A grunt gurgled out of him. His knuckles on the wheel turned white.

We drove a few blocks in silence, that finger tapping the wheel.

"Your old man," he said. "How's he making out these days?"

I heard the insinuation in the question. My old man the loser. This was how he'd hurt me. If I wouldn't tell him anything, at least he'd leave me wounded. *Go ahead, Lip-shitz. You can't touch me. There's nothing you can say.*

"Every time I see him," he said, "I can't help but think, 'What a shame. All that talent.'"

That's it? That's all you got? I've heard this number before.

"I saw him at the wake, you know. But we didn't get a chance to talk much. You didn't make it there, did you? To the wake. Anyway, your old man and I, we were pals."

He paused a few beats, as if I'd miss the great fucking irony of him repeating what I'd just said. *Yeah, well fuck you, pal.*

"Jack Daniels was his drink. But you probably know that. If it weren't for the whiskey, who knows." He shook his head. He let me take this in, too. All that drinking. Such a waste. And now he slowed himself, his words taking on a new gravity. "The two of us, we'd get plastered. And he'd tell me things. Things he never told anyone. Not a soul. I didn't remember half the shit he told me, but one time...ah, you probably know all his stories. Why he started drinking in the first place. You don't need me..."

I wouldn't turn toward him. This is what he wanted. I didn't move at all. Which may have been worse. I willed myself to look away at what we passed. The storefronts. The cleaners. The hot dog stand on the corner with pure Vienna beef. I couldn't believe how many houses had awnings. Corrugated plastic awnings. I'd never really noticed. And all the ornate gates blocking entry to gangways. When I got to California, I'd miss those Chicago bungalows.

"I mean, I'd start drinking, too, if I had to live with what he did. I mean, it was an accident and all that. But killing his sister? That's some dark shit. Pour me a double. And keep 'em coming. You know what I mean."

Was he talking about me? About me and Ellie? What the hell was he talking about?

I turned toward him. "Your dad was full of shit," I said. "And you're a bigger pile of shit."

He pulled to the curb, moved the stick to Park, and draped his arm over the seat, content he'd gotten to me.

"Someone was in that house. My old man's house. Some things are just a little off. And I intend to find out who it was. And, when I do…"

He didn't need to finish. That much he'd learned from his old man. I imagined the two of them sharing the same house all those years ago. Like two pit bulls. One would do anything to protect the other. Not unlike Nonna.

I pushed myself out, waiting for the satisfaction of slamming the door. But, as it swung shut, all I heard was, "I'll be seeing you."

25

◈

There must exist an asshole gene. Because this was classic Lipschultz. Plant a dirty mine. Then step back and wait. The satisfaction came in the suffering. But George didn't live two doors down. He wouldn't be able to witness my agony. And he didn't have the patience of his old man.

After he dropped me off, I raced to find a phone booth to warn Nonna. They're on every corner when you *don't* need one. I imagined our conversation, telling her in my best Italian, and with what I hoped was dead urgency, that she needed to lock her doors and not answer if Mr. Lipschultz's son knocked. *George. His name is George. You remember George, right?* I would have her repeat what I'd said.

Then a brief comedy would ensue.

She'd snort.

"Do you understand? Are you sure you understand?"

"You want I make bread?"

"No! No bread."

I'd tell her I would take care of everything, that there was nothing to worry about. And all she'd worry about is if I'd taken a lunch.

No phone booths. I kept moving. I didn't know what else to do. I walked the twelve blocks to work, my eyes on the lookout for a shit brown Thunderbird. Would I forever be peeking over my shoulder? *My old man had it in for you, didn't he?* The old bastard had talked to his son about the fire.

I passed three phone booths and slowed at each one but realized I didn't have any change, only a few bus tokens. Maybe I could begin my hitchhiking right now. But I was headed east, already in the wrong direction. If I would have stopped, right there in the middle of the block on Diversey Avenue, and turned, crossed to hop on the CTA, hopped off again at the bank, where I had a little savings book, not much but enough to get me started, I could begin my escape out west. I pictured hiking on roads lined with orange groves and sloping through green valleys. A clean slate. I could change my name. Tony Lazarus. That would be fitting. Maryann would've sneered. She wouldn't have approved of any of this thinking. But she wouldn't have a solution, either. Take classes! Too late for that. But I didn't turn around. I marched ahead, my shoulders hunched against the frigid air, my cheeks blistered with cold.

After a few blocks, I realized why I wasn't going anywhere. I wanted to see Alexandra again. Such a modest yearning this was. But it was enough. Though we'd only gone out once, not counting the stroll along Ashland after school that day, and though I hadn't told her much about myself, maybe *because* I hadn't told her much, a warmth filled my throat when I thought about her. We'd gone to see *The Graduate* and, on the way home—after we'd climbed off the bus, and before turning up her street, still feeling the exhilaration of the last scene—I grabbed her hand and pulled her in and asked if she wanted to go out again. She glanced down and away. For a second, I was devastated because I thought she was going to suggest that we be friends, but I was learning how to read her and spotted surprise, plain and simple surprise, and so I leaned down and kissed her. She pressed into me and haltingly took the back of my neck with her hand. If there's a better thing in this world than that—the gentle cuffing of the neck, the fingers pulling you in, welcoming you—well, I haven't found it.

Thinking about Alexandra caused a ripple of guilt, as if I were betraying Maryann, but this is what she wanted, what she'd insisted I do. Move on.

I got to work, punched in, waited for dispatch, almost forgot to head to Loading for salt since no new snow had fallen overnight, and the flakes coming down now wouldn't amount to much. Not on my shift, at least. I waved goodbye to my foreman, Big Mario, who winked at me, knowing I'd have an easy day, clearing a sewer drain here and there. If he only knew.

I drove through Freddy's territory, hoping to run into him, but he never followed any particular route. I tried his store, where Melba was still ringing up pints and sliding them into narrow brown-bag sleeves for customers, eyeing me with amusement, but no, she hadn't seen Freddy all day.

I circled my old man's apartment, stopping in front and gazing up at his window, which was closed. I tapped the top of the steering wheel like I'd seen George do that morning, deciding. I got out, left the engine running, checked a sewer grate, kicked away a few leaves, and returned to the truck. I glanced at the window again, cut the engine, and finally worked up the nerve to ring his bell.

The buzzer to unlock the hallway door rattled, and my heart seized. In a matter of seconds, I knew it was my mom upstairs pressing the button. My old man wouldn't have answered as quickly and he wouldn't have held the buzzer as long. I'd been rehearsing what I might say to my dad, calculating his reactions, but I hadn't factored in Mom. In the four months since my broken leg, I'd seen less and less of her. I imagined a graph illustrating this decline. The more swiftly I strode on crutches, the less she came around to nurse me. From what I remembered in school, from a chapter on statistics, this was a negative correlation, though not seeing me may have seemed positive to her. She'd leave me notes, explaining that she was staying at her sister's house and reminding me of doctor appointments, the orthopedist's, never the shrink's. I wasn't sure if she knew I'd stopped going. Sometimes, she'd attach a few dollars, never specifying what to buy as my father might do.

I reached the second-floor landing and turned.

"Anthony!"

The door was open a crack. She peeked out, looking small, a tentative smile spreading. She opened the door wider and came out to hug me. I hugged back and didn't ease my grip because I wasn't sure I could face her. I wanted to run downstairs and pretend I hadn't rung the bell. This was all a big mistake.

"Is everything all right?" she asked. "How did...did Daddy tell you...it's good to see you. We've been meaning to...talk to you. Come in. You're working? Come in."

"I just wanted to...I don't know...ask him some...you probably need to get to work."

Her white pants and blouse were pressed. I could hear the hiss of the iron inside and smell her pink hand lotion.

"No, not right away. Not for a while. Come inside."

She usually wore her hair shoulder length, but now it was shorter than mine. One less worry in the morning in her frantic rush to get ready. But she seemed—I didn't want to admit it— settled. Happy. Not hurried at all. The sad distance in her eyes was gone. Her cheeks were fuller, as if she'd been sleeping well. Her hair was...browner. A darker shade, maybe.

Inside, sections of *The Daily News* were scattered on the floor next to the couch. A half-filled coffee cup rested on top of the sports section. All signs of Dad. The room was mostly bare, with touches of Mom, the throw rug at the entrance, where I wiped my boots, a crushed blue carpet between the two couches, the ironing board, the white curtains on a level rod. And the radio scratching a tune from some other room. The Grass Roots singing about midnight confessions. This is what I'd been missing at home, I realized, her transistor radio on the shelf above the sink tuned to WLS. I wanted to follow the music to see if it was the same radio.

"Daddy...he's working," she said. "Believe it or not."

The only time she referred to him as Daddy was when they

were getting along. And I hadn't heard *Daddy* in a while. Though she did feel compelled to add the last little dig.

"He comes home. For a sandwich, sometimes. If you wait... if you want to wait."

We sat across from each other stiffly, as if we'd just met. She knew I expected an explanation but danced around this, asking about work and my leg and if I was hungry, something she'd never ask at home with Nonna downstairs. But this was *her* apartment, and I was her guest, and she felt an obligation to make me feel welcome.

What the hell are you doing here, Mom? That's what I wanted to ask. But what I said was, "So, you..." I swept a hand from one end of the apartment to the other, which felt like a gesture my dad would use. Though I'm not sure I actually did this. I may not have moved at all, only my eyes. Either way, she understood. But I should have come earlier, while she was ironing. She would have had something to do with her hands then. Sitting and fidgeting, she seemed like someone else.

"It's...hard to explain," she said.

I have time. The sewer grates can wait. I wasn't proud that the great city of Chicago was paying me to sit on my old man's couch, but I wasn't racked with guilt either. Freddy might've been a little proud.

She started and stopped several times, as if she'd been doing her own rehearsing about what to say, but the words weren't falling into place like she'd intended. She hadn't been expecting me, she wasn't ready to talk about whatever it was she wanted to talk about. Not today.

"You know what. Hold on."

She marched out of the living room, past a small dining area, and toward the music. I heard it turn louder and then Mom on the phone. I couldn't hear everything she said, but I could tell by the way she talked that she wasn't talking to my dad.

"That's right. Sorry for the late notice."

She came back without turning down the music, for which I was relieved. *Turn the television on, too. And the vacuum cleaner.*

"You called in sick. You never—"

Why call attention to that? What kind of asshole calls attention to that? There was a reason she'd turned up the music. A familiar restraint crossed her face. She was going to ignore what I'd said and move ahead. But she didn't. What this was, was a different kind of restraint. A new kind of determination.

"I did. I called in sick."

She paused and waited for me to meet her eyes, which didn't take as long as she expected. We were two different people sitting across from each other.

"There aren't many things I love more than my job," she said. "But there are a few."

Like Milk Duds. In a dark theater. On a Sunday afternoon. With Tony Curtis. But I didn't say any of this. I didn't say a word. She seemed a little perplexed but mostly grateful. Which emboldened her to say the next thing.

"It feels…it feels as if we've never talked. I don't know if this is the way most parents feel. I think it probably is. But I feel it especially…"

With a kind of half grip, as if something had just fallen out of her hand, she pointed to me, to herself, to us. Yes, especially with us. Too much had gone unspoken. The story of my life. And I realized by *my* unease the critical role I'd played in this. Anytime she'd tried to see how I was doing, I would shut down. There were reasons, of course. I needed my armor. But I was the one who hid. She probably thought, *Oh, I'll give him his space, he needs his space.* And then that became what we did. I thought about all the pity I'd unleashed on myself because no one cared what I thought. How could they ever know? I suppose I'd expected my mom to read my mind. Was that too much to ask?

And then another thought, out of nowhere.

"You're not dying or something, are you?"

She leaned into the couch, as if thrown back by a harsh wind. She smiled, forced yet genuine. "What—"

"I don't know. The way you're talking, like you're worried you're not going to be...like your time is..."

"No, I'm not dying. No cancer. No disease." She laughed.

"Good."

She glanced at the sports section. "But the time thing. I do feel that. Like I've wasted...you get to a certain age, and this... this urgency creeps in. Which sounds trite, I know, but it's true."

The old faraway look returned, the one that raised me. The look that said she was too preoccupied with grief and didn't have time for me, which I always understood, because I did the same, though I could never swallow my stupid resentment when I saw this in her.

"You asked me a question before," she said.

"I did?"

"What I'm doing here. That's what you wanted to know." She seemed to be making an effort to stop wringing her hands. "It's become increasingly difficult to go back to that apartment," she said.

I nodded. I understood. Though I didn't.

"Dad, he said the same thing."

She drew back, ready to explain, then stopped.

"Does it have something to do with me?" I asked.

She put up her hands and shook her head. Though she couldn't say, "No." Her eyes welled up, but she caught herself. "Daddy and I..." She cleared her throat, choking back tears. "It's confusing. We've been talking about...this is a two-bedroom and we thought maybe you could...but then we didn't know what to do about..."

"So why can't you...why can't you go back to our apartment?" I knew the answer. Why did I need her to say it?

A single tear fell now, but her voice was resolute. "I think you know why, Anthony. But it's important that you hear this. I wish I'd discovered this sooner, to think about what *you* need to hear, because it's taken…my own…what I mean is…at the hospital, I've been seeing my own…therapist." She drew in a deep breath. "I wish I'd gone sooner."

"So say it. Why can't you go back?"

"Because it's too painful."

"You think it's easy for me?" Especially now. Alone.

"I see your pain, Anthony. I know. It's as plain as day. But, for you, there's also a kind of…a kind of comfort being there. Am I right? I've felt that comfort, too, being close to the things your sister touched. I've gone into her room and picked up those things myself. That little music box she used to open just to annoy you. Her clothes, her shoes. And I imagine. But with you, it's different. I see that. You have this capacity for…for feeling. Which probably seems like a curse sometimes. But, my God, I've heard you, Anthony. I've heard you…talking to her. At first, I thought you were sleepwalking. But I realized…she was there…before your eyes. And you can't imagine my envy. I wanted you to teach me. I wanted you to tell her something from me. And even though I knew it wasn't real, it would have been real enough. If it was happening before your eyes, I could convince myself that she'd heard me, too. But I couldn't bring myself to say a word. I didn't want to spoil this…this thing you had. How could I?"

"Ellie. You can say her name, Mom."

"Ellie."

Now the tears came freely, and I moved next to her and she sank into my chest, and I thought, *What if Dad walks in right now and sees us both sobbing?* I wanted that. I wanted nothing more than for him to see that.

"She's here," I said. I wiped away her tears and pointed to my heart. "She's always here." And no, Ellie wasn't there, not in the usual way I saw her. But with my mom weeping, believing, my little sister was more real than ever.

We talked some more and waited for Dad to show. She knew about my leg, too, she admitted. The doctors had told her not to draw attention to it, which would only make my preoccupation worse. I would outgrow this "disease," they assured her.

"But they didn't know what they were talking about. And they didn't bother to find out. So I did my own searching. I'm a nurse. What did you expect?"

I nodded, waiting for her to tell me what she found.

"I did find case studies. Not many. But documented. And real. But there were no answers. And besides, I knew this…this torture you felt over your leg was tied somehow to your capacity to…to see Ellie. And how could I take that away from you?"

"And you thought the shrink would do what, then?"

She shook her head. "I don't know. You had so much going on. I thought it would be useful to you in some way."

In my head, I thanked her for not belittling my preoccupation with my leg or connecting it with Ellie, as if I were expressing sympathy pains over *her* weak leg. She remembered. She knew my obsession began well before Ellie turned sick with the first hairline fracture when I was barely seven. But maybe, just maybe, as one doctor had the balls to suggest, I was sympathizing *before* her illness struck, as if my body was foreseeing the future. I thanked her also for not suggesting this nonsense, either. The two horrible conditions—Ellie's stricken leg and my lame one—were eerily similar, yes, but this wasn't some curse handed down by a diabolical God, and my body didn't possess glorious telepathic powers. No, our troubles, or my troubles, were gloriously mundane. Odd maybe, but ground in the dirt and grit of this world.

We sat there in comfortable silence, both aware that this talking is what we'd needed long ago. But we wouldn't have been ready. We would have been a mother and a son without a language, preverbal in our grief, each unable to muster up a single word of comfort for the other.

Then she said something I'd never considered, though it sounded familiar, as if I knew it in my bones. She said, "How could I have sent her to school that day? She'd been running a low-grade fever. Maryann, too, 'cause they'd been playing together. Ellie was better by Sunday, sure, but still. She could have stayed with Nonna. Nonna would have watched over her...after what she'd gone through, the post-polio thing, you'd think I would have been more...I should have been a better mother. I've tortured myself over that. I'm getting better at not being so hard on myself. But I think, sometimes, that I didn't love her enough. Otherwise..."

And this, her mounting doubt, her anguish, is what tore me up, finally.

26

✦

And then they were both there, shoulder to shoulder, on the other side of the table in his tiny kitchen. They seemed propped up like tall scarecrows. A splinter of late afternoon sunlight slanted onto the gray Formica tabletop, illuminating the chrome edges. I envied the Herman's Hermits, who were "into something good" on the radio. One of those stupid songs that get stuck in your head.

I sat there at war with myself.

Do I tell them everything and shatter this...whatever this was...peace? The three of us in the same room. Or do I follow my instincts, which they'd taught me well, and bury what I needed to tell them, what I needed to ask?

Nonna needs your help.

I studied the wallpaper above the wainscoting over my old man's shoulder instead, though I couldn't tell you the pattern now, only that it seemed coated by a fine layer of grease. I don't have this compulsion often, but I wanted to get a soapy rag and wipe it down. I do remember my old man's shirt, an oversized button-down flannel that Mom had probably washed and ironed.

They said it might be a good idea if I moved in with them. My mom said it, actually, intimating that the two of them had been talking about this for a while, which I imagined as Mom talking and Dad nodding, whether he agreed or not. And now they were waiting to hear what I thought.

"What about Nonna?" I asked. My favorite method of stalling.

"God damn," my old man muttered.

They exchanged troubled glances.

"We talked about that," my mom said. She glanced again at my dad before adding, "We'll work that out. She could, maybe, *be* here, too."

And scour the walls.

I chewed the inside of my lip and nodded. That would solve nothing, I thought. The son of a cop would find us. Hell, my old man had probably given George his address at the wake. We all needed to move farther away. *I'll be seeing you.*

A coil of panic twisted through me, but for a different reason. I'd been trying to wean myself from Ellie. My room had become a weed emporium. But, in the back of my twisted mind, I knew I could always quit. I'd quit before and everything had returned to normal. Normal! Ha! But to leave entirely? To imagine someone else in her room? In my room?

"You okay?" Mom asked.

"No," I said. "I'm not."

"Tell us. Talk to us."

"I'm not used to this. We haven't exactly been…"

"We can start."

I wasn't sure.

I wasn't convinced they really wanted me there. What if I hadn't shown up? It felt to me as if we were having two conversations, the one in my head—ranting like a maniac with finger pointing and screaming, *Where the hell were you when I needed you?*—and the one they witnessed, me sitting with my arms folded, trying to appear defiant, which wasn't that difficult.

What if I hadn't shown up?

Yet, there we were. Talking. Mom not rushing off to work, her lotioned hands on her lap, her back straighter than usual. This is how her therapist sat and waited. At least this is what I assumed because she wasn't acting quite like Mom. There was an openness about her that seemed foreign. Later, when I'd had a chance to think about this, the irony hit me hard. She'd lost a daughter and, until now, could barely talk about this with her son. She'd been paralyzed with grief, which was understandable, but she'd never really *grieved* because of the goddamn suffocating neighborhood we lived in, which was something my shrink had mentioned one time but that I'd never understood until recently. You were supposed to make the sign of the cross back then and keep your head bowed and move on. Mom was a victim, too. But, now, revolution was in the air. She wasn't wearing tie-dyed shirts or planting daisies in her hair, but a quiet revolution had taken root within her. My shrink would have been proud of my insights.

Or maybe, and this was harder to admit, we couldn't have had this conversation at home because I would have been searching for Ellie over my shoulder, and Mom, watching me, knowing, would have been even more guarded than I was. What a pair we were.

And my old man? He studied his fingers, glanced at my mom, rocked in a steady tight rhythm that was barely noticeable. He'd stopped drinking, Mom told me. And this rocking, apparently, was one of the aftershocks. As if he were tallying the seconds he'd been sober. Or, to an observer like his merciless son, counting down the time before he gave in and downed a quick shot at the bar. Just one. Having convinced himself that, after one, he could turn and stroll back to his happy family. What an asshole I was for not believing in him. For not helping him instead.

"So, the job's going...?" I asked him.

He drifted into a more pronounced rocking. "Good. It's good. Not bad."

For three months, he'd been working as a bartender at a neighborhood tavern a few blocks south. Who knew bartending better than he did? And, for six months, he'd been sober.

"So, you think it's...okay...you think it's a good idea, you working there?"

Ordinarily, Mom would have either come to his defense—*This is a test for him, he needs to do this, he needs to face this, and give him credit, six months is six months*—or joined me in attacking him. But she held back. I could see the restraint in the twisting of her fingers.

I calculated. He'd been sober before he left. And, if Mom's version of the story was accurate, he'd remained sober. On his own. Until she joined him.

Finally, she opened her mouth, closed it, then said, "You know Dad can survive on the tips alone, right?"

I took in the kitchen that wasn't as ratty as I'd first imagined, then met their eyes. Even Dad was looking at me, waiting for a hint of a smile, because what she'd meant was that customers would tip him well because he was a charming sonofabitch and that maybe his son could find it in his heart to acknowledge some of that charm. What went unsaid was that there were deeper currents running beneath that charm, or rather, running beneath the drinking, a darkness I understood…but didn't. But I could see that he, unlike my mom, was not ready to talk about this.

I didn't smile. I turned inward. About now is when I'd have searched around for Ellie, but I knew she wouldn't be there. I should have at least said goodbye to her before hitting the weed. I didn't say a goddamn goodbye. This is probably how the two of them felt every day of their lives.

"About moving in. What do you think?" my mother asked. But, in her nervousness, it came out rushed. *Whattyatink?*

I shrugged, picked at a crumb on the table.

"We know it's asking a lot. Leaving. It's the only place you—"

I glanced up at my old man, who quickly averted his eyes and shrunk into his chair. Apparently, he knew about me and Ellie, too. And he was embarrassed to know. How many times had they talked about me?

I'm not crazy, I wanted to shout. *And, besides, I'm smoking weed. Lots of it. I've moved on.* But I didn't believe this myself.

"I don't know," I said. "I need to get the truck back."

Mom leaned back, hurt. She'd taken off work. We'd talked, really talked. And she'd broken down. We both had. Then Dad showed up and the walls had risen again. What did she expect? That I'd move in that night? That we could break down years of stonewalling in a single day?

She rubbed her temple, as if wiping off the hurt, determined to maintain her poise. Even though it was a role she hadn't quite grown into—the casual leaning, the pasted smile meant to convey great patience and unvarnished acceptance—I was grateful for the effort. Ordinarily, she would have turned short with me and said, flippantly, *Well, you better get the truck back then.*

"It's complicated," I said. I'd give them this. Room for them to probe. Room for her at least. This was agony for my old man. He wanted this to end. He needed for this to end.

"What do you mean?" *Whattya.*

Give me a piece of paper. I'll tell you what I mean. I'll fill every line. Because this wasn't only about leaving my sister, as they probably assumed, though this would *not* be a point of discussion, not with my old man there. But I couldn't talk about the rest, either.

For starters, I wouldn't be able to smoke here, and Ellie might take up residence, too. Also, Nonna would not agree to moving, and she couldn't be left alone there. I couldn't tell them why because they'd become accomplices or accessories or whatever the cops called it.

When he saw that I wasn't going to offer even a shrug, my dad shifted in his chair and began a series of throat clearings that included a fist over his mouth and a half cough. "Maybe it's time, Anthony, to move ahead," he said. "Do you think—"

"Do I think what?"

A look of resolve washed over him.

"Don't you think *she* would have wanted that for you?"

Ellie. Say it. Say her name. And to use that on me. He of all people.

"And what about *your* sister?" I said flatly.

Their eyes became pinned to each other for a second.

"What would she want?"

I had hit my target. The blood drained from his face. The slow rocking ceased.

"I don't even know her name," I said. "You say you want me to move in here. For what? So we can be a family? When did we ever have that?"

She reached for his hand. He didn't move away. I couldn't recall the last time I'd seen them touch. Such a small thing. Yet... *You can do this,* she was signaling to him.

He didn't cough or clear his throat. His eyes bored into the gray tabletop, which was dull now. With the sun nearly gone, the two coils of fluorescent bulbs from the ceiling fixture seemed suddenly harsh.

"Lucia," he said.

Three syllables. *That's a beautiful name,* I wanted to say.

"I called her Lucy. Nonna hated that. My dad, too. Not the name. But that we were here...in America. Not even that, he just missed the old country. He never came to terms with that...with leaving. He never felt he belonged here."

I didn't dare move.

His eyes traveled from the table to the casement window above the sink to his own hands. His face became longer somehow.

"All Nonno wanted was...he didn't want much. I didn't think I'd inherited that, but I did. I see that now. What he wanted was to work hard and not be cheated...and to come home to a good meal and a glass of wine and a game of cards at night with some friends."

Mom squeezed his hand. I pretended not to notice.

"He wasn't...he didn't spend a lot of time with me. He was always beat for one thing. Cutting meat all day. Those hands. If you could've seen him at work. Anyway, when I was a kid—I barely remember this but I know it's real—he'd get on the floor with me, with my army guys. Or play catch with me in the backyard, which was rare. But to have that again..."

193

He shook his head. He wasn't anywhere near to crying, but Mom was. If I weren't there, she would have taken his head and cradled it to her shoulder. I'd never seen this, but I felt as if I had.

"He'd muss my hair whenever he saw me. Before, that is. I always loved that. But that was the extent of it. Fathers back then weren't exactly, you know…involved."

No, not like today. But I buried this quickly. He was so deep into what he was saying that he didn't pick up on the irony of what he'd said.

"But, when Lucia came, something changed in him. Every time he saw her, his face brightened. It was the same with everyone who saw her. She had these big brown eyes. He'd pick her up and rub his nose in her neck, and she'd squeal, and the whole room would be laughing."

I wasn't sure he would go on. He released himself from Mom's grasp so he could fold his hands under his chin, as if in prayer.

He glanced over at me. "Nonna would dress her in these frilly dresses. Even when we were playing and running around." His eyes became distant, imagining. "She was four years younger than me and she liked to play chase."

He stopped, ran a hand through his hair.

"It's okay," my mom whispered.

"One day, we ran into my parents' room. We were usually shooed out of there, but Nonna was busy in the kitchen, and so we ran in there, and my sister, she was just about to tag me. And—"

He could use a drink. A tall glass. No ice.

"I twisted away from her. So she wouldn't touch me. Just a little twist. And she fell. In front of the dresser, she fell. I knew she would get up in a second and that I had nowhere to go. I was cornered. So I started climbing. I climbed the dresser, it was this tall thing. I knew she couldn't reach me up there. I imagined looking down, teasing her. Then I heard Nonna's voice in my head—I can still hear it now—warning me about climbing. Because I used to climb everything. I got in trouble all the time.

And then it…you know…it happened so fast. I grabbed the top of the dresser and got a good strong grip, ignoring Nonna's voice in my head, and pulled myself up. But, my feet, they kept sliding. I couldn't get any traction. So I started kicking…these wild kicks. Because I could see that she was going to get to her feet any second. Any second, she was going to tag me. And that laugh. My feet kept sliding and I got desperate, so I pushed my foot against the wall, *behind* the dresser. And, the whole thing, it started tipping. The most horrible few seconds of…there was nothing I could do, and I knew, I could feel how heavy this thing was. I screamed her name, to warn her. But she couldn't…I'll never forget those eyes, looking up. Not frightened. Just confused. I don't know if I screamed again, but I think I did because my mother came flying in, or she'd heard the crash, and she started screaming, too, and cursing and I realized that no sound was coming from under the…that goddamn stupid dresser. Just a sickening silence."

His fingers were shaking. They seemed to match my own trembling coming from somewhere low and dark.

"I wish I could say that not a day goes by that I don't think about her. But I can't. Because, after a while, I couldn't bear it, reliving that. It's an effort. It's an effort to forget. A drink sometimes helped. But I've made a mess of it. You know it better than anyone. And I know I can't make things right. Between you and me, I mean. That's off the table. It'll never happen. But maybe there's room for something."

I called up an image of a truck pulling up to our apartment when I was young. Two guys in gas station jumpsuits hauling my new bureau to my room. The reason I've kept this tucked away all these years is because of what happened next. Because it was so unusual for my old man to have a hammer in his hand. After the men left, he slunk into my room, took out the top drawer, and began banging long frame nails from inside the dresser into the wall studs. I didn't know he even owned a hammer. It took him a while to pound the nails flush because he couldn't find room for leverage inside the top of the dresser like that. His t-shirt was blotted with sweat and his forehead pulsated with heat, and then he disappeared for a few hours, which wasn't unusual. When he came back to inspect his work, rested and reeking of bourbon, he seemed content—that big bureau wasn't going anywhere—but even I could tell it was a shoddy job. And I never gave it another thought. Until now.

None of us moved. No one had a word to say.

From the tinny transistor radio, the Animals sang, "I gotta get out of this place." Any song would have taken on extra meaning then, but I could see that, at the moment, I was the only one who heard. And the meaning I imposed was not for myself but for my old man. But there was no place for him to go.

27

❖

I didn't stay.

I returned the truck to dispatch, where Big Mario told me to stick close to the horn because a big storm was coming. *The storm has already hit*, I wanted to tell him.

On the bus, the lights too bright overhead, I fingered my paycheck and decided it was time to buy a car. I was tired of being a passenger. I could still call up the trace of whiskey on my new pal's breath that morning, even though our pleasant ride seemed a lifetime ago. I kept playing back that jowly grin and the menace in his voice and wondered how the hell I was ever going to sleep. It seemed like I'd been balancing on a tightrope for months. I tried my shrink's old trick—of tensing each muscle and then relaxing—and soon found myself giving in to the jostle of the big bus, my bones absorbing the hit of each pothole, my neck swaying forward and back with the hiss of the brakes.

I tried to think of a word to describe the day, a word Miss G might come up with, one that would impress Maryann—or make Alexandra take notice, but not too much because she probably still wasn't quite sure what to make of me. Half the time I didn't know myself. *To know thyself.* We read an essay in English…junior year, I think…with that line in it. I don't remember anything about the essay. Or was it a play? But I remember the line, and daydreaming in class, and the great comfort I felt that some writer out there in some room with a desk near a window had the same doubts. You think I'd have paid closer attention, trying to learn something from this guy who'd spent time contemplating the very thing I was obsessed with. But I was off in my own world, probably thinking about my leg and how cursed I was.

Tumultuous. That's the word I came up with. A tumultuous day. Like no other. And yet, after thinking about my morning ride and my weepy talk with my mom and the nightmare my old man had kept from me all those years, what I kept coming back to was the quiet time sandwiched in the middle. The two hours spent waiting for Frank Lazzeri to come home from his bartending duties. Because, during that time, with Mom brewing coffee and then sitting with one leg tucked under the other on the couch reading Frank's newspaper, and me reading the sports and other sections I usually had no interest in, like Dear Abby, who advised a reader to follow her heart regarding an old flame, I felt protected. A blanket of stillness had descended on the apartment, and I didn't want that broken.

Like in a dream, my old man's baseball card came to mind. The card had always seemed unreal to me, like he'd gone to a novelty shop and rented the Tigers uniform and the orange and black cap. The way he fought back a smile only heightened the impression, as if he wanted you to see he was pulling a fast one on you. The card was stored in a cigar box on a shelf in my closet that included a baseball signed by Hammerin' Hank Greenberg, apparently worth a few dollars today, and a box score from one of the few games my dad had played in. The box score had been neatly clipped with scissors but would've been thrown out if I hadn't retrieved it one day from a pile of papers ready for the trash during Mom's spring cleaning—an annual event that became more frenzied after Ellie died, though we never touched her room, as if she was only away on a long trip. The last item in the box was Ellie's scapular from her communion, with a picture of Mother Mary on one side and the date of the holy sacrament on the other, its own kind of box score.

I wondered if they knew about these small treasures I'd kept hidden in my closet and guessed that they didn't. They didn't dare. They'd been through hell and needed to protect themselves from added grief. Oh sure, after the fire they wouldn't let me out of their sight, touching me as they passed, as people do after a loss. But soon we fell into our routines, the three of us occupying the farthest reaches of the apartment, sauntering around flat-footed, barely glancing at one another, afraid to shatter the delicate balance we'd built. I couldn't have known then that my old man's inward glances were filled, too, with images of his poor little sister lying under a heavy dresser. I couldn't have known that he was replaying in our apartment the same tiptoeing that had gone on with *his* mother and father. What torture that must have been, the death of his daughter tearing open old wounds that would never really heal, even without this fresh tragedy.

After a while, the walls of our apartment must have suffocated him. The far corners weren't far enough, and he had to leave. And Mom, she understood. She wouldn't try to hold him there because that would only drive him farther away. And, she probably figured, he always came back. She understood him. She understood his drinking, too. But she was helpless against that. The drinking was too big for her. But, this time around, with six months under his belt, she was determined. Something was raging inside her. Maybe she believed this was her last chance. That's how she probably laid it out for him. *This is it, Frank. I'll put my name on the mailbox, but I can easily pull off that ten-cent label, and then we'll never see each other again. Is that understood?* And my old man, he was grateful for another chance, one last gasp.

And where did I stand in all this? Had they given me much thought? Or were they so caught up in their own pain that they couldn't glimpse mine? Because I didn't cry? Because all my grief was inside? Did they assume I was fine because this is what they needed to believe?

What my mom had confided scratched open memories of long ago, especially all the sighing they did, which they must have believed was silent. I remember now…*If only*….that's what I heard in the sighs. If only we hadn't sent Ellie to school that day. She'd been feeling run down during Thanksgiving. And, though she was better, another day of rest would've been what a good parent would've ordered. Now I can add the other regret to that memory, my old man's pain, the tilting and the clawing that he must have played over in his head a thousand times. How does someone get over that? I would have started drinking, too. I would have believed, too, that I never deserved any good goddamn thing that came my way. And, when some good break did come, I would have sabotaged all my good fortune, as my old man had so expertly done. I, too, would have disguised this as modesty. This "modesty" probably seemed attractive to my mom when they first met…and then infuriated her to no end after they'd been married for a while.

If only.

All the things we could have had. That's a common refrain, what I always come back to.

A turn into a different room while playing, and we would've had Aunt Lucia. I liked the sound of that. And even though she would never be any older than two, I would start using that—*Aunt Lucia*—even if it was only in my head.

A few *more* sniffles, or a rattling cough after Thanksgiving, and Ellie would've been heading off to college last August. Which was about the time I broke my tibia. Though I may not have broken it. And there would've been no need for Nonna to be baking a friendly loaf of deadly bread for that bastard of a neighbor, who would otherwise have registered as less than a blip in our lives.

As usual, regret burned a searing hole in my chest. But, this time, I saw more than my own. Maybe this is why they never told me much. Maybe they thought I had enough to handle.

Gazing out the dirty window of the bus, I never realized how many shit brown cars there were that looked like Thunderbirds. Brief jolts of panic came and went with each sighting, but the jolts seemed distant, like only a dim reconstruction of the panic I'd felt that morning. Which gave me confidence that maybe I *would* sleep tonight. I'd already begun to distance myself, something I was good at. But, as I began to slump back in the seat, my eyes heavy again, a new terror took hold. That sonofabitch would go after Maryann…and I hadn't even warned her.

28

❖

By the next morning, we'd gotten hit with five inches of snow, the kind every kid hates because it doesn't pack well, like it's made of sand. The snow was still flaking down, with another five inches coming. The buses were running late, but I finally got to work and was reamed out by Big Mario, who asked me why I hadn't picked up in the middle of the night. *Maybe because I disconnected the phone*, I wanted to bark. Because a certain prick decided it would be a good idea to call and hang up after I'd answered. I sensed the fragrant punch of whiskey after each click, pictured his whiskers gnashing against the mouthpiece of the phone and thought I heard the bristling before the click. He may have been an amateur compared to his dad, but balls-out terror didn't require much nuance. And it took its toll. After disconnecting the phone, I strained to hear whether Nonna's phone would start ringing, too. It didn't.

I pushed out of the truck yard and stopped to call Maryann. Her mom said she'd gone out but didn't know where. Between salt runs, I searched for the places where she might be. I drove up and down Chicago Avenue, thinking she could be Christmas shopping. I lurched through the neighborhood about a hundred times, my eye out for that familiar stride of hers.

When I finally caught up with her that night, she seemed calmer than I expected. I'd been watching for her from my bedroom window and almost missed her because I'd been peering in the wrong direction. I threw on a jacket and raced down when I spotted her trudging home kicking snow.

"Of course I didn't get in his car," she said. "I'm not stupid."

"What did he say?"

"He didn't say anything. I didn't give him a chance. He tried to be all sweet."

I told her I'd been worried about her. This softened her, but she shot me a look that made it clear she wasn't coming over. Which hurt because this was not what I had in mind. This was not what I'd ever have in mind again. This quiet realization caused something like grief to ripple through me, but I knew it would pass. Not long ago, the sight of her ruby cheeks and warm brown eyes glimmering against the cold would have stirred a yearning in me but, now that she was unattainable, I wouldn't allow that hunger to even begin because I knew that would be torturous. *How quickly I can adapt*, I thought, a little proud of myself—and disappointed, too, though not sure why. Because I'd given in so quickly? Because I'd had no say in the matter? Given the chance, what would I have said back in my bedroom that night when she said goodbye to us? *We can make this work?* She knew better. She always did. I wanted her to assure me that this new way of being with each other would become comfortable and that it would last. Though maybe she didn't know this herself.

"It's freezing out here," she said.

But she didn't look like she was freezing. She wasn't even shivering. She looked like she'd been walking a single block, enough time for her cheeks to redden but not much more.

"We need to talk," she said. "Tomorrow. Get our stories straight. In case he comes around again."

She didn't seem worried. She hugged me tightly and held me for a second. So this was how it was going to be. This is what we'd do. *Don't you dare plant one on my cheek*, I thought. I didn't know if I could stand that.

"Get inside," she said. "Tomorrow."

She'd been walking home from the corner *farthest* from the bus stop. Which is why I'd almost missed her. And now I understood.

Some college boy had dropped her off. Out of courtesy to me, she'd told him she'd walk the rest of the way. She hadn't even given him a reason. Just said, "Drop me off here." As she turned, I tried to pick up a cologne scent, something acrid or musky. But the cold had killed off any scent that might have lingered on her. She waved with her mittened hand as she stepped toward her house. And I watched for a sign to confirm my suspicion, crushed when I saw it. She bounced away with her head down, trying to hold back the contented smile of something new in her life.

❖

Three more calls that night before I disconnected the cord. I still had trouble sleeping and was about to call in sick. I decided that I wanted to have wheels for the day, even if the wheels were part of an industrial orange truck that sprayed salt onto the windshields of pissed-off drivers who offered me the gift of their finger, which more or less matched how I felt toward the world, a mood I chalked up to my endless tossing and turning.

In the middle of the night, I wrote a note to Maryann and put a stamp on it, though I intended to slip it into her mailbox, because no one fucks with the U.S. mail. I hoped. In the light of morning, I reread it, hoping I wouldn't cringe with regret over what I'd written.

Hey Maryann,

This is your pain in the ass neighbor two doors down. It's 2:34 in the morning and I can't sleep and you can probably imagine why, and I don't want to call you and wake you up, so I decided to write this note because I'm afraid. And it's not what you're probably thinking. I'm afraid of something else, that after our long "talk" a while ago, which seems like forever, the two of us won't be able to look each other in the eye (not that I'm any good at that anyway, which you've made quite clear, though I've gotten better) and say what's on our minds. I mean, it always takes me a little while to get to what I want to say but, with you, I always get there. And I don't want to lose that. I don't want to become overly self-conscious around you. And I guess the reason I'm bringing this up is that last night, I saw this shyness in you. Like you were holding back. And I understand why. To spare me. To avoid hurting me. But you know what, I can take it. I can take the hurt. I have to look at this ugly mug in the mirror every morning, right? Talk about hurt. What I can't take though, seriously, is the distance between us.

What you said during our long "talk," I get it. I do. I get it I get it I get it. You thought you saw something last night out in the cold, like I was trying to convince you to change your mind about you and me—I could see that, like you were disappointed that I would even go there—but you were wrong. You're not usually. I'm the one. And you're the one who pulls me out of my stupid wrongness. But this time, last night, I wasn't trying to suggest anything. I just wanted to make sure you were okay. I was worried about you. That's all.

I know you will pursue other "interests." It kills me. But I get it. It'll take a while to get used to, that's all. Which you know, which is why you were walking home last night, right? And I thank you. Without sarcasm, I thank you. I don't know if I could have said this last night, because, like I mentioned, it takes me a while to get to what I want to say, but your walking home was a kind thing to do. I don't know if I've repaid all the kindness you've shown me for so long. My whole life. Actually, I do know. I haven't come close to repaying you. I'll need a lifetime to do that.

Anyway, I just want you to know, you don't need to walk home. I can't say it any more simply. I want you to be happy. The only reason I can express this is because I know you want the same for me. And I know that you have no reservations about this, which blows my mind. I'll work through my own reservations. With your help, I hope.

I'm going to work. We'll talk when we talk. Be safe.

Love,

Ant

I tucked the note back in the envelope, licked the seal, and considered dumping it in the trash. Even while writing the letter, I'd held back, fearing that someone else might find and read it. I'd made references only Maryann would understand and left out details that might land me in hot water. I hoped I hadn't held back with how I felt, though. When it came to those matters, I had no gauge. It was the kind of letter I'd want Maryann to check before I sent it. I did consider adding something about Alexandra, to show her I was capable of moving on, that I was doing better than okay, but I was afraid she'd think I was trying to make her jealous, which might have held some truth.

On two strong legs, I bounced down the stairs to the smell of bacon and eggs and the sound of the back door slamming. But, when I looked out, I saw no one. Maybe my mother, sneaking in and out to get something from her room. That's what I wanted to believe. Though I couldn't peel myself away from the door for a while in my paranoia. I drew in a deep breath, fearing I might catch a brief whiff of Mr. Lipschultz, not a real scent but some remnant from the tangled wires of my brain. But nothing. Just a bare trace of baked anise.

I filled my plate and soon Nonna joined me. This is what she needed. Though we exchanged few words, the indelible blood ties of family soared through me. I wasn't proud of what she'd done, but she'd done it for me, and I knew I could trust her with my life.

We ate in silence, which didn't seem at all strained. I already knew I would one day miss those quiet meal times together, which felt like a reprieve from the harshness *out there.*

I had questions. Plenty of questions. But I was fairly certain I would never ask them.

When you walked in on little Francesco screaming, after you'd told him hundreds of times not to climb, did you want to strangle him?

How many times after that did the impulse to punish him arise for her? Every day? What had she done with all her rage and sorrow?

What do you say at confession, Nonna?

I never quite understood how confession worked in the first place. You confess, the priest absolves. But what if you confess only some of your sins? Does absolution offer a clean slate, even for the sins you didn't mention? Because, as a boy, that's what I thought. That I was starting anew. The fact that I didn't deserve a fresh start gnawed at me, but that never lasted long. I tucked away the brightness of absolution in my praying hands and left the church feeling lighter and clean.

Did you tell Father Stanislaus—or whoever was on duty that Saturday— what you did with your bread?

And if she failed to mention this? Would absolution still come? If she did tell him, did she confess in Italian, the priest pretending to understand? And can God forgive such a horrendous act?

Why even go to confession, Nonna? After losing a daughter and then a granddaughter, how do you continue to believe?

This question was intended for me. What did I believe? I wasn't sure.

Why'd you do it, Nonna?

To protect me, sure. But there had to be more. Because the old bastard reminded her of old wounds? Because it was inconceivable to believe that, in her family, another brother could be responsible for the death of his sister? Was her baking a fit of passion? To squelch the old blame she could never hide toward her son? But baking? No jury could ever view baking as a fit of anything.

When you pass from this world, Nonna, where will I get fresh baked bread?

I wasn't trying to be coy. I'd discarded the fork and measuring spoon and bowl and pan she'd used that day to set the world right again, and now each piece torn from one of her warm loaves was infused with sacredness. The difference between breathing and not breathing was something I could hold.

And what do we do now, Nonna? What do we do?

29

❖

Balls-out terror? That's what he likes? We'll show him balls-out terror, Antney. You wait and see."

After he found out at the wake that my old man was bartending, the Lucky Tap on Pulaski became Freddy's new favorite tavern. He paid his tab each time, didn't expect special treatment, didn't go there to meet up with a pack of old friends. He came because he still looked up to Frank Lazzeri, who was younger than Freddy, a one-man fan club that would never be dismantled. And he was good for business, customers enjoying his pontification on city matters so much that they sank down for another beer, rather than pushing off stools to go home to their families. I'd seen the same collective shrug in bar after bar when I tagged along with him, all of them grateful to Freddy for the reminder that they worked hard *dammit* and *deserved* one more.

"You need to get back to work, Freddy?" Our running joke.

The place reeked of disinfectant when I walked in, but now I could only smell stale booze and the dried grease-salt from my own gloves in my coat pocket. The Schlitz sign in the window flickered now and then and drew my attention each time and, as I worked my gaze back to Freddy, I took in the worn floorboards that led to the center stools where we sat.

"I'm serious, Antney. We'll show him."

He wasn't drunk, not even half drunk. But I couldn't tell

if his bravado was real or if he was trying to impress my old man, who sauntered over.

"Show who?" my dad asked.

I'd been watching him. Hoping he'd overhear. He dipped in and out of conversations, leaning in, as if waiting for a sign from the catcher on whether he should linger for a while, sometimes offering an ear but more often checking on drinks and wiping down the varnished counter. I might have been the only one aware of how afraid he was to stop moving. Not the three guys to my right, one stool away, who were deep in conversation about the Bears' chances to make the playoffs. They'd taken off their coats but not their ear-flapped hats. And on Freddy's left were two singles nursing beers.

"Your pal, George. Trying to tighten the screws on your son here. But we're going to give him a little taste."

And what would have taken me weeks to reveal to my father was suddenly out there. I became intensely aware of the other men and intensely grateful that no one turned. After realizing no one else had heard, and after a jolt of envy—what if I could live my life like Freddy, head on?—I felt an unfamiliar bald nakedness. I was used to my layers of deception and half-truths and my habit of checking out the world through the corners of my eyes. I'd learned from my old man, of course, who finally stopped moving and did his own sly check of the stools on either side of us. To see that wariness brought on a mostly silent, *Oh shit,* to my lips. He didn't have to say a word to convey that his old buddy George had a crazy streak in him that would shock even Freddy, who didn't pick up on any of this.

Freddy—in a hushed voice, more for drama than privacy— explained about the ride in the Thunderbird and the phone calls and the deranged glare in that motherfucker's eyes, which Freddy hadn't seen but, nonetheless, described fairly accurately. Or maybe he *had* seen that look. Freddy had seen just about everything.

My old man turned to me for confirmation, and I nodded,

trying not to appear as sheepish as I felt. I imagined myself as an actual sheep, my eyes yearning for pity, but I looked away so he wouldn't see.

What happened next, not only in the bar, but later, astounded me. My hangdog old man, in the span of a few breaths, became a bear—his shoulders straightening, squaring off, and his chest swelling, all achieved in the way he stood with his legs apart and his weight shifting from his heels to the balls of his feet, ready to attack. He wiped the inside of a tumbler with his small towel, going over the same side again and again, not thinking yet, not deliberating, just pure rage, something mostly foreign to him. Maybe this is what he needed. He had his wife back, sure, and maybe his son. But, in time, he'd take us for granted and slip away again, if he felt we could do without him. But maybe the rage would remind him he was wrong, that we *did* need him. I didn't know if I believed any of this, but I was grateful nonetheless for the blind gleam that said he would do anything to protect his son.

I didn't stay long. I wasn't sure I could lie convincingly about why George might be after me. I could suggest he was carrying out his dad's mission to pin the fire on me, but why would that interest George? He wasn't exactly some principled son bent on honoring his father's unfinished business. I'd need time to come up with a story.

When my father asked, as I knew he would, I shrugged and waited for Freddy to drop the other shoe. But Freddy was sober enough to realize that no father wanted to hear that his son was suspected of starting a fire that killed his own sister, even if the source of the suspicion was one lizard old buddy who didn't know his ass from his face.

My old man flipped the towel over his shoulder and resumed his role as bartender. He began to slide away, still gripping the glass, as if he wanted to hurl it at the door, which happened to be about ninety feet away, a familiar distance. He stopped and turned back.

"We're going to take care of this Lipschultz business," he said. "Once and for all."

The instant I stepped outside, a cold punishing blast slapping me sideways, I knew I'd messed up. With each step, regret lodged itself deeper. I should have never gone to the bar. I was a stupid, selfish bastard. What the hell was I thinking? I was desperate for help, sure, but to bring in my old man? Given that Nonna was involved, I needed to keep him as far away as possible. The less he knew, the better, for his own good.

And the rage? Not that I'd anticipated it, but this was exactly what I'd wanted, wasn't it? Some show of paternal pride. But that would only push him closer to another drink. He'd fallen into a routine and I'd disrupted it. I'd been thinking about myself. Only myself. That much was suddenly clear. How to work myself out of this now? I'd talk to him. After Freddy left, I'd go back and talk to him. Tell him that Freddy had twisted this thing, like he always did, so he'd have himself another story. *Let's all take a breath, Dad, and back off and see what happens, and if that nutcracker of a friend comes back, I'll let you know. Let's wait this thing out. What's he gonna do? When it comes down to it, what can he do?* Maybe I'd leave out this last part and not invite my dad's imagination to run wild.

And Freddy? There was something I wanted him to do. Something that had been gnawing at me for a while. To find someone else for me. Which would distract him from George, too. Or, quite possibly, he'd already forgotten about George.

30

❖

I returned the truck to the city garage, took the bus back to the Lucky Tap, saw that my old man's rage had boiled down, reassured him I was okay, told him not to do anything, then used the pay phone to call Alexandra.

I asked if she wanted to meet me at the Hub movie theater on Chicago Avenue, feeling like a shmuck for not offering to pick her up. But I didn't want to chance someone following me there. Above all else, I needed to keep her out of this.

I got to the Hub first but didn't buy tickets because, as cold as it was, I wanted to be outside waiting so I could say, "For two," when I pushed the three singles through the arched slot in the window. I wanted to see the two tickets and my change slide back to me knowing, when I turned, that Alexandra would be there, thankful because she loved movies as much as I did. She would smile over the newness of being together, not knowing what would come next...what we both felt.

As I waited, I began to exhale through my mouth, each gray breath providing endless fascination. Surprised I'd never thought of this before, a diversion came to me. I'd look for faces in my breaths, as if they were clouds. But each breath dissolved before my eyes could latch on. I glanced up and down the street, hoping no one had caught me in my childish game. I would be twenty-one in a month. I shifted from side to side to keep warm, breathing through my nose now, as I imagined a grown

WHERE MY BODY ENDS

man would do, though I had no idea what it meant to be a man. My entire life seemed like one huge role that I was unsuited for, as if I'd missed rehearsal after rehearsal. And to drag Alexandra into this mess. I hoped she wasn't simply a diversion for me, that I wasn't using her to keep my mind off more pressing matters. Because I couldn't help but feel that watching a movie with her for the next two hours was simply an escape through some hatch and that when we crawled back onto Chicago Avenue, I'd have to go back to setting things right in my world and Alexandra would be left behind.

Maybe there was a way not to let my problems define me. My shrink would have been proud of this revelation. And then she would have sagged in her leather couch when my mind began to drift and I saddled myself with those very problems. Because they were me. And I was them. Many of them, admittedly, were self-imposed. But others...well.

One of the theater doors opened, two figures walked out, and a wave of burnt popcorn assaulted me. A bus hissed to a stop in front of Woolworth's across the street, its fumes battling with the scent of popcorn. Men, but mostly women, some with small children, scurried past me. All of them had burdens, too, their own stories of regret and shame, some darker than others, though none of this provided me with any relief. Only the thought of Alexandra turning the corner gave me any light.

A Thunderbird rumbled by. An older model, dull pewter, but my heart raced just the same. I saw George Lipschultz's big face in the cloud of the exhaust and remembered my dad's warnings just as I'd left the bar. We'd stepped outside. He wanted to fill me in, he said. Before he said a word, I knew from his more than usual stammering that what he would say to me was meant as a kind of armor, something I could use if I was cornered, but also to show what a crazy sonofabitch his old friend was.

My dad told me that when George was a baby—which was impossible to imagine, a fat, runny-nosed runt coming to mind—

he was always sick. They had to use ice mattresses in his crib to keep his fevers down. When the fevers broke, he'd sleep with his mom, and this became their habit, mom and son in the same bed, long past the normal age for this. Both his older brother and father, separately and together, were relentless in their teasing, and George had to either take their attacks or lash back. He knew he couldn't win at home, not with both of them piling on. But on the streets, and at school, he became brutal, pummeling anyone who questioned his toughness. After a while, no one questioned anything about George Lipschultz, but even a dark look in his direction could set him off.

He and my dad got into it a couple of times, but my dad was agile and able to sidestep his wild haymakers. George would get winded and abandon the punches and dive headfirst, arms flailing, but these desperate charges were even easier to deflect. Through all that, my dad earned an odd sort of respect, and the two of them became unlikely friends. An arm's-length friendship, my dad called it, because he was drawn to the danger, maybe even envied George's explosive temper, but there lurked the constant worry that his friend would turn on him. Like sitting on a keg of gunpowder—not something my old man said outright but what I thought and now felt.

Night was coming on fast now. The snow-wet streets reflected the streetlights and the brightness from storefronts. At the end of the block, Alexandra in her red winter coat ambled toward me.

"Have you ever heard anyone say 'Groovy'?" she asked. "You look frozen." She pulled me by the arm, and we turned to the ticket window and rushed inside. "I was watching the Monkees again. Stupid show, but I can't stop watching it. And they were saying *groovy*, and I was thinking, years from now, people are going to think we talked like that."

"That's how they'll learn history, you think? By watching television?"

"Don't you think?"

214

We watched the end of *A Few Dollars More*, which I'd seen already, and stayed for *Stranger on the Run*. I like Henry Fonda, but he's not anywhere near as cool as Clint Eastwood, at least not in a Western. I would have been fine with leaving in the middle, but the theater was warm and dark, and we leaned into each other like a couple and ate a box of popcorn and washed that down with a box of Dots.

After, we walked to the bus stop without saying a word about the movies, except that we wished the order were reversed and we'd seen all of *Dollars* and less of *Stranger*.

"Do you ever think about leaving?" I asked. "Just taking off?"

"You mean running away?"

"Yeah, I guess."

"What are you running from?"

I grabbed her mittened hand. "You're avoiding the question."

"I have to know what you mean before I answer," she said. "I mean, I run away every day. I sit under a tree. I read. I go to the movies with a boy who wants to run away, maybe really run away. But no, I don't feel any deep desire to—"

"You sit under a tree?"

"In the summer, sure."

"Do you really, or is this something you imagine yourself doing? Because it's a nice image, but when you really look…I can't remember the last time I actually saw someone sitting under a tree."

"Well, I guess you haven't really looked. Or you would have seen me."

"Then I'll look. I guess."

"And, when you see me, you'll join me?"

"I'm not sure. Because it sounds like you go there to be alone."

"You can bring a book," she said. "And sit on the other side of the trunk. That way you won't see me and you can still believe that no one sits under a tree."

We reached the bus stop. I peered down Ashland for the bus, while Alexandra searched for something in my face. When I met her eyes, she looked to the street.

She coughed into her hand and held it there for a second. "What are you running from, Anthony?"

"I was being hypothetical. Westerns get me thinking."

"You weren't being hypothetical," she muttered. "Talk about avoiding the question."

"Is that what you think?"

"Yes." She met my eyes this time. "You haven't told me anything about yourself. Not really. And I don't think it's out of shyness or anything like that. I get this feeling that you're trying to protect me, maybe. Am I right, Anthony Lazzeri?"

"You think I'm hiding something? That I have deep dark secrets?"

"Do you?"

"I guess I was hoping—"

"Hoping what?"

"That we could see a few movies and I could walk you home after and maybe get up the nerve to tell you that I like the way you look down when you smile..."

She looked at her shoes and smiled and said, "And everything would be nice...and happy."

"What's wrong with that? Everybody deserves that."

I searched again for the bus and suggested we walk to the next stop to keep warm. But I just wanted to move. I could think better when I was moving.

"Nice is good," she said. "Happy is good. But if I don't know you, then—"

"How about this? How about if I tell you a thought I had the other day. If you knew my thoughts, you'd know me, right?"

"I suppose." She tucked her hand under my arm.

"I was thinking...this is hard to explain...I've never said this. When things happen, big things—"

"Tragic things. Or good things?"

"Tragic, I guess. At least that's when I think this. Anyway, I feel this odd contrast. Like I'm invisible. Like I'm a speck in this vast universe. Separate from everything. At the same time, it feels like the universe is staring at me. Mocking me, maybe. Like this is a big joke on me."

She grinned and pulled me down to her and kissed me on the neck. "I feel like that every day," she said. "So tell me. What's making you feel so small?"

31

❖

When I got home, I found minestrone soup in the fridge and this letter on my pillow.

Dear A,

I was trying to think of something encouraging to say, like, You'll land on your feet. But I realized what a poor choice of words that would be, in so many ways. You and I may be the only two who understand why. I picture you snickering right now and maybe missing me and all our little jokes, and I want you to know that I miss that too, as surprising as this might be to you. You're right, it was a little awkward between us last time. It might just take a while. But we are like old shoes to each other, which is a stupid analogy, but you know what I mean. I'm still trying to think of something encouraging to write, but I can't because no matter what I come up with, I imagine you picking it apart like you do, like we both do, because sometimes there just aren't any words. Well, maybe there are a few. Because, apparently, you've forgotten. As painful as this may be to hear again, we have to move on. Greener pastures and all that. But I love you. I will always love you. (Go ahead, say it. "Why do you have to be so goddamn mature?")

I miss you.

Maryann

So, this is how we'd get along, writing letters, as if seeing only shadows of each other. The thing she left out was the most striking. I will always love you...*like a brother.* She'd finally sensed my own old reluctance about being with her. Or maybe she'd always sensed it but I was just too goddamn irresistible. That's what I would try to believe...and fail to believe.

I sat on the bed, expecting to see Ellie. Mere habit. I hadn't said goodbye to her before taking up pot, though every time we spoke seemed like the last time. I'd said everything I needed to say to her, so much so that her appearances had become ordinary. She always knew how I felt.

"I have to move on," I said aloud. I said it again, louder, and thought I spotted movement in the hall, but it was a play of light from outside, a passing car maybe, a flickering streetlight.

I took in my room, which didn't seem like mine anymore. Baseball pennants frayed at the tips. Dusty trophies. A record player on my dresser. Albums scattered. A thick Herman Wouk war book with a bookmark near the middle, though I couldn't recall a single detail of what I'd read. Nonna must have come in and picked up after me because the floor was clean of laundry. I'd been careful to smoke my joints near an open window to avoid her wrath.

One day, someone else would inhabit this room, gaze out at the street below, unaware of all the history here. I felt like I should leave some marker, a note in a bottle, a diary stuffed under a loose floorboard, my old man's baseball card tucked inside the baseboard in the closet with a tiny triangle of a corner sticking out. If I left a note, what would I say?

A baseball playing gimp, who brought on the gimpiness himself (long story) used to listen to records in this room and talk to his sister, who would console him for years after she died in a fire at Our Lady of the Angels school (another long story) that you can almost see from the front window, the school that is, and then he

had to move on because this is what life is about, he'd been told, by
his sometime girlfriend next door, who is like a sister to him now.

That would be enough to preserve some part of me here.
I wouldn't need to add anything about some bastard of a neighbor,
who got himself killed finally by his own nastiness, though that
would also shed light on who I am. And my parents? I should
leave behind something about them. The burdens they carried?
Because who they were, before and after the fire, helped stitch me
together into who I am, not quite whole maybe, but enough for
me to make a life of my own. And Nonna? Maybe if I described
her hands, the determination on her lined face. She's a part of
me, my conscience maybe. I carry her with me. Which is why
I needed to ask her if she would be by my side for the next thing
I needed to do. Because I didn't think I could do it alone.

32

❖

I pictured his face many times, round and thick, which left you with the impression that he had no neck. But I had never imagined that moment, standing across from him. All it took was a single call from Freddy to one of his cop buddies, who had gotten me an address, which turned out to be a tiny bungalow on the South Side of Chicago in Bridgeport, not far from Comiskey Park. From what Freddy could make out, he lived with his mother.

I didn't call ahead. I didn't have to knock more than once. And he answered the door himself. I pushed aside the realization that I'd been waiting nine years for this.

Over the years, his face had become one big puddle, the spidery veins in his cheeks going nowhere. His straw hair was matted, his gaze steady and direct, as if he had nothing to conceal, no shame to deflect, which caused me to reevaluate what I was doing there in the cramped basement of his mother's house. But his eyes didn't penetrate, didn't connect with anything outside himself, they were simply tracking movement, getting him from one end of the basement to the other. His army-green t-shirt sagged but didn't hide the weak shoulders and the flabbiness of his gut. I knew I wouldn't like him, but I didn't expect to view him as pathetic. A stab of pity snaked through me.

We sat across from each other on cushioned chairs, and the plop into mine stirred up the acrid aroma of weed. My old buddy, the other prime arson suspect from Lipschultz's file, was stoned.

I just needed to be sure he'd done what I thought he'd done all those years before, and I needed not to rouse him, to make this seem like not such an extraordinary visit. I thought maybe I'd suggest we light up. He would jump at any excuse to get high. But we'd settled into an easy calm.

"It's been a long time," I said.

"Crazy long. So, whattya been up to?" He meant to strike a relaxed pose, but his legs were crossed too tightly, and I could tell from the forced casualness of his words that he didn't have any friends, that he was speaking in the way he believed friends spoke to each other.

I kept up my side of what *I* thought *he* thought friends talked about. I told him I pitched and that I missed baseball, and he glanced at my arm, as if he expected me to produce a ball and throw a fastball at a lamp or something.

"Listen," I said. "We can't stay."

He glanced at the door, then back at me, puzzled.

"I just needed to ask you something. Something that's been bothering me for many years. When I woke up, after the fire, I was in the hospital. But I don't remember anything. What happened, how I got there. So I've been going around, asking everyone who was there, so that maybe I can, you know..."

He smiled and tried to suppress the smile, a knowing look filling his eyes. Like he'd been expecting me. He nodded, bursting with importance. But he fought this and began to shake his head, pretending now that he couldn't help me. He was practiced at pretending.

"We used to see each other sometimes at the end of the day. Remember? You know, taking down the waste baskets. It's just that I don't remember taking mine down that day. Like I said, I don't remember anything."

He sank lower in his chair. I'd put him in a pleasant state of mind, with this memory of all the days before the fire. But he wiped off his contentment and shook his head again. He was tired of people asking him questions about that afternoon.

I leaned toward him, telling myself to move slowly. I opened the binder I'd brought, pulled out the manila file that contained Lipschultz's timeline of where we were that afternoon in December, being careful to touch only the corner of the file, as I handed it to my old friend.

He didn't think twice about reaching. He had the file in his grubby hands, his prints all over it.

"What's this?"

"I have a neighbor. He's a cop. He might've been one of the cops who talked to you. Way back when. I assume they talked to you because they talked to me. He's been...I don't know what you call it...building a case. Reopening it actually. And I thought I should warn you, that's all. And I was thinking..."

"Holy shit."

"That's what I thought. It's like, evidence. Real evidence. It got me shittin' in my pants. And I was thinking...that maybe you and I should get our stories straight, because if they come asking questions... But *my* problem is, I don't remember."

Wait, I told myself. *Wait. Let this soak in.*

His fingers were like pink sausages. I searched for signs of panic. I needed panic.

"My boss," I said. "He knows people. He talked to one of his cop friends. And I guess they have a witness. And the witness is ready to...you know...talk. To say we were there. Right before the fire started. That's all I can think about lately and..."

He closed the file and tapped it with the back of his hand.

"This...this person...he saw me go into the boiler room?"

And there it was. Culpability, I think they called it. Fucking *guilt*.

I glanced at Nonna, who would not meet my eyes. But she grasped her rosary more tightly because we knew we'd heard what we'd come to hear. For years, I'd refused to believe that the fire was sparked intentionally. Otherwise, I don't think I could have gone on. But the stricken fear in his eyes, the only emotion he'd shown, convinced me otherwise. A slow surge of revulsion began to work its way up from some dark place in me. But still I sat there, taking in slow breaths. I would have thought that revulsion would crowd out any chance for calm, but I was wrong again.

Nonna stroked Ellie's downy hair. I wasn't surprised to see my sister there. She didn't need to hear a confession, but I needed her by my side one last time. She had on her school uniform, a plaid skirt with a white blouse and a scapular around her neck, which is not something she'd be wearing with a uniform, but the combination seemed fitting. She seemed serene, patient, not at all flimsy, as I would have expected.

Nonna couldn't keep her eyes off of Ellie. Seeing them together was dizzying. Yet right. Though something about Nonna was off. A corner of a sparkling handkerchief poked out from her blouse pocket, and her eyes were more luminous than I'd ever seen them, though she still wouldn't look at me.

"Yeah," I said. "One witness...one witness saw. I don't know if it was a he or a she."

Whatever terror he'd felt drained from his face, replaced by something like relief. For nine years, he'd been glancing over his shoulder, and now maybe it was over. He flipped the folder onto the end table between us.

"So what do I tell them?" I said. "Or just tell me what happened and we'll figure this thing out...together."

I picked up the manila folder, carefully fingering it on the same corner I'd held earlier, and gently returned it to the binder.

"What you said...the wastebasket, man. That's all."

"What about it?"

He scanned the room, as if expecting the cops to bust in.

"There were some old rags laying around. In the furnace room. And one of them caught fire that's all."

"And the waste basket?" *Your waste basket.*

"I don't know. That caught, too."

"It just caught?" *On its own? At the exact second you were there?*

"Pretty much."

Pretty much. This was a confession, as close as I would get. Over nine years, he'd probably convinced himself that the fire began on its own.

"And then what?"

"Then I left."

"You left?"

"I got scared."

Which was a lie. I could see the old thrill return. His voice pitched higher.

I took in a slow breath to calm myself. "And me? Where was I?"

He shrugged.

"I wasn't there?"

"No, you weren't there. Not yet."

"What do you mean?"

He chewed his bottom lip and fixed his gaze beyond me.

"I was waiting by the outside door. Watching. I thought maybe the fire alarm would go off. And then you came down the stairs with your basket. And you went right in. I saw all this smoke pouring out, so I waited. And you didn't come out. I waited some more. And, when I finally went to check on you, you were on the ground...passed out, I guess. And the flames..."

And, with that, I finally saw a trace of regret.

"So I dragged you by your arms and pulled you out. And left you by the grass."

"And then what?"

Did you look for an alarm, you sonofabitch? Did you yell, "Fire"? What the fuck did you do?

"I ran home. I was scared."

"You were scared."

"I didn't think—"

"It was goddamn two thirty. You wanted to get out early, didn't you? And you thought a little fire would... You couldn't wait fifteen fucking minutes? You know how many kids died that day? How many nuns? Did you know that—"

Ellie leaned forward, Nonna trying to console her. I turned to them.

"Did you hear that, Nonna? He ran home. He was scared. Goddamn scared."

He searched around, rose slowly to his feet, retreating. "You're crazy, man. You're touched. Who the fuck are you talking to?"

And now fury, as I charged him and unleashed a single tight fist to his jaw. I expected his jowly face to provide some cushion, but all I felt was bone on teeth. And it wasn't anything like in the movies, where I would have sent him reeling across the room. Instead, he collapsed into himself, falling into a sweaty crouch, holding his jaw and moaning. I stood over him. A single punch, and my breathing was labored, my knuckles sore.

I'd kept trying to tell myself that this wasn't about him, that this visit was for Ellie, for her memory. But, in the end, hurting him was all I wanted—to kick him in his side, to crush his round face with the heel of my work boot. But I didn't. Though I had the overwhelming sense that he was *waiting* for another blow, that he wanted me to hit him again.

"Let's get out of here, Nonna."

Still sprawled on the ground, he barked, "Fucking crazy bastard."

Nonna stomped on his finger and I felt the sting in my own heel, the sharp, white pain radiating up my cursed leg.

I turned.

Ellie was gone. I was fairly sure I'd never see her again. Which stopped me cold with a sudden torrent of grief.

Nonna stood beside me, ghostlike, with stark eyes distant, filled with grief and worry, finally looking at me. Waiting. *I'll be okay*, I assured her. *I'll be okay. But I need to move on.*

Maryann

❋

I always imagined us growing old together. Only because I couldn't imagine us apart. I envisioned the two of us gray and hunched as we settled into comfortable chairs on a sunny screened porch. But that's the only scene that ever came to mind, as if we were actors pretending. I never imagined what came between, the marriage and children and the struggle to pay rent.

In order to stay with Anthony, I would have needed to take care of him, appease him, submit to his needs, which is unpopular these days. "Backward thinking" is how one of my trendy, bow-tied professors put it, falling over in apology for every door held open for the weaker sex (for these last words he'd added those stupid air quotations with his fingers). I wanted to raise my hand and explain that I didn't feel weaker when a door was held open and didn't believe that was the intended message by men, that there was no message, just a passing kindness, which we didn't need to pause to discuss in class because there were more substantial inequalities that came to mind. Such as the things he didn't say but were rumored and that I chose to believe—that his pandering was intended to send unsuspecting girls to his office—or maybe they did suspect, and hoped.

No, I could have taken care of Anthony. I wanted to. But I was forced to realize, obvious to me now, how destructive my helping would turn out to be. But destruction happens in whispers, barely detectable, until the day you see yellow police ribbon flapping in the wintry wind around your neighbor's house.

Backward thinking? More like stuck thinking. Because there's no getting past the fire. Time does not heal. Distance deceives. There's never any true healing. That much I've discovered.

Would I do anything differently? Would any of us, knowing where our deceptions would get us? Because the deceptions, coming as they did in small doses, never seemed extraordinary. I made minestrone soup. Placed it in his grandmother's fridge. I picked up after him, dropped his clothes in the hamper. No big deal.

Trace this back to the beginning, just after the fire. Anthony was eleven. Or, "fucking eleven," as he would say. Though he wouldn't put himself in the third person. Or maybe he would. I'm stalling now. Because to remember…I hate this. Not as much as Anthony. But he doesn't need to…remember, that is. I'll give him that. While I do. I need to remember, to keep me grounded, literally, on the streets and not in some pale mint psych ward.

He was eleven. In the hospital. Of course we had to tell him. His mother, father, and Nonna stood around the bed. They wanted me to be there. I wanted to be there. His mother held one hand, his father right behind her. I held his other hand, with Nonna by my side. He asked about Ellie, and we told him. Not with words, but with the squeeze of his hands and the tide of tears, convulsive sobs that his mother and I tried to hold back for Anthony's sake, which seems strange now because if there ever was a time for unchecked grief, that was it. We huddled closer, and all the air went out of the room and, when we caught our breaths, our eyes fixed on Anthony, we waited. But he couldn't speak. He wiped a line of wetness from the corner of each eye and nodded and pasted on a crooked smile like people do at times like these, a reflex of incomprehension.

I remember looking at his legs under the sheets. This was a child's bed and he barely fit. A wave of self-pity washed over me as I wondered why no one had come to my bed to console me like this, why no one was asking me how I was doing. They must have seen a strength in me that I didn't feel, which provided the strength, I suppose, and guided me toward what I needed to be.

For weeks, Anthony was mute. And, by his side, I became mute as well. I understood. There was nothing to say. We dragged two chairs to the window in his bedroom and gazed out endlessly. Sometimes I would touch his arm, take a lock of his hair between my fingers, just to let him know I was there. Neither one of us was encouraged, or maybe even allowed, to go the wake and funeral, which was fine with us. That view of scudding clouds and rooftops and water towers receding in the distance was enough for us. My mind was more or less blank, and I relished the numbness. For Anthony, I suspect he was already busy calling up his sister. He had an extraordinary capacity for extending his imagination, where he didn't quite know where his body ended and where the world began, as he liked to say. And mostly I envied this.

They wanted to know if we cared to go to back to school, as had been arranged, so we could finish out the year. They were parceling everyone out to different sister schools. They actually used that term, no one catching the cruel irony of "sister." Anthony heard it, I'm sure. I went back in mid-February, Anthony followed in March, on a cold, rainy day that I remember because I shared my umbrella with him.

At the vaulted entrance of the school, a dark monstrosity of bricks with a flat roof, nothing like the ornateness of Our Lady of the Angels, he asked, "Now what?"

I didn't answer because I didn't know. The next day, we paused at the same spot, and I answered, "Geography." And that was the first real smile I'd gotten. I threaded my fingers through his, but not for long, because we were headed inside.

Months later, Nonna passed suddenly, on a weekday morning, while we sat at our desks learning about the Louisiana Purchase or decimals or maybe space exploration. "Her heart gave out," is how my mom phrased it, and that made sense to me. But how to break this to Anthony? We had to tell him, of course. Though insisting, instead, that she fled to Italy did come to mind because I'd heard the whispers. Nonna still had a sister there. And poor Anthony. If they could have figured out a reason for her leaving without saying goodbye, I think this would have been the story. She could then die in Italy when Anthony was less fragile. That this idea was entertained helps explain what happened next.

Anthony's eyes turned blank when he was finally told. He nodded, his only indication that he'd heard. I'd been dragged into the middle again. We sat in Nonna's kitchen. His mom and dad must have thought this would provide comfort. They could point to the St. Anthony calendar on a nail next to the fridge and suggest that Nonna was with her favorite saint now. They could feed him something she used to prepare for him—her homemade ravioli, left over from the night before, or her green and red bell peppers, marinated, served with homemade bread that he could tear apart to dip into the pool of vinegar and oil and oregano. These things would surely provide comfort to him. Which they did.

But Anthony couldn't accept this news. He retreated once again, not into muteness this time but toward a kind of sleepwalking. This time, I did go to the wake and funeral. But not Anthony. He probably just read, because, after I got back and slipped out of my funeral dress, I stopped over and he was curled around a Green Lantern comic book, which I think he liked because the Green Lantern wasn't the most popular superhero. I picked up another issue off his stack and read alongside him into the afternoon, until supper.

Everyone began to tiptoe around him. And, when it became clear that he wasn't going to let Nonna go—he'd show up at her table at dinner time, he'd bring down his laundry hamper to her washing machine, he'd leave her mail in the usual basket near the phone and one time answered her phone and said to the caller that she was not home—his mother became resigned. Maybe desperate. She didn't want to send him to some shrink. Not yet.

Instead, she dropped by Nonna's good friend at the end of the block, Mrs. Mazzolini, and asked her how to make stuffed peppers, baked lasagna, and all the other dishes she and Nonna had shared over the years. And bread, especially bread. For Nonna and Mrs. Mazzolini, it wasn't enough to enjoy the meals. No, they had to have endless discussions *about* the meals, each one envying the other and testing out the other's version of the same dishes. Mrs. Mazzolini was more than happy to guide Anthony's mom, who couldn't tell the difference between store-bought spaghetti sauce and homemade red gravy, a sin of utmost proportions. And then Anthony's mom taught me, and my mom, too. Between the three of us, we supplied endless meals and placed them on Nonna's table. Not every day, not even every week. Just enough to sustain the illusion. His mom and my mom eventually stopped, but I never did. Not completely. I didn't have the heart, and even asked Anthony about Nonna from time to time, mainly to see if he was any nearer to letting her go.

We did nothing outright to encourage Anthony. No one said, "Nonna will have supper ready soon," but no one tried to pierce through his delusions, either. He was eleven. This would pass. Time would heal. I won't pretend to understand how things became entangled in his mind, how his actions became hers. I suppose if you think about something long enough, that thing attains substance and heft, and evidence to the contrary is pruned away branch by wilted branch. And I won't pretend to understand how in Anthony's mind Ellie is gone, but here, too, and how Nonna never left. Sometimes there are no explanations.

Anthony's mom didn't understand, either. She only wanted to console her son, like she'd never be able to do again with her little girl. Even recently, after she left, she hired Mrs. Mazzolini to supply meals and clean Anthony's room every so often. An odd kind of consoling, maybe. And it's easy to judge her. Parenting by the path of least resistance. But, maybe, after all these years, she saw this as her only choice.

Another mystery perplexed me for the longest time. How Anthony got Mr. Lipschultz to eat the bread he baked. Then it came to me. I felt proud of myself for figuring it out and sickened by my pride. It wasn't some brilliant plan Anthony dreamt up. It wasn't a plan at all. Anyone staring out a window all day, paranoid about getting thrown in jail, could have come up with it. Most people would have dismissed the idea, but Anthony got caught up. And lost himself. At the window, he saw Mrs. Mazzolini dropping off bread to Mr. Lipschultz almost every day. One night, I'm guessing, Anthony broke in and exchanged one of her loaves with his, the weight of this deed too heavy to keep as his own. On that night, he knew exactly where his body ended and where Nonna's world began. Because that is what he needed. And Perez's gift, the LSD dissolving under his tongue, played its part, too, I'm sure.

Now what? I wish the answer were as simple as "Geography." But the question is different now. Awful things have happened. Anthony needs to know what he's done. Though I'm not sure I can break it to him.

In the end, I hate to admit it, maybe all the things I've done for Anthony, I really did for myself, to keep *me* sane. When I went to Miss G, for instance, I convinced myself this would be for Anthony's benefit. I knew he was becoming too close to her, that she wouldn't be good for him, so I asked her to set him up with one of her students, that he needed this...that this was critical, in fact. What I left out was, *This way, he'll forget about you, Miss G.* But, the truth is, Anthony with another girl would help him forget about *me*. Because I needed a break. I needed a life away from Anthony.

33

B alls-out shot. Nothing to lose.

"Do you have any houses for sale?"

Big grin now.

George Lipschultz, fake fountain pen in hand, stopped filling in his numbers and gazed up at me over his reading glasses. An instant change swept over him, what you might imagine a wary animal doing, his snout becoming compact, his breath coming in short, hot spurts. I didn't get near enough to find out if his breaths were in fact hot, but there was no mistaking the boarish glare.

He wouldn't say anything. But his jaw was working. And he was thinking, *What the fuck you doing here?*

"Don't dick with a man's livelihood," Freddy had warned me.

"Can we talk about houses?" I asked.

His eyes shifted, taking in his coworkers, most of whom were working the phones. One man was absorbed in his coffee and newspaper. The metal-sided desks were lined up in two long rows, half of them occupied. On either side of the desks were private offices. George gestured with his head toward the office closest to him.

This was where he parked his ass each day for important deals, yet I felt like I was the more assured one this time, as if his fury had subtracted some edge from him.

Nothing to lose.

"At school, I had this class my senior year," I said. "Great

Thinkers of the Twentieth Century. It turned out to be a philosophy class."

He crossed his arms in disbelief. *Who the fuck is this kid coming in here talking like some professor?*

"You know, the typical dilemmas. If a tree falls in a forest and no one is there to hear... It still makes a noise, right? Of course it makes a noise. Don't be stupid. But when you think about it, you start to second-guess yourself. I remember starting to second-guess just about everything in my life. We talked about Freud. Not such a great psychologist, but a great philosopher. He had this idea that all boys want to kill their fathers. Because the father, you know, he *has* the mother, and so the little boy, he gets furious about this. But I think it works the other way around, too. If the mother and son are too close, you know, like spending too much time together, the father is the one who gets all jealous, and maybe, I don't know, he wants to hurt the son somehow. Maybe not kill him, but hurt him real bad. With names and shit. I know, sticks and stones and all that, but the teasing can be brutal, if you know what I mean."

I paused but only to catch my breath. I studied the changes in his face, which was far from pokered. I needed to soften his glare.

"I've never been a father, so I can't say how a father feels, but I've been a son...I *am* a son, and I remember times when, yeah, I wanted to hurt my old man. But, if someone else hurt him, that would be a different story. I'd become all protective, you know what I mean. I mean, if someone is going to destroy my dad, it's going to be me. It would piss me off to no end if someone else did what I wanted to do. But I guess there's another way of looking at it...that maybe...at least for me...I don't have the balls to hurt my dad and, if someone else came along and put my old man in his place, maybe I should be grateful in some strange way. But not really. I know I'd never admit to that. Some people might say the gratitude is unconscious. A lot of anger is misplaced. You're really angry at yourself for not destroying your dad before someone else did. I don't buy any of this, by the way. I just bring it up as a way to understand me and my old man, and I know the two of you are close...or were, and...what I'd most want to do, though, if someone hurt my dad, is to get even. Right?"

I was talking at a clipped speed, and I didn't know if any of this was making sense because I was barely thinking about what I was saying. I just wanted to get to this next part.

"Anyway, I went to see an old friend today. Not really a friend. And I thought you might be interested. I beat the shit out of him. And that's what I was saying before. Don't get all pissed off at me for beating the shit out of him, because it's probably something you want to do yourself. But you can't. You've got this job, and you can't go around beating up guys my age because then you'd lose everything. The reason you want to beat up this kid—but you don't have to because I took care of it for you—is he was the one"—deep breath—"who broke into your old man's house. You were right. Someone broke in. But it wasn't me."

George unfolded his arms and leaned toward me. He seemed skeptical but ready to hear more.

"After the fire, your old man, he interrogated me and this other kid. But, with me, because I was a neighbor, it never seemed like an interrogation. He was just asking questions. And I wanted to help, but I couldn't remember much because I was...like... passed out from the smoke. But, this other kid, not a scratch. He was the first one out of the school. So, your old man, I guess he never really dropped the case in his mind. Not too long ago, he went back and interviewed him, this loser. And the kid, he panicked, and broke in to see what he could find. This kid, he's a stupid kid." It took great effort to leave out, *I'm pretty sure he left his fingerprints all over the place. Or at least on a file folder that's in the closet. Check the closet!*

"This kid's name?"

I reached into my pocket for the slip of paper on which I'd written his name and address. The sacrificial goat.

"I'm not saying he did anything to your old man. But he was in his house."

Again, with great effort, I didn't add, *And he found your dad's notes in the closet.*

"So, why'd you beat him up?"

"I think maybe your old man was right about him and the fire."

"He told you this?"

"Not in so many words. But, yeah, he did it."

He'd been interviewed so many times by the cops, though nothing ever came of it. There was no evidence linking him to the fire. Otherwise, he would have been arrested already. But, if he went to jail for breaking in and maybe killing Lipschultz, I wouldn't lose any sleep. Backward justice.

George tapped his thick fingers on the desk. He wasn't buying any of this. Not yet. But he'd be calling his dad's cop friends, who'd be bringing over a fingerprint kit. That I was certain of. And I was also certain they'd find prints on a certain file folder. And if they found mine anywhere, well, he used to invite me in from time to time. We were neighbors, after all. Pals.

I pushed back my chair and sprang up because I wanted to remain in charge. I didn't need this asshole standing to excuse me, staring down at me with his bulldog snarl. He knew this game and didn't budge. His hand became a fist, then a pointed finger that he began to raise in warning. He fixed his gaze on me. He wanted to unleash one last threat. Before he opened his mouth, though, I slapped my palm on the desk as I imagined Freddy would do—nothing to lose—and announced, "Gotta go," then turned and felt my balls-out assurance draining with each quickening step.

34

❖

I had this thought...that I would write a book. I already have the title: *Blame This.* They can shelve the book in the philosophy section, to guarantee that no one will read it. This book, that I will never write, will be about how stupid we all are. How, if we believe we're not good enough, we spend every waking minute building a case against ourselves. Which gives us a kind of perverted pleasure.

I didn't light the match. Though at times I pictured one. I pictured a stick of plied paper with a drop at the end the color of blood, which would require several scratches before it flashed. But I never had matches. In fact, from what I've gathered, I tried to smother the fire, attacking it with whatever was near. There's a chance I fanned the flames. I'm not happy about that. I've been punishing myself for my stupidity. But that's not where the blame comes in. I didn't know about oxygen feeding fire. I couldn't be blamed for not knowing.

But I could have run out of there. Out of that dingy boiler room, which I can picture from all the other times I emptied the waste basket. Vault-thick doors on the sooty boiler, blue licks of flame pushing out behind the iron grates. Cement floor. A tangle of pipes overhead, hissing. It was exciting entering that room, dark and warm, a glimpse into the underbelly of the school that most had never seen.

When I saw the flames rising from what I assume now was a wastebasket like the one I would have been carrying, gray metal and ridged, I could have shouted. I could have let loose a cry that would have reverberated beyond the walls of that blackened room. The entire city would have heard. My old man would have pulled his truck over, my mom would have paused before reaching for the thermometer in her nurse's pocket, Nonna would have wiped her apron, but most importantly, Ellie would have recognized my cry and vaulted from her classroom and shouted, "Fire!" with her lungs full and clean, and those skinny legs of hers, one weaker than the other but strong, strong enough, would have taken her room to room, warning everyone, not because she was a hero but because she wanted to do the right thing. Which I could have shown her.

I should have screamed.

I stayed too long.

It's my fault.

I know the more reasonable answer. I know where blame should be laid. Instead of screaming and running around himself, that sonofabitch used precious minutes dragging me out of the school. And, because he was frantic, about *me*, maybe I interfered with what might have become a sequence of thoughts in his head, where instead of saving me, he could have thought, *This is not what I had in mind, this is out of control. I can still scream, I can pretend I walked in here and the fire was already going, and I can say, "Holy shit, Sister Anne—sorry, holy shoot—I couldn't believe what was happening, I knew what I had to do." And maybe everyone will finally look at me as someone smart instead of thinking about all the trouble I always cause, I can show them, finally, who I am.*

This is what I may have interfered with. Which brings the blame back squarely on me, as illogical as that may be. Which is why, maybe, I couldn't let my sister go.

Yes, my logic may be twisted. But I'm afraid no one can convince me otherwise. That can be chapter two of my book. How we push aside reality for the sake of certainty. I'm an expert.

Freddy tells me that my old friend from school, the one who saved my life by dragging me out of an inferno of his own making, was arrested, so maybe he'll finally have to face reality, as well. Nothing will probably come of the arrest, other than maybe a conviction for breaking and entering, but to make him sweat is satisfying. Maybe, under pressure, he'll confess to the involuntary manslaughter of ninety-two children and three nuns rather than to a particular murder he didn't commit. Maybe this will ease his conscience. More twisted logic.

Chapter three will be about second-guessing everything. Amid the certainty. Which only cements the blame.

What if I had walked a little faster to the boiler room that day? And arrived before that twisted sonofabitch. Or what if I had arrived thirty seconds *later* than I did? The fire would've already been blazing and—and I'm no hero, either—I would've run. The world knows now that there were no fire alarms in the building, as impossible as this is to believe, but I could have been the alarm. *Get out now! Hold the prayers.* Fire doesn't give a shit about prayers. Fire pays no respect to nuns or priests or the pope or Jesus himself. *Get the fuck out!*

I'm usually able to set these doubts aside. Because they dizzy me. What I can't stop asking, though, is, *Why Ellie and not me?* There are no other questions.

But I know, finally, that asking gets you nowhere.

Every day, bodies are flown back from Vietnam. Every day. Right now, thousands of mothers and fathers are asking, *Why my son?* But asking gets you nowhere. Bullets and bombs are like fire. *Get out now!* That's the growing chorus.

Perez is alive. Each morning, I wake up and think this and hope that it's still true. Last month, he survived what the papers called the Tet Offensive. Freddy's son survived, too. He suffered minor wounds, after a mine exploded during a march. His bunkmate was not so fortunate. Alexandra's brother is also alive, though she refuses to celebrate. *Not yet*, she says.

I'm grateful for the good health of all three of these men, but why have they survived and not others? And will their turn come up next?

It's a maddening question. You just have to learn to let go. Move on. A lesson I've always been reluctant to take in. My family recognizes this. Which is why Nonna left suddenly without a goodbye. My parents insist she returned to Italy to care for an ailing sister. She appears to me now and then, as if in a dream, so I'm not so sure.

I'm not sure of anything anymore. It's like when you're driving and can't remember how you got home. *Did I stop at that light back there? Did I turn?* My whole life has been like that. A fog-shrouded cruise, but the fog is inside the car, inside my head. The subject of Nonna troubles me most, because I can't recall her sitting in the passenger seat of my truck weeks back when I visited my arsonist friend. I can't recall leading her to the door, glancing back to check on her. Or seeing her move across the room and falling into the chair in the basement of that sonofabitch who has been haunting me for nine years. But there she was, sitting stiffly, stroking Ellie's hair. That I will never forget. As real as the back of my hand. As real as my cursed left leg. None of this certainty consoles me, of course, because I know that Ellie is not alive, just as I know Nonna is, which doesn't reconcile. In order to get there, I would need to admit to things I've seen and done that are incomprehensible, and I've reached the conclusion that some discoveries are better left buried. Not an idea I'm proud of, but there it is. The car arrived at its destination and there's no use in fretting about how it got there. I may have to think about the stops and turns tomorrow, but there are many tomorrows. And Nonna is gone. Safe in Italy. No one will bother her there.

My old man and my mom are sleeping now, and I'm sitting in my new bedroom in their apartment at a makeshift desk, getting down these thoughts. I know I won't be here long. I don't want to interfere with their wary happiness. But, for now, this is what I need.

This morning, Maryann helped me move the last of my things from my old bedroom. I didn't have as much as I expected, but I still felt like I was shedding a great weight. The truck was packed, and we went inside the apartment for one final check and then stood on the front stoop, taking in the sweep of houses on either side and the skeletal branches that would soon be leafy and full.

"You know, right?" she asked.

"That you will always love me. Yeah, I know."

She squeezed my hand.

I imagined warmth on my face, but the sky was overcast, a muddy gray. I squinted up to where I thought the sun might be.

Gazing skyward, I imagined other things, as well. I imagined Alexandra standing beside me, her shoulder pressed into mine, weakening me with the milky scent of her skin. My old man and my mom appeared, too, worry lining their faces, but together, with hands touching. Nonna was there, and Ellie. Nonna's scowl had flattened into a startled grin, and Ellie, she couldn't keep her eyes off her grandmother. She fingered Nonna's black shift skirt, as if it held velvety secrets. I glanced at old Lipschultz's house, and he was puffing away, making smoke rings with his cigarettes, not bothering to turn in our direction.

I gave Maryann a return squeeze, released her hand, and wondered where we were headed, the two of us. And how we'd make it back to each other when we needed that. I knew I'd been a hindrance and a burden to her but that I'd also helped her through. She needed to take care of someone. And I no doubt needed help.

I don't know if Alexandra and I balance each other as well, but we're about as serious as two people can be after four months. We've talked about following Miss G to Pasadena, where she plans to move at the end of the school year. Talk of leaving helps Alexandra forget about her brother stuck in some foxhole, so *actually* leaving would be foolish, I think. We will stay, and I will reluctantly fill her in on the maddening muddle of thoughts and visions I've had over these many years and hopefully have left behind. And if she stays, after hearing about the fires raging in my head, after hearing about who I am, I will count that as a small miracle.

Author's Note

When you work on a novel that centers on a particular historical event, you want to get the facts right. When the event is horrific, as in the case of the fire at Our Lady of the Angels School in Chicago on December 1, 1958, you feel the pressure acutely and agonize over every detail. You want to honor the lives of the ninety-two children and three nuns, lost far too soon. For these reasons, I am indebted to the fine reporting found in the newspaper archives at the *Chicago Tribune*, and to John Kuenster and David Cowan, authors of the definitive account of the fire, *To Sleep with the Angels: The Story of a Fire*.

I did need to take some liberties with the facts, of course. While the neighborhood in 1958 included many Italian-American families, the Lazzeri family is entirely my creation. And, while I hope I captured the voice and character of columnist Mike Royko, he didn't utter any of the lines I ascribe to him, though he did belly up to the bar at the kinds of taverns I describe. As for the person who allegedly started the fire, speculation abounds, so that character, while based on that same speculation, is fictional.

More critical than historical accuracy for me was emotional precision. Just mention the fire to anyone of a certain age in Chicago and watch that person's eyes well up instantly, even now, decades after the fire. I'm too young to have that direct response, but I grew up in Chicago, and it *feels* as if I can remember the fire. I've heard the stories over and over, and my emotions have become visceral. I realized, after writing this book, that I was paying tribute to those witnesses and their stories. No, they were not *eye*witnesses, but they may as well have been.

My main storyteller was my mother-in-law, Marilyn, who attended the school but graduated years before the blaze. Her younger brother, though, *was* a student at the time of the fire, but he'd been excused from class minutes earlier to help unload a truck. Many of his classmates perished that day.

What I heard from Marilyn, time and again, was grief. Fervent and unresolved grief. This was a tragedy she would never forget and never quite come to terms with. I didn't set out to write this book with Marilyn in mind, not consciously at least, but her spirit pervades every page. She lost her own mother when she was only eight, the defining event of her life. Her mother's death bestowed upon her a mission: to lessen the pain of others, especially children. Which began at home—she would cover for her older sisters when they snuck in late at night, and she would watch over and protect her younger brothers throughout the day. Grief still gripped her, but nurturing others became her calling. She would have made a good nun, herself. Which is why the fire at her old school hit her so hard, I think. There was nothing she could do. She had to carry that sense of helplessness with her.

That is the emotional resonance I wanted to capture in this book. To what depths will one plunge to deal with unbearable pain? How much can one mind and body take? Does time really heal? Or does grief continue to grip us and shape the way we live our lives?

❖

Editor's note: A wealth of information on the
Our Lady of the Angels Fire can also be found at
www.olafire.com.

❖

For more information on Tony Romano and his books, visit:
http://www.tonyromanoauthor.com/

Acknowledgments

Gratitude for me usually has no priorities, but in this case, my thanks flow first to everyone at Allium Press, especially founder, Emily Victorson, a thorough and thoughtful editor, who nurtured this book along as if it were her own. I'm happy to call her a friend. Thanks also to friends and readers of early drafts of this book, Gina Enk and Sabra Gerber, whose constant encouragement means more than they'll ever know. Thanks to the roundup of usual suspects, who through their support nudged me to think of myself as a writer: my first editor Fred Gardaphé and teacher Tom Bracken, along with friends and reliable readers Henry Sampson, Maria Mungai, Gary Anderson, Kevin Brewner, Daniel Ferri, and Billy Lombardo. Thanks to my girls, Lauren, Angela, and Allie, who always make the world a richer place. I couldn't be prouder of them. Thanks finally to Maureen. My love grows deeper every year.

ALSO PUBLISHED BY ALLIUM PRESS OF CHICAGO

Visit our website for more information:
www.alliumpress.com

THE EMILY CABOT MYSTERIES
Frances McNamara

Death at the Fair

The 1893 World's Columbian Exposition provides a vibrant backdrop for the first book in the series. Emily Cabot, one of the first women graduate students at the University of Chicago, is eager to prove herself in the emerging field of sociology. While she is busy exploring the Exposition with her family and friends, her colleague, Dr. Stephen Chapman, is accused of murder. Emily sets out to search for the truth behind the crime, but is thwarted by the gamblers, thieves, and corrupt politicians who are ever-present in Chicago. A lynching that occurred in the dead man's past leads Emily to seek the assistance of the black activist Ida B. Wells.

◆

Death at Hull House

After Emily Cabot is expelled from the University of Chicago, she finds work at Hull House, the famous settlement established by Jane Addams. There she quickly becomes involved in the political and social problems of the immigrant community. But when a man who works for a sweatshop owner is murdered in the Hull House parlor, Emily must determine whether one of her colleagues is responsible, or whether the real reason for the murder is revenge for a past tragedy in her own family. As a smallpox epidemic spreads through the impoverished west side of Chicago, the very existence of the settlement is threatened and Emily finds herself in jeopardy from both the deadly disease and a killer.

◆

Death at Pullman

A model town at war with itself...George Pullman created an ideal community for his railroad car workers, complete with every amenity they could want or need. But when hard economic times hit in 1894, lay-offs follow and the workers can no longer pay their rent or buy food at the company store. Starving and desperate, they turn against their once benevolent employer. Emily Cabot and her friend Dr. Stephen Chapman bring much needed food and medical supplies to the town, hoping they can meet the immediate needs of the workers and keep them from resorting to violence. But when one young worker—suspected of being a spy—is murdered, and a bomb plot comes to light, Emily must race to discover the truth behind a tangled web of family and company alliances.

◆

Death at Woods Hole

Exhausted after the tumult of the Pullman Strike of 1894, Emily Cabot is looking forward to a restful summer visit to Cape Cod. She has plans to collect "beasties" for the Marine Biological Laboratory, alongside other visiting scientists from the University of Chicago. She also hopes to enjoy romantic clambakes with Dr. Stephen Chapman, although they must keep an important secret from their friends. But her summer takes a dramatic turn when she finds a dead man floating in a fish tank. In order to solve his murder she must first deal with dueling scientists, a testy local sheriff, the theft of a fortune, and uncooperative weather.

◆

Death at Chinatown

In the summer of 1896, amateur sleuth Emily Cabot meets two young Chinese women who have recently received medical degrees. She is inspired to make an important decision about her own life when she learns about the difficult choices they have made in order to pursue their careers. When one of the women is accused of poisoning a Chinese herbalist, Emily once again finds herself in the midst of a murder investigation. But, before the case can be solved, she must first settle a serious quarrel with her husband, help quell a political uprising, and overcome threats against her family. Timeless issues, such as restrictions on immigration, the conflict between Western and Eastern medicine, and women's struggle to balance family and work, are woven seamlessly throughout this mystery set in Chicago's original Chinatown.

◆

Death at the Paris Exposition

In the sixth Emily Cabot Mystery, the intrepid amateur sleuth's journey once again takes her to a world's fair—the Paris Exposition of 1900. Chicago socialite Bertha Palmer has been named the only female U. S. commissioner to the Exposition and she enlists Emily's services as her social secretary. Their visit to the House of Worth for the fitting of a couture gown is interrupted by the theft of Mrs. Palmer's famous pearl necklace. Before that crime can be solved, several young women meet untimely deaths and a member of the Palmers' inner circle is accused of the crimes. As Emily races to clear the family name she encounters jealous society ladies, American heiresses seeking titled European husbands, and more luscious gowns and priceless jewels. Along the way, she takes refuge from the tumult at the country estate of Impressionist painter Mary Cassatt. In between her work and sleuthing, she is able to share the Art Nouveau delights of the Exposition, and the enduring pleasures of the City of Light, with her husband and their young children.

THE HANLEY & RIVKA MYSTERIES
D. M. Pirrone

Shall We Not Revenge

In the harsh early winter months of 1872, while Chicago is still smoldering from the Great Fire, Irish Catholic detective Frank Hanley is assigned the case of a murdered Orthodox Jewish rabbi. His investigation proves difficult when the neighborhood's Yiddish-speaking residents, wary of outsiders, are reluctant to talk. But when the rabbi's headstrong daughter, Rivka, unexpectedly offers to help Hanley find her father's killer, the detective receives much more than the break he was looking for. Their pursuit of the truth draws Rivka and Hanley closer together and leads them to a relief organization run by the city's wealthy movers and shakers. Along the way, they uncover a web of political corruption, crooked cops, and well-buried ties to two notorious Irish thugs from Hanley's checkered past. Even after he is kicked off the case, stripped of his badge, and thrown in jail, Hanley refuses to quit. With a personal vendetta to settle for an innocent life lost, he is determined to expose a complicated criminal scheme, not only for his own sake, but for Rivka's as well.

◆

For You Were Strangers

On a spring morning in 1872, former Civil War officer Ben Champion is discovered dead in his Chicago bedroom—a bayonet protruding from his back. What starts as a routine case for Detective Frank Hanley soon becomes anything but, as his investigation into Champion's life turns up hidden truths best left buried. Meanwhile, Rivka Kelmansky's long-lost brother, Aaron, arrives on her doorstep, along with his mulatto wife and son. Fugitives from an attack by night riders, Aaron and his family know too much about past actions that still threaten powerful men—defective guns provided to Union soldiers, and an 1864 conspiracy to establish Chicago as the capital of a Northwest Confederacy. Champion had his own connection to that conspiracy, along with ties to a former slave now passing as white and an escaped Confederate guerrilla bent on vengeance, any of which might have led to his death. Hanley and Rivka must untangle this web of circumstances, amid simmering hostilities still present seven years after the end of the Civil War, as they race against time to solve the murder, before the secrets of bygone days claim more victims.

Honor Above All
J. Bard-Collins

Pinkerton agent Garrett Lyons arrives in Chicago in 1882, close on the trail of the person who murdered his partner. He encounters a vibrant city that is striving ever upwards, full of plans to construct new buildings that will "scrape the sky." In his quest for the truth Garrett stumbles across a complex plot involving counterfeit government bonds, fierce architectural competition, and painful reminders of his military past. Along the way he seeks the support and companionship of his friends— elegant Charlotte, who runs an upscale poker game for the city's elite, and up-and-coming architect Louis Sullivan. Rich with historical details that bring early 1880s Chicago to life, this novel will appeal equally to mystery fans, history buffs, and architecture enthusiasts.

◆

The Reason for Time
Mary Burns

On a hot, humid Monday afternoon in July 1919, Maeve Curragh watches as a blimp plunges from the sky and smashes into a downtown Chicago bank building. It is the first of ten extraordinary days in Chicago history that will forever change the course of her life. Racial tensions mount as soldiers return from the battlefields of Europe and the Great Migration brings new faces to the city, culminating in violent race riots. Each day the young Irish immigrant, a catalogue order clerk for the Chicago Magic Company, devours the news of a metropolis where cultural pressures are every bit as febrile as the weather. But her interest in the headlines wanes when she catches the eye of a charming streetcar conductor. Maeve's singular voice captures the spirit of a young woman living through one of Chicago's most turbulent periods. Seamlessly blending fact with fiction, Mary Burns weaves an evocative tale of how an ordinary life can become inextricably linked with history.

Set the Night on Fire
Libby Fischer Hellmann

Someone is trying to kill Lila Hilliard. During the Christmas holidays she returns from running errands to find her family home in flames, her father and brother trapped inside. Later, she is attacked by a mysterious man on a motorcycle...and the threats don't end there. As Lila desperately tries to piece together who is after her and why, she uncovers information about her father's past in Chicago during the volatile days of the late 1960s...information he never shared with her, but now threatens to destroy her. Part thriller, part historical novel, and part love story, *Set the Night on Fire* paints an unforgettable portrait of Chicago during a turbulent time: the riots at the Democratic Convention...the struggle for power between the Black Panthers and SDS...and a group of young idealists who tried to change the world.

◆

A Bitter Veil
Libby Fischer Hellmann

It all began with a line of Persian poetry . . . Anna and Nouri, both studying in Chicago, fall in love despite their very different backgrounds. Anna, who has never been close to her parents, is more than happy to return with Nouri to his native Iran, to be embraced by his wealthy family. Beginning their married life together in 1978, their world is abruptly turned upside down by the overthrow of the Shah and the rise of the Islamic Republic. Under the Ayatollah Khomeini and the Republican Guard, life becomes increasingly restricted and Anna must learn to exist in a transformed world, where none of the familiar Western rules apply. Random arrests and torture become the norm, women are required to wear hijab, and Anna discovers that she is no longer free to leave the country. As events reach a fevered pitch, Anna realizes that nothing is as she thought, and no one can be trusted... not even her husband.

FOR YOUNGER READERS

Her Mother's Secret
Barbara Garland Polikoff

Fifteen-year-old Sarah, the daughter of Jewish immigrants, wants nothing more than to become an artist. But as she spreads her wings she must come to terms with the secrets that her family is only beginning to share with her. Replete with historical details that vividly evoke the Chicago of the 1890s, this moving coming-of-age story is set against the backdrop of a vibrant, turbulent city. Sarah moves between two very different worlds—the colorful immigrant neighborhood surrounding Hull House and the sophisticated, elegant World's Columbian Exposition. This novel eloquently captures the struggles of a young girl as she experiences the timeless emotions of friendship, family turmoil, loss...and first love.

A companion guide to *Her Mother's Secret*
is available at www.alliumpress.com. In the guide you will find
resources for further exploration of Sarah's time and place.

◆

City of Grit and Gold
Maud Macrory Powell

The streets of Chicago in 1886 are full of turmoil. Striking workers clash with police...illness and injury lurk around every corner...and twelve-year-old Addie must find her way through it all. Torn between her gruff Papa—who owns a hat shop and thinks the workers should be content with their American lives—and her beloved Uncle Chaim—who is active in the protests for the eight-hour day—Addie struggles to understand her topsy-turvy world, while keeping her family intact. Set in a Jewish neighborhood of Chicago during the days surrounding the Haymarket Affair, this novel vividly portrays one immigrant family's experience, while also eloquently depicting the timeless conflict between the haves and the have-nots.

A companion guide to *City of Grit and Gold*
is available at www.alliumpress.com. In the guide you will find
resources for further exploration of Addie's time and place.

CPSIA information can be obtained
at www.ICGtesting.com
Printed in the USA
FFOW03n1137141217
43948566-43063FF